EVENT
1000

A novel by

DAVID LAVALLEE

HOLT, RINEHART AND WINSTON
New York   Chicago   San Francisco

Published simultaneously in Canada by Holt, Rinehart
and Winston of Canada, Limited.

Library of Congress Catalog Card Number: 73-138881

First Edition

DESIGNER: BERRY EITEL

SBN: 03-085969-7

Printed in the United States of America

To shipmates on and under the sea.

AUTHOR'S NOTE

The characters in this story are fictional and in no way refer to individuals in the U.S. Navy now, or in the past. The submarine *Lancerfish* described herein does not exist and does not represent any current class of attack boat. However, the event that befalls the *Lancerfish* could happen to one of our operational nuclear powered submarines one day.

Our Submarine Force has always been keenly aware of the particular danger to its calling—men trapped in a submarine that is stranded on the bottom. To prepare for such an eventuality, the Navy trains submarine personnel in techniques for individual escape and for rescue by a chamber from the surface. Some years ago, the operation order that covered search and rescue of submariners was identified *Exercise 1000*. If the actual disaster struck, it could no longer be termed an exercise and would then be designated *Event 1000*.

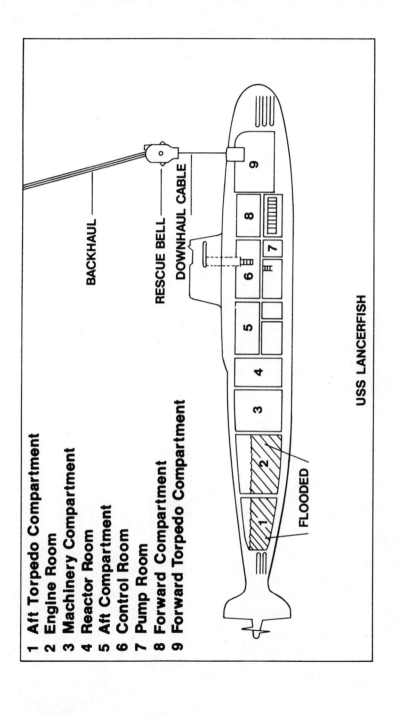

1 Aft Torpedo Compartment
2 Engine Room
3 Machinery Compartment
4 Reactor Room
5 Aft Compartment
6 Control Room
7 Pump Room
8 Forward Compartment
9 Forward Torpedo Compartment

BACKHAUL

RESCUE BELL

DOWNHAUL CABLE

FLOODED

USS LANCERFISH

DISASTER

1 – MAY FOURTEENTH

A HUNDRED MILES southeast of Ambrose Light, off New York City, the sea deepens from the shallow water of the continental shelf into the abyss of the Atlantic Ocean. Long swells rise and heave against the great buttress of the continent. This is the demarcation that mariners call the hundred-fathom line. Here the sea changes color from dark green to a deep cobalt that has something of the night in it.

Nearly sixty miles seaward, a deserted expanse of water was broken by the abrupt emergence of a periscope. The slender shaft rose into the darkness of a moonless night and left a boiling wake, sparkled with phosphorous. It made a slow, cycloptic survey of the horizon as it rushed through the water. Then more of the periscope appeared, followed by a black, glistening superstructure. The monster bow broached the surface, and there was a great upheaval from the depths as a submarine came into view. Now added to the sound of a light wind on the face of the sea came the muffled whine of turbines and the hiss of water along sleek sides. The vacant bridge was quickly peopled by dark figures, and the strange monster became a human contrivance.

In the red light of the control room other men of the watch moved about like devils in some imaginary inferno. The helmsman, his impassive face reflecting the light from the console, shifted position in his bucket seat and adjusted to a new course. Illuminated dials clicked to the heading. The sonar operator stared into space as he listened to the reverberating pulses of sound probing the miles of water. At the rear of the compartment the captain bent over a chart with the navigator and penciled in the surfacing position. The submarine was approaching the New York sea lanes and was scheduled to moor at Hudson River pier the following morning, May fifteenth.

The captain climbed to the bridge and gratefully filled his lungs. The fresh air reminded him of mowed grass or sliced watermelons. Overhead, the stars winked mysterious messages from a black void. A clear and quiet night; he was pleased. The long fleet exercise was over; tomorrow they would enter port to celebrate Armed Forces Day in New York. He thought of his wife, who would be there to meet the boat, and a warm anticipation came over him. They would have four days together; shows, concerts, and sleeping late every morning, a real holiday after weeks of separation.

Lieutenant Hayman, the officer-of-the-deck, and two lookouts came to the bridge for their watch. The junior officer exchanged a few words with his captain and received his orders for the night. They were out of the submerged submarine transit lane and would proceed into port on the surface. It was expected that Ambrose Light would be sighted about 0500, and they would enter the harbor on the morning watch.

Captain Hascomb tarried a moment, reluctant to leave the quiet darkness of the bridge. Tomorrow would be full of formalities and protocol, and he would have to be up early. Soon after arrival he had to pay his respects to the Admiral, the Commandant of the Third Naval District. Then he had to wait aboard for the Admiral to return the call. Generally, this tradition was dispensed with by the Admiral's Chief of Staff, who would tell the sub's commander that all calls were considered made. But this case was different. The Admiral was a submariner and would want to see this latest class of nuclear attack boat. It would be afternoon before Captain Hascomb could get away and join his wife. He took a final deep breath of salty air, let it out with a sigh, and went below.

Hayman settled into the routine of the watch. He was at home on the bridge of a submarine. He propped his tall angular frame against the bulkhead and regarded the empty sea, a blackness merging with the sky. He pushed back the cap that accentuated his thin face and relaxed, happy the old man had gone below. He had never been at ease with the Captain or with any officer who had the special aura of the Naval Academy.

Hayman checked the bridge compass repeater and noted it was off course a degree and a half. The dial remained motionless; the helmsman was obviously doping off. He leaned over the speaker that connected him to the control room. "Who's got the helm down there?" he asked casually.

"Dirksen, sir."

"Okay, Rowboat, let's keep this thing pointed in the right direction." A comradely "yessir" answered, followed after a moment by "steady on three-zero-seven."

Hayman stretched and resumed his slouch on the bridge. The submarine seemed suspended between the two great elements of water and air, not moving forward at all. He gazed into the depths of the sky, picking out the familiar constellations and stars. There was Orion, the Great Hunter, and Vega, alone emitting a steady yellow light. Against this backdrop of night he could see the faint outline of the periscope swaying gently. The watch, the night, were like many others he had experienced. Routine reports came

5

to the bridge and the lookouts were rotated, like an overly rehearsed play. There was a significance in this watch, though; it was his last on the *Lancerfish*. In the morning he would leave for a new billet, and this time he would be reporting as an officer qualified in submarines. There would be a strange crew to get to know, a new skipper, and, above all, a different exec. That had been the only unpleasant part of his duty on the *Lancerfish*—Lieutenant Commander Crawford, the executive officer.

Near 2000 Lt(jg) Langworthy came to the bridge and stared about sleepily. "Ready to relieve you, Robbie, but give me a minute to get used to this awful darkness." He sipped at a steaming cup of coffee and peered ahead. "New York, New York," he sang softly and smiled. "God, it'll be good to get ashore."

"Channel fever?"

"Yeah, I'd like to see something besides hairy sailors and smell 'My Sin' instead of hydraulic oil."

"That's another kind of fever," Hayman said dryly. He was impatient to get off watch. "I assume you've read the Night Orders. We're on course three-zero-seven gyro, speed fifteen and answering bells on the reactor. The boat is rigged for dive, but we're going the rest of the way on the surface." Langworthy accepted this information without interest and said conversationally, "Your last watch on the old *Lancerfish*, huh, Robbie?"

"Yeah. We'll be running into more shipping as we near the coast, so keep alert. All contacts are past the beam, so for the moment you've got no problems." He handed Langworthy the binoculars and returned his languid salute.

"Okay, Robbie, I've got it." He pushed the speaker key and said to the quartermaster below, "This is Mr. Langworthy. I've got the deck and the conn."

Hayman came down from the bridge and stopped in the control room to write the log for his watch. He was the

6

one with "channel fever," he thought. He was to be detached in New York to proceed to his new duty assignment in Key West. He had eighteen days leave coming and would be able to spend some time with Judy, a girl he had met only last Christmas but who now took up much of his time. He hoped she would be on the pier when the boat warped alongside in the morning. It had been six weeks since that weekend. That first, special weekend. Nuclear powered boats would be all right if they didn't operate so much. The *Lancerfish* had been a good tour of duty, but he was glad it was over. His new berth was an old conventional diesel-electric sub, a rebuilt veteran of the war. Not as glamorous, but it would have a better operating schedule. Instead of top secret missions all over the world, the old fleet-type submarines generally stayed around their home port, rendering services as a target or school boat. At least he would be able to get ashore on weekends.

He checked over his brief entry, which described an uneventful watch, signed at the bottom, and closed the log book. Everything he did now was for the last time. He took off his parka and looked about the control room. The compartment was darkened for night cruising, with only red lights illuminating the diving stand and main ballast blow manifold. The echo sounder chirped rythmically as it drew a profile of the sea floor on slowly turning graph paper. Rows of dials, valves, and vents gleamed dully behind the auxiliaryman on watch. Across the compartment the chief-of-the-watch noted air bank pressures and checked the green and red buttons of light on the closure panel over his head. Periodically the steering motor growled as the helmsman corrected course with the aircraft-type controls. The silhouettes of three men were gathered at the combat command island in the center of the compartment, where the quartermaster hung over the handles of number two periscope. They spoke quietly of their plans for liberty in New York City the next day.

Hayman ambled back to the dinette of the crew's quarters and heard the blare of a movie sound track. The dinette was dense with cigarette smoke, and a score of faces reflected the light from the screen. The background music underscored a tender love scene. Hayman regarded the faces of the audience, which showed rapt attention as they projected themselves into the story. The sequence flicked to a close-up of a girl speaking fervently.

"John, I've waited . . ." a portentous pause *". . . so long for this moment; to know the feel of your arms."*

Violins swelled with passion. From the transfixed audience a rough sailor's voice commented, "Someone's gonna get laid."

"Shut up, Seapig, the only thing you've ever laid was Titless Terry at the *Blue Dolphin.*"

"Aw, take a flying . . ."

"Pipe down, you guys," a chief spoke from the rear.

Hayman sat through the movie with little interest and when it was over headed forward to his stateroom. He swung through the watertight opening to the forward compartment, fumbled past the curtained door to his quarters, and turned on the desk light. His suitcase and handbag stood by the empty wardrobe, ready for his departure in the morning. The last night aboard, he thought again. It was always a bit sad to leave a boat, whether it was a good tour of duty or not. Something of himself would be left behind in the accumulation of weeks and months of living in the same environment. The experience gained and eventual qualification had given him confidence. It had not been easy. Days of learning the submarine, studying each compartment, the myriad systems and procedures had been required. Days of making diagrams of the ballast tanks, air banks, and all the complicated circuitry that made up one of the Navy's fastest, deepest diving and sophisticated submarines. Hayman knew the *Lancerfish* better than he would ever know another boat. It was the sub in which he had

8

finally qualified and earned his gold dolphins. He undressed and turned in, stretching in the comfortable bunk. The submarine rolled lazily and peacefully, and sleep overtook him.

Langworthy's long night watch wore on, and he passed the time by plotting the positions of increasing numbers of ships. All seemed to be heading north or south, well clear of their track. He huddled in his duffle coat and squirmed against the cold Atlantic air. More than an hour to go before being relieved, and he was chilled through. At 2310 the port lookout reported a light on the horizon dead ahead. Langworthy keyed the speaker and ordered the radar operator to acquire and track the contact. The operator should have had that on his scope before the lookout picked it up, Langworthy thought, but withheld a reprimand. He stepped to the target bearing transmitter and sighted on the pinpoint of light. He noted that the range light was now visible and showed that the ship was on a reciprocal course. Probably outward bound, he thought. The bridge speaker clicked. "Radar reports contact bearing three-zero-one, range twenty-seven thousand yards. Designated Skunk Kilo." The minutes passed, and the radar operator reported again in mechanical tones, "Skunk Kilo, bearing three-zero-one, range twenty-one thousand yards. Angle on the bow, zero. First estimated course, one-two-one, speed now fourteen. Constant bearing."

Damn, thought Langworthy, we'll have to maneuver clear, and just about the time I'm due to be relieved. He watched the bearing on the TBT. No change. Under *International Rules of the Nautical Road* both vessels had the responsibility of opening the passing distance by altering course to starboard. He decided to wait until the contact closed them more before taking action. The ship was still over ten miles away.

At fifteen thousand yards the bearing was still constant, which indicated a meeting situation. Langworthy called Captain Hascomb and made his report, describing the maneuver he intended to make. At ten thousand yards he would come right twenty-five degrees, which would provide a distance of two miles between tracks. To Captain Hascomb this seemed to be proper and in ample time to avoid embarrassment to the other vessel. Still, he had better go to the bridge. Langworthy had only recently been designated an underway OOD.

Hascomb hoisted himself through the upper hatch and groped his way out on the dark platform. He put his binoculars to his eyes. "What's the range?" he demanded as he observed the ship ahead was still bow on.

"Eight thousand yards, sir."

"Well, you had better start coming right, he's closing fast. Looks like a small merchantman."

"I've changed course already. We're on three-three-two."

Hascomb accepted the information with an automatic "very well," but a sense of danger nudged his thoughts. The other ship had a slight starboard bow angle. She had changed course too, but in the wrong direction. Most likely picking up a transatlantic sailing route and couldn't be bothered by some little vessel over three miles away. Hascomb snapped into the speaker, "Radar, range to Kilo."

"Six thousand, five-double-oh," came the reply. He thought for a moment. If he came left now there was the possibility the other ship would suddenly adhere to the rules and turn to starboard, toward the submarine.

"Has the bearing started to drift?" he asked, and could see before the answer came that it had not.

"Five thousand yards," radar reported. Two and a half miles, still plenty of sea room.

"Come right again, Mr. Langworthy." That should take them across the course of the oncoming ship. "Use full rudder and sound one blast on the whistle," he added.

There was still no bearing drift at 3000 yards. The ship must have again altered course, but to port, adamantly holding to her track. There was distance to turn to the left and not get in the path of the freighter. The dark mass of the vessel was now plainly visible in addition to the running lights. As the submarine commander peered into the gloom, he became apprehensive. Better take no chances and come left; they were getting into extremus. Captain Hascomb barked into the speaker, "I've got the conn. Left full rudder." He sounded the sub's whistle five times, the international danger signal.

The bow of the *Lancerfish* commenced swinging rapidly to port. Langworthy jumped to the TBT and called out bearings. It appeared they would clear. "Range, twelve hundred yards," crackled the speaker. Hascomb voiced his thoughts as he watched the looming hulk. "Stupid sonofabitch, nearly got us." As he followed the ship's increasing bearing, he saw that the silhouette of the bridge had changed. He froze. She was turning to the right, toward the submarine. Range four hundred yards.

Captain Hascomb sounded the collision alarm. In horror he watched the high bow of the merchantman coming about like a lumbering beast turning on a tormentor. The sound of the propeller was distinct, thrashing half out of the water. She must be empty and riding high, he thought irrelevantly. In a quick movement he sounded the diving alarm. "Clear the bridge! Dive! Dive!" he shouted. The response was instant. Air roared from the vents. Maybe they could get under her, or at least submerge enough to save the pressure hull from being ruptured. Langworthy and the lookouts had gone below.

Too late to duck the other ship. Hascomb looked up helplessly as the forecastle blotted out the stars, and for an instant he saw a face staring down at him from the high bulwarks. The water between the two vessels diminished rapidly and disappeared.

The shock of impact knocked Hascomb to the grating. There was a screeching, tearing noise and *Lancerfish* rolled hard to port. He tried to struggle to his feet, but his knee was wedged between the deck and the side of the bridge. As the submarine sank under him, he wrenched at his pinned leg, but it would not come free. In the terror and noise he heard a voice shouting to him from the hatch. It was Langworthy. The hull had disappeared and water slopped onto the bridge.

"Shut it!" the captain bellowed, but the words were swept away by a wave.

The submarine slanted under and the icy weight of water surged around him. Now he was underwater, his breath stopped in his throat. Pain, then numbness suffused his body, and a cold fury pervaded his thoughts. It was senseless, stupid. Goddammit, why? A terrible, relentless pressure closed around him, and for the last conscious moment he thought of his wife.

Hayman awoke when the *Lancerfish* began the frantic maneuvers to avoid the merchant ship. He opened his eyes and tried to evaluate the purpose for the increased speed. He could feel the vibrations quivering through the bunk. He swung his legs over the edge and sat listening. At the sound of the collision alarm he was galvanized into action. He ran to close the watertight door leading to the torpedo room. Then he heard the diving klaxon and the jarring collision caught him, slamming him from side to side in the narrow passageway. There was the sound of breaking glass and heavy objects falling on the deck, and over it all the hysterical, whooping scream of the collision siren.

Hayman latched the door and spun the handle to the closed position. The air was thick and hot as it compressed from the inrush of water somewhere in the boat. Then he shut the ventilation flappers on the bulkhead, bracing himself against the giddy list to port. He looked through the glass peephole and saw that the torpedo room wasn't flooding. They must have been hit aft. Men in underwear scurried about securing the compartment. He headed for main control, the deck was taking a downward slant. Other officers spilled out of their cubicles, dazed with sleep. The Exec was ahead of him and reached the watertight door leading aft. He crouched quickly to glance through the peephole, then undogged the hatch and climbed through the small opening. Hayman followed, barking a shin on the high coaming. He was aware of some frenzied effort by the watch in the dim compartment.

"Rig for white!" Hayman identified the Exec's crisp voice. The control room was suddenly stark with light. His eyes went to the large depth gauge; ninety feet and sinking. Langworthy was on the control island giving orders to the men on the hydraulic and air manifolds. "Shut all vents; blow all main ballast . . . blow bow buoyancy . . . engine back emergency . . . give me hard rise on the planes!" The submarine wiggled as high pressure air thundered into the ballast tanks. The hand on the depth gauge slowed as it passed 120 feet, then crept to 125, paused, and hung motionless. The Exec noted the Captain was not there. Langworthy, white and shaken, met his glance.

"The skipper is topside. . . . We couldn't wait."

"After torpedo room doesn't answer." The telephone talker's voice was shrill. His eyes widened as he accepted more information. "The engineroom reports flooding out of control, they request permission to evacuate to machinery compartment!"

Crawford snatched a handset from the bulkhead, "Machinery compartment, this is the Exec. What's the water level in the engineroom?" As he listened his face darkened. Two feet above the lower edge of the watertight door. Personnel could not evacuate the compartment. The depth gauge showed they were sinking again. Crawford took command. "Blow auxiliaries to sea," he yelled. "Have the ma-

13

chinery compartment open internal salvage air to the engineroom and after torpedo room." He had to stop the water entering the boat. If the rupture was low enough they might be able to force out sufficient water to regain positive buoyancy. He looked at the fathometer and saw that the depth of water was over 300 fathoms. "Right full rudder, ahead flank," he ordered, then turned to the chart desk. He measured off their approximate position from the last loran fix. They were over the Hudson Canyon, nearly eight miles from the hundred-fathom line. If they could keep the *Lancerfish* going for a few minutes longer, they would make shallower water. If they bottomed here, there would be no hope for survival. "Steady on three-fiver-zero," he commanded, which would head them for the nearest shoal water.

The telephone talker had been trying to get damage reports from the other spaces. He turned to the Exec.

"No answer from the engineroom or Tubes Aft. The reactor compartment is secure, we're getting main and auxiliary power."

The men in the control room were frozen in postures of attention as they watched the depth gauge. The distant palpitation of the screw felt reassuring, but their stern heavy angle was increasing.

"Fifteen degrees up bubble with hard rise on the planes, I can't hold her," sang out the helmsman, casting a quick glance over his shoulder at the Exec. Crawford, as though hypnotized, kept his eyes on the gauge and acknowledged, almost casually.

"Very well, Saunders, mind your course and leave it at full rise."

The dead reckoning plot showed five miles to the hundred-fathom curve. Their depth was 450 feet. The *Lancerfish* was settling slowly with all tanks blown. The machinery compartment reported main ballast tanks five and six were not holding air; they had been holed by the collision. The manifold operator was ordered to secure the blowing on these tanks. The hand of the depth gauge was moving faster now: 610 feet . . . 625 . . . 650.

"Machinery compartment reports screw has stopped!" the telephone talker shouted in Crawford's face. They were all turned toward the depth gauge and the hand that moved so inexorably.

Salvage air still whistled into the engineroom and after torpedo room. The survivors in those compartments were finished struggling now. The tremendous pressure of the sea at that depth had no doubt extinguished all life aft of the machinery compartment.

"Passing one thousand feet," the quartermaster reported. "Bottom is coming up." The speed diminished rapidly now. It was obvious they would not make the continental shelf.

A bump, then another, this time jarring them violently and rattling equipment consoles. The bow came down slowly and the deck heeled to a port list. As though by command, the men lurched forward from the decrease in momentum. From outside the submarine came the muffled screech and groans of the hull plowing through mud and sand. Depth 1235 feet; the *Lancerfish* was on the bottom.

"Secure the air," Crawford ordered. All their blowing would have no effect now, except to send billows of bubbles to the surface. Most likely the two after compartments had been opened high along the hull, Crawford surmised, and they were almost completely flooded. The submarine was several hundred tons heavy. Now he had to conserve whatever air there was left in the banks.

As the noise of rushing air subsided, a deadly quiet settled over the boat. No one spoke for a moment, then an awed voice broke the silence.

"Mother of Christ, look at the depth!"

The men looked at one another, then at the Exec. The *Lancerfish* shifted slightly and again there came a distant growling sound. The deck canted twelve degrees to port and had an up angle of six degrees. Crawford looked over the damage control form. The engineroom and after torpedo room were crossed out and labled simply "flooded." All other compartments were secure and taking no water. The nuclear reactor was maintaining the auxiliary electrical load. The life support system which purified their atmosphere and produced oxygen was functioning. Crawford searched the faces of the men gathered around him. He singled out the chief-of-the-boat, Guy Harris, and gave him instructions to take a muster to determine who was aft and to set up a security watch to check bilges.

"Chief, I want an electrician on watch at all times on the life support system."

"Aye, sir, if that craps out we're good for only two or three days."

Crawford then ordered all officers to inspect spaces and equipments they were responsible for, and report back to the wardroom.

Hayman ducked into the torpedo room. Several men were perched on their bunks, which were tiered aft of the tube nest. A voice whispered, "There's the torpedo officer," and all heads turned toward him. McGovern, Torpedoman first class, came from between the two rows of tubes, his trousers wet and smeared with grease from crawling through the lower flats and bilges.

"All secure, Mr. Hayman, taking no water." Hayman acknowledged and ordered that flares be laid out. A young nonrated man who had reported to the *Lancerfish* just before the sub had sailed, hung his head over the edge of a bunk and asked, "Do you think they can get a bell on us, Lieutenant?"

"Yeah, I think so," Hayman answered, making his voice as casual as possible. "We're on a pretty level bottom, though deep. The rescue bell is designed for only eight hun-

16

dred and fifty feet, but I think it can be modified to get down to us."

"Mr. Hayman, have a look."

McGovern was standing behind the signal ejector, looking at it with disgust. Hayman saw that water was seeping around the edge of the breech door. The brass barrel, which angled upward to the top of the pressure hull, was beaded with moisture. It was flooded. The exterior muzzle door would not seal, making it impossible to send up flares. He went aft to report to the Exec.

Lieutenant Commander Crawford stood at the end of the wardroom table clutching an emergency flashlight as the officers came in. His broad face and light blue eyes regarded them as they took positions around the table. Their faces had the blank stare of shock and disbelief. Only a short time before they had been on the surface heading for port, anticipating shore leave in New York City. Now, suddenly, they were trapped in their submarine, men were dead, and their routine had been shattered by disaster.

No one spoke as they filed in. Some gazed at the sweating pressure hull, and others with their heads turned toward the Exec waited for him to speak. It was strange not having the Captain there. Crawford noted that Hughes, the electrical officer, was not present. "Where's Hugh?" he demanded. Young Tom Evers, the navigator, said bluntly, "He was aft, commander," and looked at his hands.

Chief Harris stuck his head into the small compartment and handed the Exec a piece of paper. Crawford scanned it quickly. It contained the names of the men lost in the after compartments. Out of eighty-three men, twenty-one had died there, and the Captain was unaccounted for. Crawford hoped the merchant ship had picked him up. He turned to the others.

"I'm afraid the after torpedo room and engineroom are completely flooded and main ballast tanks five and six were breached. All reserve buoyancy is gone, we can't surface,

17

and—" he paused, looking hard at each officer—"we're lying in over twelve hundred feet of water." No need to tell them that individual escape from such a depth was out of the question. "Our only hope," he continued, "is the rescue chamber."

Lt(jg) Evers broke in. "But Commander, the rescue bell has an operational depth of eight or nine hundred feet. Aren't we too deep?"

"I know, but those chambers have a design safety factor of three. The downhaul cable which we will float up with our messenger buoy is about fifteen hundred feet in length." He turned to Hayman. "How about it. Torpedo Officer, that's your responsibility. Did you verify the length of the downhaul cable during the shipyard overhaul?"

"Not personally." Hayman felt the eyes of the officers on him. "Those cables are made up especially for submarines and are required to be twelve hundred and seventy feet in one continuous length."

"Even so, the depth of water over the forward messenger buoy is about twenty-five feet less than keel depth," Crawford said. "That gives us about sixty extra feet of cable."

The operations officer, Lt. John Fitzgibbons, spoke up. "We're all dead, it's only a matter of time. We'll live until the air gives out," he said in a soft, morose voice. "That bell will never make it to this . . ."

"Hold it!" Crawford banged the table with the flashlight. "In the meantime we're alive, and I think something can be done. Knock that kind of talk off. We have a responsibility to those guys." He gestured toward the control room. "The odds look bad, but what do you want to tell them, lay down and die? We've got the reactor and the life support system to sustain us until something is figured out topside. I think we'll make out." He paused, relaxing somewhat, and turned to Hayman again. "How about that new rescue submersible the Navy's been working on? What's it called?"

18

"Deep Submergence Rescue Vehicle," Hayman said, smiling slightly. "DSRV for short. The first one was launched last year but still isn't operational. Anyway, if it was ready, we aren't. The boat has to be modified to mate with it."

Crawford heaved a sigh and got up. "Release the messenger buoy now. Even if it doesn't reach the surface, it might be picked up on sonar. All of us must look at the situation positively," he said, looking at Fitzgibbons.

Crawford instructed the supply officer, Lt(jg) Roche, to inventory their provisions, including the emergency rations. He returned to the control room to check the security watch Chief Harris had set up. He hoped it would not be too long before there were Navy ships over them.

2 – THE SEARCH

MAY 15-17

IN THE OPERATIONS room of the Third Coast Guard District headquarters, in lower Manhattan, a lone radioman sat contemplating the early morning. He had come on watch at midnight and was still logy with sleep. It looked like an uneventful watch. The weather was good all along the eastern seaboard, and merchant shipping was light. The message traffic had been filed, and now he sat with his coffee looking out the window at the empty streets of New York. He could see up Broadway, almost to City Hall. Not a living thing moved. The traffic signals changed from green to red and back again, giving commands to deserted streets like a memory. A fragment of newspaper caught the wind and sailed along the sidewalk, glided to the gutter, then shot up precipitously in a sudden draft.

One of the teletype machines ranged along the wall came to life, breaking the stillness of the room. It whacked out a few letters, paused, then commenced a syncopated run of typing, hesitated, and picked up the measured beat again. The radioman waited until the message was completed, then tore it from the machine and read the brief, electrifying announcement. Collision! He hurried down the hall to the duty officer's room, gave a short knock, and entered, turning on the light.

"Sir, an emergency relay from Cape May, picked up on five hundred kilocycles." He waited for the lieutenant to awake. A mumble came from the narrow bed, and the officer sat up, squinting in the harsh overhead light. He looked at his watch, then took the dispatch and read:

EMERGENCY FROM SS OCEAN BELLE X IN COLLISION WITH UNIDENTIFIED SUBMARINE X SUB DOVE IN POSITION 39 DEGREES 25 MIN NORTH LATITUDE AND 72 DEGREES 03 MIN WEST LONGITUDE X STANDING BY IN CASE OF SURVIVORS X NO SHIP CASUALTIES X MODERATE DAMAGE TO BOW TAKING SOME WATER IN FORWARD VOID X TIME 2355 LOCAL.

"Get the rest of the watch up, alert cutter two-one-nine to get underway soonest for collision site. Get me a message form."

The officer looked at his watch again—0010. Have to get search and rescue ships there fast, there may be men in the water, he thought, slipping quickly into his trousers. In the Operations Room he deftly picked off the coordinates of the collision area on the chart. The sub was hit in the shipping lanes over a hundred miles off New York. The officer was fully awake now. He sent an Operational Immediate message to the Commander Submarine Force, U. S. Atlantic Fleet, requesting verification of U. S. units. Twenty-five minutes later the answer came back:

BELIEVE TO BE USS LANCERFISH SSN 919 X HAVE INITIATED OPERATION SUBLOST X RESCUE VESSEL DISPATCHED.

At the Submarine Base in New London, Connecticut, there was considerable activity in the early hours of May fifteenth. The air was periodically shattered by the emergency horn. Its aggrieved bellow carried across the Thames

River to the Coast Guard Academy, floated over the campus of Connecticut College, and disturbed the sleep of a farmer in Gales Ferry. A steady stream of automobiles moved through the main gate of the base, and the windows in the headquarters building cast anemic light in the advancing dawn.

In the SubLant operations room Captain B. C. Holmes, Commander, Submarine Squadron Two, thumbed through the message file. The last communication from *Lancerfish* was her surfacing report, four and a half hours before the collision message from the *Ocean Belle*. He moved to the chart table and stepped off the position again. The dividers looked small and fragile in his thick fingers. A young officer came up and peered over his shoulder.

"Radio reports the *Lancerfish* doesn't answer on any frequency, Commodore. That must have been her."

Still studying the chart, the older officer said quietly, "Yes, thank you," and read the depth inscriptions plotted around the area. Over 300 fathoms! Holmes thought of the *Lancerfish*'s skipper, Joe Hascomb, who had been with the squadron less than a year. Was he sitting on the bottom of the Atlantic waiting for what looked like an impossible rescue? Or perhaps the submarine had gone into one of the deeps close by and the hull had crushed, and there would be no survivors.

Earlier that morning ComSubLant, Rear Admiral Thomas Calhoun, himself had called Holmes to break the news. "One of your boats is down, Captain. Looks like *Lancerfish* was clobbered offshore. I've initiated op order Event 1000. I want you to take *Barnett* to the scene. I'll brief you when you get here."

It had taken Holmes less than thirty minutes to get to headquarters. *Event 1000,* he had thought as he sprang up the steps to Operations. How many times they had practiced this emergency procedure, which for training was referred to as Exercise 1000. But now it was the real thing, an *Event*.

Now, as he prepared to get underway, Holmes took a final look at the soundings on the chart. The shallowest depth in the area was well beyond a thousand feet. Well, no point in dwelling on that, he thought. First the boat had to be located and a determination made whether or not anyone on board was alive. He headed for the Admiral's office for a short meeting before departure.

The destroyer *Barnett* waited at pierside for Commodore Holmes to come aboard. Her mooring lines were singled up, and her boilers were under a full head of steam. Five hours had passed since the initial report from the Coast Guard concerning the collision. The submarine rescue vessel *Kingfisher* had left at 0230, as soon as most of her divers were aboard. Destroyer units and aircraft were combing the area for survivors, or debris that might indicate where *Lancerfish* had gone down.

Holmes hurried across the gangway and made his way to the bridge, where the C. O. of the *Barnett* waited for him. The men in the pilot house visibly stiffened when Holmes' large form stepped out on deck. He wore his familiar blue windbreaker with the name "Barney" stenciled across the back. This was what he was called by contemporaries. Subordinates referred to him in private as Barnacle Bill. Up river the black, sinister shapes of submarines were moored at the finger piers. On their after decks men were beginning to group for morning muster.

The *Barnett* backed into the Thames River, pivoted, and stood downstream at standard speed. When clear of the channel entrance, full speed was rung up and a course set to clear Montauk Point. A freshening breeze set the water of Long Island Sound into a frenzy of small white caps. It would be rough in the open sea.

The *Kingfisher* and *Barnett* arrived on station almost simultaneously, due to the slower speed of the rescue vessel.

23

Holmes ordered the other ship to haul clear while the destroyer commenced the sonar search. A reference buoy had been dropped by the Coast Guard on the position where the collision had occurred. Lookouts were instructed to be alert for the bright orange messenger buoy that the submarine would release if she could. By late afternoon the wind had increased to twenty-five knots, which in turn was building up the waves. Visibility was excellent, but the rough seas slowed the search and hampered the sound equipment. Holmes, braced on the starboard wing of the bridge, gazed at the deep blue waves flecked with foam. He watched the wheeling seagulls dipping in the destroyer's wake, their pealing cries casting a funereal sound in the air. A sudden spread of flying fish skittered in front of the bow, their silver bodies flashing in the sun. Somewhere under this sparkling scene of life rested the dark hulk of *Lancerfish*. Even now, he thought, what silent fish peers at the submarine, an intruder in its world, then aimlessly moves away? Holmes turned his attention to the sonar repeater, but there were no contacts.

Near sunset two small ships were sighted bearing in from the west, heading for the search area. When they were within a mile of the *Barnett*, the Coast Guard cutter intercepted them and radioed to stand clear. One was a charter boat out of Briele, N. J., and the other was a sleek seventy-foot cabin cruiser, both carrying newsmen. They lay to and Holmes inspected them through his binoculars. On the pilot house of the charter boat he saw a huddle of figures. The American press had arrived to describe the tragedy of the *Lancerfish* to their public.

A radioman came out on the windswept bridge and handed a message-board to the officer-of-the-deck, who quickly passed it to the Commodore. It was a dispatch from ComSubLant addressed to him, designating Captain B. C. Holmes as the "on scene" commander for search and rescue. He smiled briefly. It was ironic. Old Tom Calhoun must have thought so too, if he remembered their past encounters on the subject of submarine rescue. Holmes recalled his outspoken criticisms in the past of the Navy's lack of rescue systems for the new deep boats. Recently there had been a heated conference with the Admiral over a magazine article Holmes had published. In it he had cited the lagging development of the Deep Submergence Rescue Vehicle as "a Navy application of 'benign neglect,' to use a popular term of the times." Calhoun had cautioned him to pull his horns in.

"You've got a point, Barney," the Admiral had said. "I don't deny that, but funds have been chopped, even for operational requirements and fleet modernization. And anyway, it's been over twenty-five years since a submarine accident in which the crew had to be rescued."

Holmes had stomped from the Admiral's office with the parting remark that if one of the new subs was sunk, they had better hope there would be no survivors waiting for rescue. "Because," he had said, "we can't get them out with the gear we've got now, and there would be one hell of a public howl."

Evidently his bitching hadn't shaken the boss's faith in him, Holmes reflected, reading the message over again. But first the *Lancerfish* had to be found, which was proving more difficult than he had anticipated.

Darkness closed on the search operations, and a sense of futility replaced the earlier atmosphere of urgency. Two more destroyers joined the *Barnett* that night and circled the area, alternating in sonar ranging and passive listening. Holmes went below to dine with the C. O. Their conversation was filled with conjecture about finding the submarine.

"Sonar conditions are poor, too deep, and there's a thermal layer at two hundred feet," Captain Johnson said as he helped himself to the platter of meat and potatoes offered by the steward. "Really, not much chance of locat-

25

ing her unless she sends up a buoy, and that won't be spotted at night." Holmes nodded and the captain regarded him steadily. "You know the depth of water here. If we find the sub and anyone is alive, how will you get them out?"

"Let's find that out first, Harry. Give me just one problem at a time."

During their coffee the message-board was brought in. The same radioman who had been on the bridge stood patiently as Holmes read through the file. One dispatch was from the Commandant of the Third Naval District in New York. It requested that two correspondents be put on the *Barnett* to pool releases about the search operations. Holmes scribbled a short reply at the bottom of the message. "Permission granted to embark media reps. Ensure newsmen are accredited." He instructed the radioman to make ComSub-Lant information addressee to both messages.

"Well, here we go. The press will be with us soon, and I can almost hear their questions," Holmes said, looking grim.

The next morning was dark and cloudy. The wind had shifted to the northeast during the night, bringing cold slanting rain. There was a low moaning in the halyards and antennae of the *Barnett* as she came about and took the seas head on. The bow rose slowly, then dived into a white-capped wave; the hull vibrated and a plume of spray trailed off her forecastle. Holmes had been on deck for two hours of the morning watch. He was cold and a little irritated. One of the destroyers had dropped out of the search because of a sonar casualty. Now the weather seemed to be against them too. He went to the chart room, aft of the pilot house, to read the latest weather advisory.

"Messenger, tell a steward to get me a cup of coffee—black and sweet. I'll be in the chart house."

Holmes studied the chart overlays penciled and smudged by many tracks and positions which traced their

26

search operations the night before. He tapped the barometer and noted that it had fallen another two hundredths. The quartermaster handed him another weather forecast. "Doesn't look so good, Commodore. I think we're in for a squally day."

During the previous day and night the search had covered the area established around the datum buoy several times, with no results. Twice during the midwatch there had been false contacts which caused some excitement. Now the *Barnett* was heading for the launch that carried the newsmen from New York. When they were within a quarter of a mile of the white boat, the officer-of-the-deck signaled them to come alongside. Holmes watched the operation from his high perch on the bridge. He leaned across the coaming on folded arms and saw the two civilians grab awkwardly for the jacob's ladder that had been lowered. The other reporters looked tired and miserable as they rocked gaily on the launch. Cameras, a tape recorder, and a large black box were handed up to the sailors on the *Barnett*, and then the launch pulled ahead and cleared the side.

"Have them taken to my quarters," Holmes called down to the officer escorting the reporters. "I'll be down in a moment." He wanted to speak to them privately and give them a briefing on the situation.

The cabin was small but comfortable. It belonged to the ship's captain, who had moved to his sea cabin near the pilot house out of deference to the Commodore. There was a large bunk with drawers under it, a desk, and a wardrobe. In the middle of the cabin was a round table with a green cover. The two journalists sat facing each other at the table. One was tall and thin with sharp features accentuated by a neat moustache. Dressed in an expensively tailored tweed suit, Leonard Wright was correspondent for the combined television networks. Next to him on the deck was a rugged black case, scarred and labeled by many travels. He sat regarding his fellow newsman with urbane amusement. Edgar

Lewis was a tall man too, but fleshy with a big face that blended into an almost neckless body. He was the representative for UPI, and he was unhappy and seasick from the long, rocky ride aboard the launch. He wore his slightly faded blue topcoat and hat, as though at any moment he would get up and leave. He shook his head.

"Jesus, the older I get, the tougher the assignments. During the war I spent eighteen months in the Seabees. Now every time there's a job that has something to do with water, I get tapped by the assignment editor."

The cabin door opened and an immaculate steward carried in a tray with coffee decanter and cups and set it in front of the men.

"Well, this beats that canoe we came out on," the heavy reporter observed. He leaned against the table, looking from side to side confidentially. "Do you think we'll sleep here?" he asked hopefully.

"We'll be lucky if we get the chief's quarters. This is the Old Man's stateroom. We're on what the Navy lovingly calls a greyhound of the sea, Ed, not one of the luxury queens. Space here is taken up by a million dollars worth of electronics. No posh comforts."

The door opened again and Holmes entered. He took an unlighted cigar out of his mouth and introduced himself perfunctorily. A trace of a smile pulled at his wide mouth.

"I guess it was a bit uncomfortable in that spitkit you came out in. We'll fix you up with some breakfast, as soon as Captain Johnson comes down from the bridge. In the meantime I'll give you a rundown on the operation so far." He heaved off the duffle coat and sailed his cap to the bunk.

Wright made the introductions for himself and Lewis. He was impressed by Holmes's size. The wide shoulders and massive chest blended smoothly into the trunk of the Commodore's body, giving him a stately portliness. The face was broad, almost ugly with its frog-like mouth and protruding hooded eyes. The coarse, dark complexion accentuated the

28

full white hair. An imposing figure, Wright thought—what one imagined an old seadog to look like.

"Later I would like to get some sixteen-millimeter footage of you on the bridge," Wright said. "The launch can rendezvous with us to take the film back to the city, when convenient with you, of course. Also, we'd like to use one of your radio circuits to file releases, if possible."

Holmes regarded him reflectively. "That may be some time—a rendezvous with the launch, I mean. The weather is picking up and I think we're in for a blow. Your launch will have to beat it back to port." He took a chair between the two newsmen at the table. The ship was beginning to roll about more. Instead of short, slow swings from side to side, there was now a pronounced wallowing. Occasionally the steel deck and bulkheads shuddered faintly as they pitched into the sea. Holmes steadied the jiggling cup the steward had placed before him and continued. "We're now heading back to datum—the point where the collision occurred—to run another fathometer profile of the bottom."

Holmes went on to explain the procedures being used to locate the sunken submarine, and the negative results thus far. As he talked he studied the correspondents. He wanted to know what kind of men they were and the type of news they were looking for. From them the public would learn about the disaster, and care had to be taken not to give wrong interpretations. Families of the lost crewmen would be anxiously scanning the news stories, looking for whatever hope there might be.

Leonard Wright was known to Holmes; he appeared frequently on television news features. Wright seemed overly solicitous and smoothly respectful. His lean, carefully barbered countenance was attentive yet somehow veiled. He frowned slightly, and frequently would lean back in his chair with one arm cocked behind his head and stroke his hair. From time to time he would write something in a little notebook as Holmes spoke. No doubt forming his first re-lease, Holmes thought.

Lewis, on the other hand, seemed hardly to pay attention. He sat sideways to the table with one leg up resting an ankle on the other knee. He was interested in the photograph of Captain Johnson's wife and children which was on the desk. He asked the steward for more coffee and shifted around in the chair, putting both forearms on the table.

"Captain, is there anything like dramamine on this boat?"

The steward disappeared with an order to get the pills from sick bay, and Holmes continued. "So, you see, our search has been made more difficult with such an uneven bottom. Where the *Lancerfish* went down the sounding is over three hundred fathoms. From there the sea floor begins to shoal steeply with outcroppings, which gives us false echoes on the sound gear."

"What are the chances of anyone being alive, Commodore?" Wright asked.

"It depends upon how quickly the sub flooded. If there are dry compartments; if the crew was able to get the watertight doors closed between them and the flooding, there is a very good chance that there are survivors."

"And if you find them, what then? Can they get out?"

Holmes sipped at his coffee, holding the cup like a bowl. He set it down carefully.

"They will have to come out by the rescue bell. The pressure is too great for individual escapes."

He knew too well the problems that would have to be faced once the sub was found. If they were able to release the messenger buoy, it would not reach the surface. But the cable might be picked up on sonar, and he would send a diver down to attach more cable. The problem then would be to get a bell beyond the messenger buoy. He did not mention this aspect to the reporters and hoped Wright would not pursue the point.

"How long can they last?" Lewis suddenly asked. He directed his full attention now to Holmes. "Those guys down there—how long can they keep going?"

"It's hard to say until we make contact. I don't want to conjecture on the possibilities now."

Wright offered an answer. "Ed, if that atomic bomb they have for a power plant is still working, and they can make air, they can last forever. Or at least until the food runs out." He closed his notebook with satisfaction. The steward commenced laying the table for breakfast. Wright looked at Lewis benevolently. "At last, Ed, we eat."

Lewis got up, took off his coat and hat, and hung them on the back of the door. He picked up the capsule of dramamine and swallowed it with coffee, then lurched to the porthole and stared at the grey waves freckled with rain.

"Jesus," he breathed.

News of the submarine disaster flashed quickly across the country. The morning editions of the New York newspapers carried the headlines: "Feared U. S. Sub Sunk Off Jersey Coast." Later, extras on the street before noon announced in screaming type: "Submarine Lancerfish Sunk." Ironically, one paper failed to pull a short notice in the back pages concerning the arrival of the *Lancerfish* and stated that the submarine would be open for public visiting on Armed Forces Day.

Radio and television programs were interrupted when the bulletin came in from Washington: "The Chief of Naval Operations has announced that at approximately eleven forty-five Friday night the nuclear powered submarine USS *Lancerfish* collided with the steamship *Ocean Belle* off New York and sank with her crew of eighty-three officers and men. The Navy is speeding search and rescue vessels to the scene to locate the doomed submarine and to pick up possible survivors."

The first full news report on the accident was filed from New London, Connecticut, and appeared with a recent photograph of the *Lancerfish* underway in Long Island Sound. The inside pages had pictures of the captain, the executive officer, and some of the crewmembers. One bylined article interviewed the wife of Torpedoman First Class C. T. Rodgers. A photograph accompanying the story showed Mrs. Rodgers and three youngsters staring blankly into the camera. At the end of the story she was quoted: "I know Claude will be all right. I have faith in God and the United States Navy."

It was two days before active searching could be resumed because of the storm. Four destroyers were now on the scene in addition to the *Barnett,* but they could do little except steam at eight knots and continue sonar pinging. Holmes was anxious for the weather to abate so he could put to use a side scanning sonar. He hoped the sub had released the messenger buoy. With this new acoustic device they might pick up the cable.

On May seventeenth ComSubLant radioed that the submarine *Striker* had been dispatched to assist in the search. This sub was of the same class as the *Lancerfish* and would make submerged sonar searches when thermal layers obscured the sound transmissions of the surface vessels.

The *Barnett* had returned to datum and was lying to, rolling in the trough of the sea. The wind and waves were calming, and Holmes was again trying to communicate with the *Lancerfish* by the underwater telephone. He was convinced that the submarine had not completely flooded, which meant men were alive on board. This had been determined by a radio conversation with the mate of the *Ocean Belle,* who had been on the bridge at the time of collision. Also, one seaman had witnessed the final moments before the bow of the freighter crashed into the stern of the submarine. He described seeing the black hull swinging desperately to port and hearing the collision alarm. Seconds later he had heard the two honks of the diving klaxon and the roar of air from the tank vents. Holmes, knowing how fast a crew could close up a boat, estimated that the forward section was saved. One bit of information that he had gotten during that long radio conference disturbed him. The *Lancerfish* had been swinging to a southeasterly direction when hit. This would head her for deeper water.

Holmes sat in the dark, muffled silence of Combat Information Center. He waited for the OOD to tell him that the *Barnett* was over the position he had designated on the chart. He had stepped a distance of 1500 yards in the direction of 160 degrees true, the most probable location where the *Lancerfish* would have bottomed.

The CIC was manned by the three men of the regular steaming watch. The radarman sat at his console monitoring the line of light that swept around the scope, painting yellow dots of ships in the force. Ghostly lighted status boards and the "surface plot" showed up in the darkened room like illuminated spiderwebs.

The door opened momentarily, letting in the hard glare of daylight, and Wright entered. Holmes acknowledged his presence with a brief "morning," and continued to stare into the darkness. Captain Johnson in his bridge parka and binoculars was standing by the underwater telephone. An electronic voice broke the stillness.

"Combat, Bridge—we're on station."

The radarman spoke into a speaker, "Combat, aye," and looked to the captain. Captain Johnson held a small microphone to his lips.

"Hello, *Lancerfish*; *Lancerfish*; *Lancerfish*; this is *Barnett*. Do you read, over."

He turned up the gain on the panel, and all listened intently to the hissing noise level coming from the loudspeaker. He repeated the call several times. Finally Holmes said, "If they do hear us, Harry, they certainly can't make a reply." He got up and stood behind the radar console and vacantly watched the repeated smear of light, as though he might divine some answer to his thoughts there. An amplified voice startled the quiet. "*Lancerfish*; *Lancerfish*; this is *Barnett*. Do you read? Over." For an instant Holmes' pulse quickened, then he turned to where the words had come. Wright was bending over his little battery-powered tape recorder, smiling thinly. "This will add a little drama to my taped commentary going out tonight," he said. Holmes, annoyed, walked out, saying to Captain Johnson, "Let's make another run. Let me know when the *Striker* gets here."

Wright went below to the wardroom, where he found Lewis in the lounge area carefully handwriting his release. One end of the large compartment had been designated as their "press room." Lewis looked up.

"Nothing, huh?"

Wright poured a cup of coffee from the Silex on the buffet and sat down. "Nope. Personally I don't think they will find them, but the Commodore feels there are survivors down there." He tasted his coffee thoughtfully and leaned back in his chair. "I wonder what he thinks he can do if the sub *is* located. I asked him how long the search would go on and he said, 'until we find them.' "

After lunch Holmes went to his quarters where he met Wright for an interview. The reporter had set up his recorder and was waiting for him. After settling themselves at the table Wright launched into the interview with a short introduction.

"Take one. May seventeenth, aboard the USS *Barnett* in the collision area of the submarine *Lancerfish*. With me is Captain Barnaby C. Holmes, United States Navy, the task force commander for search and rescue operations on the sunken submarine. Captain Holmes is a veteran submariner and salvage expert. Under his command are five destroyers; the rescue vessel *Kingfisher*; the submarine *Striker*, a sister ship of the *Lancerfish*; and aircraft from the New York Naval Air Station. For the past two days this fleet has been comb-

34

ing the sea in hopes of finding some trace of the lost nuclear-powered submarine. High seas and winds have been a handicap in these operations, but now the weather is moderating, and it is hoped that some clues may turn up to indicate exactly where the *Lancerfish* rests."

As he spoke Wright would look up from time to time, as though a television camera were focused on him. His voice was assured and well modulated. He turned slightly towards Holmes.

"Commodore Holmes, you said earlier that you believed men are alive in the submarine. Will you explain your reason for this assumption?"

Holmes thought for a moment and then recounted the conversation he had with the crewmember of the *Ocean Belle,* and his interpretation of what had probably happened. He described how the men would react upon hearing the collision alarm and that most likely only one or two compartments had flooded. Under such conditions, with ruptured ballast tanks and the weight of water-filled compartments, all reserve buoyancy would be gone. As he spoke he imagined himself on the bridge of the submarine and what his reactions would have been. Once he saw that collision was imminent, he would have sounded the alarm and dived. In his mind he saw the control room, the frantic blowing of tanks after the collision, which for a time would slow the sinking. Then, ahead full . . . flank speed . . . hell, yes! Ahead flank, try to maintain as much positive buoyancy possible with speed, and haul ass for shallower water. He jumped up, startling Wright, and dashed for the door.

He mounted the ladder to the bridge wing two steps at a time. "Officer-of-the-deck," he bellowed, "how far to the datum buoy?" and before he got an answer, ordered, "make for it!" He went to the chart house and laid off a course from the point of collision to Ambrose Light. "At Datum come to course three-three-zero," he ordered. "When three

35

miles out from the buoy, slow to six knots and start echo ranging. I want continuous fathometer soundings."

Hell, yes, he thought again. The *Lancerfish* could make thirty knots submerged under normal conditions. The skipper would naturally use all the power he could get from the reactor to get him out of deep water and head him toward that nearest shallow sounding to the north.

Holmes stuck his head into the pilot house. "Messenger, ask Captain Johnson to come to the bridge, please. On your way back get me a black and sweet." The frustration and fatigue of the previous two days seemed to evaporate.

3 – FIRST DAY

During the first hours on the bottom the crew of the *Lancerfish* had carefully calculated the time it would take before surface contact would be made. It was expected that sonar communications would be established with someone the first day. After that it would only be a matter of hours before a rescue vessel moored over them and hooked into the downhaul cable.

Those of the crew not on watch in the reactor room or tending the life support system in the machinery compartment were gathered in the torpedo room, confident in their rescue and ready for departure through the escape trunk. By 1000 on May fifteenth every man knew the length of the cable which was their only link with the world above. It had been decided by Chief Harris that the downhaul was not only the required 1270 feet, but that it was most likely even longer. He said that he seemed to recall seeing 250 fathoms stenciled on the reel. That would be 1500 feet, more than enough to reach the surface.

The Exec tried to prepare the men for the eventuality of delays, yet urged them to maintain their morale and optimism. He perched himself on the chart desk in main control and spoke to them over the general announcing system. He talked reassuringly, in terms of the exact time when the rescue vessel would be overhead and the first group would embark in the bell. In the meantime alert watches had to be maintained on the reactor which furnished the electrical power for the oxygen generator and air purifiers. Failure of this energy source and life support machinery would shorten their survival to about forty-eight hours. They must be prepared should sea conditions on the surface postpone the rescue attempt.

Lt. Delmore Ritter, the engineering officer, listened to the Exec's voice coming from the speaker over his head in the reactor room. His eyes roved over the pressure and temperature gauges on the stainless steel control panel. The reactor had always been the center of his mechanical domain. Its huge, shielded bulk hummed softly with the harnessed power. It lived through the constant generation of colliding atoms that released infinitesimal sparks of energy. Heat flashed water into steam, which under pressure drove the turbines and armatures of motors. It lived almost without supervision and functioned exactly. He looked at a pressure gauge, tapped it with satisfaction, and thought as long as it lives, we live. How much more important this great machine was now. Miles of highly polished steel tubes coiled in a network of mechanical intestines carried the life force generated by the great burning heart.

The engineman on watch drew a water sample carefully, like a doctor extracting a blood specimen, and put it through the analyzer. He noted the results in his log. "Specific gravity normal, no contamination, Mr. Ritter. She's in good shape."

Ritter listened abstractedly, plucked at his nose, and muttered, "Yeah." As he bent over the machinery check-off lists, he thought about their predicament. He didn't expect rescue immediately. If any of them were ever to get out, it would be after a long wait, he felt sure of that. Five of his men were already gone; they had been the engineroom watch. A couple of nonrated men had managed to jump through the opening of the watertight door before it was shut and dogged. He remembered the vivid description given by the watch in the machinery compartment. The doomed men were in the after part of the flooding engineroom struggling helplessly in the torrent of water.

Ritter looked up as chief auxiliaryman George Benson came into the compartment. The chief had just completed a personal check of all bilges to determine if there was an increase in water accumulation. Ordinarily, leakage around sea-stop valves presented no problem, as excess water was easily disposed of by the bilge pump. However, the pump was now inoperative. Probably the overboard discharge line was blocked by mud.

The chief was a fat man, and he was breathing heavily from the exertion of climbing up and down the ladders to the lower flats of compartments. He mopped his red face with a rag.

"We're getting a small amount of water from two sea-stops, but nothing to worry about. Sanitary tanks one and two need blowing, but Christ, we'll have to be careful with that because of the pressure at this depth. It'll mean a lot of inboard venting too, which will stink up the boat something fierce." He squatted on the trash can next to the control console and wiped the back of his neck reflectively. "Sure taking a long time for anyone to come looking for us."

The Exec was thinking about this too. They should be making some sort of contact with the surface. The sonar was out of commission for the time being, so they could not hear the sounds of approaching ships. He had made several transmissions on the underwater telephone with no results, which was not surprising because of the short range of this voice equipment. He was anxious for some outside contact; the suspense of waiting was bad for morale. The men huddled in groups, talking. A strange noise, such as a dropped tool or the closing of a locker door, would suspend all conversation and they would listen carefully. It was better now with the ventilation going again. The unearthly silence when everything was shut down for collision quarters had been unnerving. Once the damage reports were in and the spaces inspected for watertight integrity, it was possible to open the bulkhead flappers between the compartments. Now the accustomed soft howl of blowers gave a feeling of normality.

By tapping on the after bulkhead of the machinery compartment it had been determined that the engineroom was more than two-thirds full of water. The upper portion of that space had an air pocket created by blowing the water level down to the rupture. The *Lancerfish* would never surface again, she was there to stay. A chilling prospect, Crawford thought, but it didn't mean they must share this fate. Something surely could be done, the Navy wouldn't just leave them there. The fact that no submarine rescue had ever been attempted so deep made him a little apprehensive. If they got out it would be a record, no doubt about that. Once they could talk to their rescuers and let them know the condition of the boat, action would start. For now, they had to endure the worst part, the waiting. He looked at his watch and thought about his family. They must have the word at home now. He wondered how his wife was taking it. Once the sub made contact with the surface, there would be some comfort for the dependents. For a few of them it would be the end of hope.

The breech door on the signal ejector now had clamps holding it against the tremendous sea pressure. Lt. Hayman inspected the installation carefully. If that inner door failed, water would explode into the torpedo room at more than 500 pounds per square inch. It would take only a short time to flood the compartment, and their sole route of escape would be cut off. If the rescue bell could reach them, it would have to seat on the upper hatch of the escape trunk, which was in the overhead of the torpedo room. Hayman pictured the steel cable that stretched from the top of the hatch up through hundreds of feet of black water. He hoped the buoy was bobbing on the surface now and not still underwater. He doubted the chief-of-the-boat's claim that there was more than 1270 feet of cable on the payout drum. Hayman had heard of instances of new reels being delivered with the even amount of 200 fathoms. Being 70 feet short was not a serious matter for a rescue system designed for an operational depth of 850 feet. There was a pretty good chance that their cable was the regulation length and would reach the surface. The depth of the *Lancerfish* was 1235 feet by the deep gauge. There was a difference of 25 feet between the keel and the top of the hatch. That gave them an extra 60 feet; the buoy must be on the surface. Then an unpleasant thought occurred to him. If there was a current, even a moderate one, the buoy would be carried by it. Two hundred fathoms is a long reach and the resultant cable angle tending in the current would mean the buoy was still submerged.

Hayman went aft to the control room, where the Exec was standing by the underwater telephone.

"Commander, got a moment?" He gestured to the unoccupied side of the compartment, wanting to speak to Crawford privately. He described his evaluation of the messenger buoy and cable and drew a pencil sketch on the bulkhead. Crawford listened tolerantly and said, "Chief Harris says he's pretty sure there was fifteen hundred feet of cable on that reel when it was delivered."

"That's wishful thinking. The chief *wants* to believe. . . ."

"I've got quite a respect for that chief, Hayman. Anyway you were probably spinning your wheels on something else that day."

41

Crawford smiled condescendingly, but his light blue eyes were hard. Hayman was infuriated and his old resentment welled up. He was a "mustang," an officer who had come up through the ranks, and all of his sixteen years in the Navy had been in the submarine service. Yet the Exec always favored Chief Harris with more professional respect than he gave to him. Hell, Hayman thought, he had been a chief-of-the-boat at one time too, before his commissioning, and yet the Exec treated him like some green ensign. Harris too, in his quiet, self-assured manner, didn't quite take to having an ex-enlisted man giving him orders. Those times in the past when Harris won the Exec's support over Hayman, the chief would roll his chewing gum, smile slightly, and turn casually away, smug in victory.

Johnson, the leading sonarman, approached them, interrupting the conference. "Commander, no dice on the sonar, the casualty is in the transducer topside." Crawford sighed and sidled past Hayman and returned to the underwater telephone by the chart desk. A vague consternation showed in his face as he looked at his watch again.

Hayman moved off toward the wardroom, still rankled by Crawford's brush-off. He supposed many regarded him as an imposter, because he had not thrown his cap in the air at Annapolis. Maybe he was overly sensitive and identified too closely with the enlisted men. Sometimes he was deliberately crass in order to be accepted by the crew. He never felt that he belonged in the forward compartment—Officer's Country. Crawford had once made a laconic remark at the wardroom table after Hayman had purposely used some sailor obscenity. The Exec had observed, "You can take a man out of the crew's quarters, but you can't take the crew's quarters out of him."

Well, the hell with them, Hayman thought, he did a better job than the other junior officers. He took the Navy more seriously. Hayman comforted himself with the knowledge that he was a "professional," he lived with the Navy and believed in it. It was his career, whereas reserve officers like Fitzgibbons and Langworthy seemed to think the forward compartment was a fraternity house. College kids, Christ! And yet with them Crawford displayed some deference and accepted them as officers. On the other hand, he treated him like an enlisted man, refusing to recognize his commissioned status. When Crawford had first reported to the boat as the new executive officer, he habitually called him by his surname. He seemed to enjoy singling him out to underscore some wardroom gaffe or reprimand him for an insignificant offense, such as failing to write his log immediately after a watch.

Hayman found Langworthy in the wardroom going over a diagram of the oxygen generator. The fold-out pages of the manual were spread on the table, and the assistant engineer sat hunched over them, reading intently.

"Ritter wants us to constantly trouble shoot on the oh-two jenny," Langworthy said. "We've got to anticipate breakdowns before they happen." He mimicked Ritter's mannerism of stroking his nose with thumb and forefinger. "What a ball of wax, huh?"

Hayman sat on the upholstered bench that formed seats for one side of the table. Langworthy continued.

"Man, if I get out of this bind, you know what you can do with submarine duty. If nothing else, I want to get out of here just so I can testify against that idiot who hit us. You never saw anything like it, Robbie, it was as though he *tried* to nail us." His face sobered with his thoughts, then he mused aloud, "Wonder if they picked up the Old Man."

The black, willowy silhouette of Rumford, the steward's mate, came into the wardroom wearing his white jacket. He waited for Langworthy to clear off his manual so he could set the table. Rumford's six-foot, two-inch height and skinny frame had provided him with the nickname "Totem." He had a perpetual stoop from living aboard submarines and continually ducking overhead valves. As he spread the heavy linen tablecloth, set out the napkin rings and silver, it occurred to Hayman that Rumford only remotely understood the predicament they were in. The young steward went about his duties as he had always performed them. The fact that the *Lancerfish* was actually sunk, stranded on the bottom, did not seem to pertain to him. That was for the officers to worry about. They handled the submarine and somehow things always worked out. Hayman studied the Negro's expressionless face.

"What's for lunch, Totem?"

"Pea soup, sir, an' cold cuts with the cherry pie from last night." He grinned cheerfully.

Some of the other officers began to appear at the door and look around the compartment. John Fitzgibbons, the operations officer, dropped into his customary seat, his round face had a vacant, slightly worried expression. "Where's ouah leader?" he drawled to no one in particular. Hayman regarded him with some annoyance. He didn't like the chubby Southerner who seemed always to have something to say, no matter how inane it might be. Fitzgibbons felt compelled to talk, to keep up a constant chatter and comment on every remark, action, or mood that took place around him. At other times in the wardroom he would add his exasperating giggle to almost anything that was said. With the enlisted men, however, Fitzgibbons maintained a haughty condescension, and was disliked by them. One of his collateral duties on the *Lancerfish* was the assignment as the "Moral Guidance Officer." His particular qualifications stemmed from the fact that for a brief period he had studied for the ministry. In this capacity he sometimes conducted lay services on Sundays, when the sub was at sea. His evangelical enthusiasm once inspired one of Hayman's torpedomen to refer to him as "John the Baptist." Fitzgibbons, overhearing it, promptly put the man on report.

Other officers crowded into the small wardroom, took their places, and waited for the executive officer. When Crawford joined them at the end of the table, he refused the bowl of soup and asked only for a sandwich. To Hayman, the Captain's absence was accentuated by this gathering for the noon meal. Small things, too, reminded him of the terrible reality of their plight. Earlier, when he had passed the Captain's cabin, he had noticed the bunk light was still burning and the khaki uniform hung still and empty on the back of a chair. The brown, regulation shoes were beside the bunk where the captain had kicked them off before turning in. He must have gone to the bridge in just his slippers and bridge coat. Also, when Hayman had made his tour of the compartments and come up to the tightly dogged door leading to the flooded engineroom, a terrible apprehension had overwhelmed him. The door and its heavy steel handle were covered with an icy moisture.

They had been on the bottom more than twelve hours now, and there was no sign of anyone searching for them. A big disappointment had been the loss of the sonar with which they could have heard propellers of search vessels, even if they had been some distance away. Crawford spoke to Lt(jg) Evers.

"Tom, when you finish lunch, relieve Chief Harris in main control and start transmitting on the underwater telephone every two minutes. Now is the most likely time a search vessel might be in the area."

"Aye, sir."

The rescue vessel could possibly be on station even now. Maybe they're attaching to the downhaul cable, Crawford thought. No, it would not be this soon, they have to put down a deep moor, and that kind of rattling around on the surface would be heard. If they had found the buoy, someone would have tried to get them on the underwater telephone. Suppose Hayman is right and the messenger buoy didn't make it all the way up? He looked at the torpedo officer eating pensively at the end of the table, his skinny shoulders hunched forward as he wolfed his food. He often clashed with Hayman, generally over minor incidents. There was an antagonism, a challenge to his authority. They were near the same age, though he had a half stripe more in rank. Crawford had gone a different route for his commission, and he felt he had worked harder for it. It had been a struggle during those years at the university, working at night to help pay the way. Then he had joined the NROTC program, which eventually got him a reserve commission. Near the end of his obligated service he had decided to make the Navy a career and had applied for a regular appointment. Hayman had served more than ten years as an enlisted man before getting his commission. He had taken the highly competitive examination for Officer Candidate School and after selection spent only four months of intensive training to achieve his unrestricted status as an officer. It hardly seemed fair.

There was no doubt in Crawford's mind that Hayman had most likely been an exceptional man. But, as frequently happens when the Navy rewards superior enlisted service this way, they replace a good sailor with an unexceptional officer. He hoped Harris was right about the length of the downhaul cable. But, even if it was short, additional wire could be added somehow. The weather forecast of the previous night wasn't encouraging, though; winds, small craft warnings, that would slow rescue too.

"It's quiet as a tomb down here."

Fitzgibbons' drawl interrupted the stillness. "Guess that wasn't a good analogy," he added. He looked at the Exec and gave a short laugh. "My daddy used to say that when you find yourself in a tight spot, keep a good sense of humor." Hayman cast an impatient look at Fitzgibbons.

"Yeah, Fitz, I notice you're always delighting us with yours." He bit deeply into his sandwich.

There was something different in Fitzgibbons' expression. His eyes had a restless awareness, like that of a cornered animal. His quips and running comments were completely automatic, as though his thoughts were elsewhere. Scared out of his wits, Hayman guessed.

The assistant operations officer and navigator, Lt(jg) Evers, edged out of his seat and moved toward the passageway. He sucked in his stomach as he eased around the Exec's chair, swelling his football player's chest. He was a large, athletic youth two years out of the Naval Academy. His short, blond crewcut accentuated the clean, regular features. Generally, Evers was an affable and happy member of the wardroom, but now he wore a sober, concentrated expression.

"I'll relieve Chief Harris now, sir," he said to the Exec, as though about to perform some extraordinary duty.

He's scared too, Hayman decided, but he's making the most of being the dedicated *naval officer*. I guess we're all a bit shaky. Wonder what my face looks like.

Lt. Ritter came into the wardroom and took Evers' seat at the table. Before sitting down he held the palm of his hand to the outlet of the supply vent, testing the airflow. He spoke to the Exec without looking at him. "I'm bleeding a few more liters of oxygen into the air. It should be enough, nobody's working hard. Considering that number one scrubber isn't up to snuff, the CO_2 isn't bad." He snapped his napkin from the ring and glanced from side to side along the table to see what the noon fare was. "Totem, I'll have some of your soup," he called through the serving window into the pantry. He turned to the Exec and said sprightly, "Everything clicks, Bob, conditions normal on the reactor." Ritter was the only officer outside of the Captain who called the Exec by his first name. Hayman liked Ritter and admired his self-confident efficiency. They had been friends for two years, and now Hayman was proud of his shipmate. Old Del wasn't scared, by God.

"Quiet!"

The Exec stopped chewing and held his sandwich in front of him like an offering, his head cocked to listen. They all turned to stare at him as they listened too. Hayman heard nothing unusual, but he waited with breath held. Crawford relaxed. "Thought I heard something from outside," he explained and went on eating.

In the after compartment there was a similar atmosphere of restraint and preoccupied tension. Nearly half of the survivors were gathered in the crew's dinette near the warmth of the galley. Some sprawled on the mess benches, and others huddled around the galley door watching the cook and one seaman produce sandwiches. Two large pots of soup bubbled on the electric range. The air was comfortable and steamy with the smell of food. Under normal conditions the dinette was the social center for men off watch. Between meal periods the crewmembers collected there to play cards, write letters, or just sit over coffee cups and talk.

It was a large compartment decorated in warm yellows and browns. The table tops were various pastel colors, and the benches were covered with a red vinyl. The dinette was more reminiscent of a modish ice cream parlor than a compartment in a submarine, except for the emergency vent valves that protruded from the bulkhead like small steering wheels. The decor was what the Navy termed "environmental habitability." On the port side were a television set and stereophonic tape recorder, which at other times played almost continuously. The atmosphere was different now; a sober anxiety dominated conversations. There was no snap of pinochle cards or the rattle of dice on the acey deucy board, or even the usual muted hubbub of brusque voices. The men exhibited a constraint and unusual politeness to one another. There was little gregarious horseplay.

Seaman Cruthers sat with his feet up on a corner bench, his back pressed to the curve of the bulkhead. He was built small, though with fine proportions. At first glance his shortness and tidy frame suggested a young boy not yet in his teens. His very blond hair and undeveloped features emphasized his physical immaturity. The crew called him "Mouse," a name that he had resisted indignantly during his first months aboard the *Lancerfish* but which he now accepted with resignation. He leaned sideways across the table toward Dirksen.

"Gimme a butt, Rowboat, before they put the smoking lamp out again."

Dirksen ruefully shook out a cigarette and complained, "You're always bumming," and sat down across from him.

"What do you think, Mouse, maybe we'll get out of here today? Chief Harris says he knows there'll be no problem once a rescue ship finds our buoy. Damn, I don't want to spend the night here."

Cruthers dragged on his cigarette and shot the smoke in front of him. "Don't bet on it. A moor has to be laid first, and that could take a whole afternoon. We'll get out of here sooner or later."

Dirksen fiddled with his pack of cigarettes, deep in thought, his fatty frame hunched forward on the table. "Man, I want to get out of here. How long's it going to take?" He was young, less than twenty years old, and had been in the submarine service just over a year. He had not completed his qualification, though Lt. Hayman had been nagging him to speed up his studying to earn his dolphins. He was large, but there was something soft about his size. His milk-white Nordic skin made him look almost womanish. Now his blue eyes stared vacantly at the pack of cigarettes that he tapped from side to side.

"I don't mind telling you, Mouse, I don't like it, I want to split." He looked around the compartment to see if anyone else had heard him. "Screw this."

"You're not alone, Babe, take it easy. Look at it this way; we're watertight, the reactor is cooking, and we've got air. So, all we have to do is sit here and wait 'til they get the bell fixed up to start pulling us out. When we hit the surface we'll get a new seabag, a thirty-day survivor's leave, and we'll be heroes. Now we just gotta sweat it out."

Dirksen relaxed a little. "Yeah, I guess so, but man, I hope that oh-two jenny doesn't crap out."

The cook carried out a tray piled with sandwiches and placed it on a table. "Okay, sailors, chow down. Get your soup from the galley." The men crowded around and the pile shrank. Cruthers took a sandwich and peeked at its contents. "Horsecock and cheese," he commented dryly. "What's the matter, Bartolla, you mad at the crew again?"

The dinette filled with men, some wearing foul weather jackets, for it was damp and chilly in the torpedo room. Soup bowls had to be held to prevent them from sliding along the table, because of the port list. The fact that the *Lancerfish* was heeled over twelve degrees and hard aground was a constant reminder of their plight. There was no heave and thrust to the deck, or vibration from the reduction gears. It was too quiet, immovably solid, and too permanent. Some of the men, the ones that had been on watch at the time of the collision, still wore their orange life vests.

Cruthers had no doubts about eventual escape from the submarine. It was not so much unshakable optimism as it was his training and confidence in the *Lancerfish*. Everything he had been taught at the submarine school and later during "school of the boat" sessions was predicated on disaster. If a salt water line gave way, a stop valve could be shut. Or, if an electrical distribution panel shorted, the load could be shunted elsewhere. Every system was backed up by an emergency measure of some sort. Even now, the predicament of the *Lancerfish* was nothing more to Cruthers than an example of damage control. With all reserve buoyancy lost by the flooding of the engineroom and the main ballast tanks ruptured, they could not surface. So, now they would get out by the rescue bell. Hell, he thought, all he would lose would be some dirty dungarees. It was only a matter of time. He finished his sandwich and drank off his cup of canned orange juice in one long breath.

"Yeah, Rowboat, all you gotta do is keep a tight ass and wait. By tomorrow the rescue ship will be here. But even if we don't ride the bell up, we can go out with escape hoods. We're only five minutes away from the surface by buoyant ascent."

Chief petty officer Timothy Ryan, the *Lancerfish*'s hospital corpsman, listened to this innocent appraisal tolerantly. The chief had been a diver before joining the submarine service and knew the problems of deep-sea diving. When he had been with the Navy Experimental Diving Unit, testing new techniques, they had thought 600 feet to be nearly maximum for a diver. Some of the new equipment permitted deeper dives using mixed gases on various schedules. There had even been some simulated dives in the laboratory to 1000 feet, but open-sea diving was very different. The chief paused over his soup and remarked to the air in front of him, "Forget it, can't be done."

"Why not, chief?" Cruthers twisted around in his seat. "Look, if you put four or five guys in the escape trunk at a time, charge them up fast, they could be on their way up in a couple of minutes. Might burst an eardrum or two, but what the hell."

"Can't do it, Mouse." Ryan wiped his mouth and turned to the young seaman and spoke authoritatively. "In the first place, we haven't got a mixed gas to breathe. On compressed air you'd get oxygen poisoning at this depth. You'd pass out or go into convulsions before the escape trunk could be equalized with sea pressure. Anyway, if you could hold out until the pressure was built up and headed out, you'd have explosive bends before you got to the surface. The only way out of here is by the rescue bell, and at that, twelve hundred feet is pushing it. That chamber is the only way. If it doesn't work, you'd better start talking to your Buddha." The chief's words left a silence in the compartment, with each man lost in his own stark thoughts.

During the early part of the afternoon watch the Exec set up a schedule for underwater telephone transmissions. At first it was every five minutes, then it was shifted to a series of calls every fifteen minutes. At 1500 Crawford tried the telephone himself, as though his authority would give a greater range to the sound impulses.

"Hello, any station, any station, this is *Lancerfish,* can you hear me? Over."

His voice, amplified on the speaker, sounded mechanical as it squawked and echoed into the depths. There was no reply except for the hiss and crackle of the speaker.

On the surface, nearly five miles away to the south, the ships of the rescue force pitched and rolled in their fruitless search.

4 – WAITING

CRAWFORD SAT AT the wardroom table drawing on the back of a navigational chart. Slowly he laid off a profile of the *Lancerfish*, referring frequently to a diagram in the Ship's Characteristics Manual. He had sketched the sea floor, shoaling steeply, and an outcropping on which he supposed the submarine rested. He darkened the after section and printed "flooded" under it. From the torpedo room escape hatch he drew a cable with a buoy on the surface and the legend "1235 feet."

He paused and studied the drawing. He was beginning to feel optimistic about their situation. He could think of no reason why the rescue bell could not make such a deep dive. After all, it probably had a wide safety margin designed into it. Mooring the rescue vessel in such deep water would be a problem, might even take a couple of days, but eventually their nightmare would be over.

He consulted the status reports of machinery and supplies. The life support system was functioning, except that number two CO_2 analyzer and one air purifier were out of commission. Del had his engineers working on the gear and had predicted the scrubber would be back on the line within a few hours. The fresh water distillation units were producing only a fraction of their normal output, but they had 1800 gallons on hand, more than enough for several days. Still, they had better start rationing, and he jotted on a scratch pad. He made another notation to keep personnel as quiet as possible to reduce carbon dioxide build-up and conserve oxygen. Off-duty crewmembers would either turn in to their bunks or remain in one location to minimize physical effort. As he thought of each requirement for survival, he added it to the list. One problem that at first caused some consternation was the fact that there had been a continuous increase of water in the torpedo room bilges. The bilge pump was completely inoperative, as was the trim pump, which could have been cross connected to the drain line. This was most likely caused by the fact that the exterior sea chests were buried in the bottom. The increase was slight and probably would present no real problem if they didn't have to spend too many days in the boat. If it really became necessary to get rid of the water, it could be bailed and dumped into a sanitary tank, which when filled could be blown to sea. Rumford poured the Exec another cup of coffee and peered at the drawing on the table.

"We going to use the rescue bell, Commander?" He cocked his head for a better view.

Crawford sat back contemplating his drawing and answered, "It's the only way." Hayman and Fitzgibbons had come into the wardroom, sliding into seats opposite Crawford. Hayman looked over the crudely sketched diagram and observed without looking up, "Yeah, Totem, it looks like your weekend has been messed up."

Crawford sent Rumford to round up the officers for another conference. He wanted to promulgate his list of instructions and give them a reassessment of the situation. Then he would speak to the crew again over the loud-speaker system. He added one more note to the list, to release oil from the auxiliary fuel oil tanks in the morning.

This would create a slick on the surface which might be spotted by a passing ship.

"You don't really think that will do any good, do you, Commander?" Hayman said, his thin mouth smiling cynically. "What with all the existing pollution, a ship would think it pretty routine."

The disappointment of not having made surface contact during the first day on the bottom eased somewhat. The men began talking more hopefully, and even joked about their predicament.

"Hey, Rowboat," Cruthers called out during the evening meal in the dinette, "Chief Harris says you've been designated to stay behind when the bell comes, to act as security watch." Dirksen grinned at the scatter of laughter and said with a full mouth, "Yeah, up yours, Mouse." There was a lively, almost normal ambience in the compartment. Chief Ryan ate methodically, thinking about the days when he served as a diver on the rescue vessel *Tringa*. He added nothing to the conversation and felt less hopeful than the others.

Hayman lay awake that first night on the bottom and fought a dread feeling that repeatedly crept up on him. The thought that for the moment there was no way out of the *Lancerfish,* and might never be, would swell to near panic. He had never felt the pangs of claustrophobia until now. The fact that he was sealed and trapped until outside help came was terrible. Somehow he could not evoke any confidence in the rescue bell, even if the buoy was on the surface. There must be a reason why it had only an operational capability of 850 feet. Then he would argue his thoughts down and think about the surface efforts that were most likely being pursued at that very moment. Once they were found, and the Navy knew there were men alive on the *Lancerfish,* they would use everything at their disposal to get

55

them out. He stared into the almost darkened little stateroom, wishing that Hughes, the young electrical officer who shared the quarters, had not been in the engineroom when it flooded. His absence was a constant reminder of death, perhaps his own fate soon. Hayman closed his eyes and thoughts chased back and forth, preventing sleep.

Shortly after midnight Hayman heard a loud exclamation in the torpedo room, then another excited voice: "I heard it too!"

Propellers!

Within minutes the entire crew had the news, which was verified by other men who had been awake. A ship had passed over them. Those that heard the beat of the propellers agreed they sounded like a destroyer. The sound had first been picked up in the relative quiet of the torpedo room. It was a fast, thrashing sound that galloped closer and closer, then quickly faded. The ship must have passed directly over them. Most of the crew stayed awake the remainder of the night, and their talk took on a confident tone. Even Chief Ryan felt a little relieved. At least someone was up there. Underwater telephone transmissions were made for the next twenty minutes, though it was doubtful such a fast moving ship would pick up their signals.

At 0730 on Sunday, May sixteenth, number two auxiliary fuel tank was blown to sea and the crew of the *Lancerfish* sat down to breakfast, believing that this was the day they would be found. Later in the morning the Exec again sent out UQC transmissions and interspersed them with the release of air from negative tank. During lunch of this second day, the men in the wardroom and crew's dinette were in much improved spirits. They even accepted the possibility that another day would go by before rescue. Crawford looked at the faces of the officers busy eating and talking. They appeared a little tired and their faces were darkened by two-day-old beards, but they were animated.

The hours dragged by and the day slowly progressed while the crew waited for something to happen. In the afternoon Ritter called the Exec to the reactor room where a problem was developing. An overboard discharge pump was overheating and producing a pulsing squeal. Ritter had consulted with his chief auxiliaryman, Benson, and decided the pump was overloaded by the tremendous back pressure of the sea. Probably the outlet was blocked by mud.

Crawford lowered himself through the small hatch going into the reactor room. The baking heat surprised him; he felt out of place among the gauges and pipes. On the control panel rows of status lights flickered mysteriously, indicating the internal condition of the atomic pile. Ritter moved close to Crawford and shouted over the noise of the pump. They would have to shift to an emergency pump for a while to let the other cool. Then it would be dismantled for inspection and replacement of the impeller, if necessary. The problem, of course, would not be solved, but there was nothing else to do. It would then become a matter of switching from one pump to the other as they heated up.

"And what if they both finally seize up, Del?" Crawford peered questioningly at the engineering officer, hoping he would have some ready alternative.

"We'll have to shut down the reactor." Ritter met Crawford's concerned look, and a semblance of a smile touched the corners of his mouth. It was a look of philosophical acceptance. "And that'll be the ballgame," he said, plucking at his nose.

Crawford made a quick calculation; if the reactor failed, they could shift to the battery, which would provide power for perhaps thirty-six hours. After that the oxygen reserve in the flasks and the lithium hydroxide abosrbent on hand would carry them for another ten to fifteen hours. A little over two days altogether. Crawford nodded to Ritter.

"Okay, Del, get on with it. Keep me informed of progress."

Crawford was sweating when he returned to the control room. He was glad to escape from the small compartment and its heat. The control room with its diving stand and the periscope island looked more familiar to him. He supposed that during the nineteen months he had been aboard the *Lancerfish* he had been in the lower section of the reactor room only half a dozen times.

Fitzgibbons was writing in the ship's log, having just completed his watch as officer-of-the-deck. Chief Harris leaned over the chart table and studied the Exec's diagram of the submarine, which was displayed for the benefit of the crew. He looked up when Crawford addressed him.

"How's it going, Chief?"

"Bit of good news, Commander. Lt. Langworthy figured our actual depth to be less than twelve hundred feet. He took pressure readings from the torpedo room and control room, averaged them out, then corrected for salinity and temperature. He says the top of the escape trunk is about eleven hundred and ninety-five feet from the surface. Sounds better than what the gauge reads. But the water is up another three inches in the torpedo room bilge since last night. Some of it is condensate, but the gag on the signal ejector now has a steady dribble."

Crawford nodded and glanced over the check-off list. "We'll start bailing in the morning if we have to. In the meantime have the bilge inspected every half hour."

Fitzgibbons read over what he had written in the log, shut it, and put his pen back in his shirt pocket. His face wore a look of gloom as he went forward to the wardroom. Crawford opened the log and turned to the page dated May fourteenth. It read like thousands of other logs he had seen in the past, with stock phrases such as "underway on the surface as before," or "answering bells on the reactor." After the 2300 routine entry there followed two pages of Langworthy's small script describing the tactics used to avoid the merchant ship, the collision, and the frantic efforts to restore buoyancy after diving. At the end of this long account was a list of the men lost in the after part of the boat, giving name, rank, and serial number dispassionately and according to regulations.

Crawford frowned when he came to the freshly written remarks by Fitzgibbons on the next page:

1200–1600: Sunk as before in 1235 feet of water in position 39° 28′north Lat. and 72° 07′ west Long. It has been forty hours since the collision and indications of search and rescue operations. The reactor is providing auxiliary power and the oxygen generator is delivering O_2 make-up. It is doubtful that a rescue bell could be brought to this depth, even if we are found. The life support equipment in *Lancerfish* can sustain us for weeks, perhaps months, but it is only prolonging the suffering. At the end of the waiting is death, the only escape. May God give us strength until He comes.

This superfluous entry in the official log annoyed Crawford. But what worried him most was the frame of mind Fitzgibbons was displaying. The Exec had observed him earlier, sitting morosely on his bunk, lost in thought. He seemed to avoid the others and seek isolation in order to brood about the unequivocal horror of their predicament. Fitzgibbons was sure they were all going to die there on the bottom. He had no hope, and this angered Crawford because he considered their situation with more optimism. After all, the *Lancerfish* had made it to shallower water where rescue was possible. If they had gone down where they were hit, they would be in a much worse fix and probably would not be able to get out. Or one of the sea valves might have blown in at those depths, flooding the rest of the boat. Hayman, too, seemed a bit pessimistic, a little too ready to believe the worst about the cable. But at least he wasn't mooning around, muttering predictions of doom. The attitude of the men in general was good. They were hopeful, even confident in some cases. He couldn't let Fitzgibbons' mood spread to the other men. Perhaps he would have a talk with him.

For now, however, he had to prepare the men for another night of waiting. Crawford hoisted his stocky frame onto the chart table and pulled the microphone of the general announcing system to his mouth.

"This is the Exec. I know this waiting to be found is becoming a strain. There are some good reasons why no one has picked us up yet. The weather indications at the time of collision were deteriorating and there's probably a storm blowing topside. Also, and most important, after we were hit we went ahead at flank speed to make shallower water. That put us nearly four miles away from where we dove. This means the search force must cover a pretty large area in order to locate us. Naturally, the ships would make their first sweeps in the immediate vicinity of the accident. It may take a day or two more before they work their way to where we are. The main thing now is to take it easy. We're quite secure, for the moment." Crawford felt as though he was apologizing for not having been found.

While the Exec was talking, the men suspended all activity and listened attentively. The speaker clicked off and a murmur of voices resumed in the crew's dinette. Cruthers put a reel on the tape recorder and adjusted the volume. The music was startling at first, but it imparted a warm, optimistic quality to the atmosphere. Talk died away as the men turned to listen. The music was a collection of popular folk and protest songs, quite familiar to them all, because they had been frequently played during the cruise.

Hayman stopped by the coffee urn and filled a regulation cup, and leaned against a table. Two more songs, then a melancholy guitar throbbed some chords and a girl's voice, pure and sweet, filled the compartment. The words of the ballad were melancholy and dominated the men sitting on the mess benches. Cruthers stirred uncomfortably. He pushed a button and the reel spun rapidly away from the depressing song, stopping in the middle of a trumpet solo.

Hayman put a foot up on a mess bench and leaned on

his skinny knee. He looked about the cheerful, brightly lit dinette. The men seemed to have each drawn away to their private thoughts. On some of the faces he glimpsed unguarded fear. The lyrics of the song had caught them unawares. Their reaction was so unanimously sudden and terrible that it uncovered the desperate fear that lurked in Hayman's subconscious as well. The palms of his hands were wet and a chill ran from the base of his skull down his spine and into his legs. The whole established order of the Navy evaporated. They were all one and the same, frightened human animals. There was no division of rank and ratings, seamen, petty officers, chiefs. Even his lieutenant bars were suddenly meaningless and belonged to another world. He had to say something, bring some rational perspective back to the group. He called to Cruthers, "The Exec says we can have a movie tonight. What's left we haven't seen?"

The young seaman took a small bundle of program folders from behind the television set and spread them like a poker hand. "The only one we haven't shown twice is *The Bible,* but it's too long; six reels of miracles in cinemascope." Cruthers thumbed through the grimy, well worn stack. "How about *Return to Paradise,* Mr. Hayman? That's not bad, it's got some good-looking—" he paused, looking at Hayman in his innocent, choirboy manner—"chicks in it."

Hayman dumped the remains of his cup in the sink. "Okay, Mouse, let's set it up after the evening meal." He headed forward to the wardroom.

As he passed the radio cubicle in the control room, Hayman saw Schoenberg, the first class radioman, sitting at his console. His earphones were on the desk in front of him and a message form was wound in the typewriter. The scene was so familiar and normal that for a moment Hayman found it difficult to believe the *Lancerfish* was actually sunk. It was as though they were cruising on the surface and Schoenberg was ready to copy the schedules, or transmit a diving message. Hayman climbed through the short water-tight door to the forward compartment and moved along the canted deck. The heavy green curtains of the staterooms on the starboard side hung into the passageway because of the list to port. As he passed the Exec's room he noted Fitzgibbons sitting in the desk chair and Crawford sprawled on his narrow berth. They were talking earnestly, and Hayman wondered what the private conference was about.

Hayman found Langworthy, Evers, and Roche talking in the wardroom. They were at one end of the table, which was littered with dirty cups and empty juice cans. Langworthy was describing the air supply and revitalization system.

"The problem is keeping the CO_2 down. The oxygen generator can stay ahead of consumption, but one of the scrubbers isn't working and the carbon dioxide is building up in low spaces. It's not serious yet, and the chief is working on it, but we can't let it get ahead of us. Personnel will have to be kept quiet, to reduce further accumulation."

"We're bound to be found soon," Evers commented, "then we can get out of here. I wonder how long they would keep up the search if they didn't, though." He looked across to Hayman. "What do you think, Robbie?"

Hayman leaned forward, his elbows on the table and one fist cupped by the other hand, and meditated briefly. It pleased him to be consulted and recognized as an authority because of his experience. After all, he reflected, he had been a submariner before they were in high school. He spoke confidently, as though he felt the conviction of his words.

"The Navy knows we have an almost unlimited endurance submerged. They know that if the reactor and forward compartments were saved we could last for God knows how long. I'd say they would search indefinitely."

"We might have the air," Roche said, "but I know we can't last indefinitely. We're low on provisions." He smiled wistfully. "That would be ironical; starving instead of suffocating on the bottom of the sea."

Hayman regarded the junior officer. In spite of his youth Roche had an aura of mature sophistication. Hayman had always been vaguely intimidated by him. Roche was the only child of a wealthy family who had given him all the benefits of their affluence as he grew up. He had gone to the best schools, traveled extensively abroad, and as a young bachelor squired the daughters of other influential families. Yet what impressed Hayman the most about Roche was his unaffected, casual attitude toward his wealth and social position. On a few occasions Hayman had glimpsed his other life, the one in which he really belonged. Once, at a flag reception given for a visiting French submarine in New London, he had observed Roche chatting urbanely with a *capitaine de corvette* in flawless French. At another time, during a port call in Washington, Roche had brought aboard a U. S. Senator, a friend of his family. Hayman had been impressed when he heard Roche call the legislator by his first name.

Roche continued matter-of-factly, "Certainly, we'll be found eventually, which will be some comfort. But, Robbie, even if your buoy *is* on the surface, it's doubtful that a rescue bell can reach us at this depth."

"They'll modify it, if necessary," Hayman said, though he felt less optimistic than his words. It was going to take a lot of time and there were many things that could bring their continued existence quickly to an end. If they could not repair the scrubber and the carbon dioxide rose to a lethal percentage, or if the reactor itself had to be shut down and oxygen could not be made, it would be over in a couple of days. Long before any new rescue device could get to them, they could all be dead. The permanent heel to port and the awful immobility of the submarine seemed to mock whatever confidence Hayman could sometimes muster. The *Lancerfish* was down forever, only some of her organs still

63

functioned, like a mortally wounded animal that was slowly dying. The horror of lingering on, the futile waiting for an impossible rescue, oppressed him once more.

The human comfort Hayman sought from his fellow officers was no help to him now and his fear again swelled uncontrollably. So, they could live until the food ran out, or one of the life support systems failed, then death. Yet he couldn't show this fear, or speak of it to the others. The façade of human perseverance and indomitable spirit had to be kept up. The ego and Navy Regulations did not permit revelation of personal terror. He wondered if the others felt this appalling fear and were only hiding it. He remembered years ago reading about a scientist who was preparing for a deep bathysphere dive. The scientist had considered taking a pistol with him, in case the cable broke; he was not prepared to face death any longer than necessary.

Fitzgibbons came to the wardroom and took a seat on the couch under the curve of the hull. His face was slightly puckered in a gloomy pout, as though he alone suffered this disastrous consequence; their situation was a personal affront to him. Hayman was mildly surprised that his natural dislike for the man still existed under the circumstances. He felt he should be more tolerant and forebearing, and accept the weakness and annoying characteristics in Fitzgibbons. After all, the poor bastard was scared too.

The presence of the others was beginning to pall on Hayman. The constant talk about the situation and prospects of eventual rescue depressed him. He left the wardroom and sought the isolation of his stateroom. Only the desk light was burning. He sat on his bunk, which had been neatly made by Rumford. He wondered how many days would pass before the steward stopped making the bunks each morning and setting the wardroom table for meals. Again, Hayman tried to thrust the morbid thoughts out of his mind, but they persisted. How was Judy taking this? They had known one another for just a few months, yet their relationship had developed rapidly and with a certain inevitability. She had even obliquely talked of marriage, though he was not quite prepared to take that step. There was something in Judy that disturbed him when he thought about being married to her. She seemed a little too gay, almost superficial. Whenever they were at the officer's club, there was a group always around them. She knew everyone, of all ranks.

And now, did she have any hope for his survival? Was she already grieving, adjusting to his loss? Was he facing inevitable death and had not accepted it yet? Was hope, or whatever optimism he could at times call forth, simply a psychological reaction? Was he in fact going to die, slowly, fearfully, and for just a stupid mistake? It was Sunday, and he should be with Judy in New York having a fun weekend.

Hayman unzipped his handbag and took out his writing portfolio. On the inside cover was a photograph of a pretty, dark-haired girl, smiling incessantly. A thin scrawl at the bottom said, "To My Sailor—Forever, Judy." Forever? How meaningless were such words as "forever," or "always." Nothing is that. She will be sad, he mused, maybe even a little anguished for a while, but her memory of him would slowly fade. He would become intangible, a tender thought once in a while, as though he had always been dead. Then, someday, there would be another man in her life. In a month, maybe less, because it is natural to get away from tragedy as soon as possible. How would she be then? Would she smile nostalgically, a bit sadly, when his memory was called up? Dammit, they had to get out!

The curtain to his room suddenly shot back and Fitzgibbons hung in the doorway. "What you doing, Robbie, writing a letter?" He gave his short snicker and eased into the tiny compartment, taking the single chair. Hayman did not answer. He was resentful of this intrusion and felt vulnerable with his thoughts. The light from the desk lamp

65

spread over Fitzgibbons' khaki bulk but left his face lost in shadow.

"Y'all mighty quiet, Robbie. You thinking what I am?"

"Depends, Fitz. Usually it's easy to tell what you're thinking. What's bothering you?"

"I think the Exec is pretty optimistic about us getting out of here, let alone being found. He keeps talking about what 'they' are doing, or the weather's bad on the surface, or anything to avoid the facts. I'm in agreement with you, Robbie, I don't think the buoy is on the surface."

Hayman could not see Fitzgibbons' face in the gloom. He flicked on the bunk light.

"What do you think he should tell us? What else can he do?"

"Be a little more realistic, prepare the men."

"How?"

"Well, give them something to hang on to, maybe more spiritual guidance." His voice lowered and a grave importance urged him forward in the chair.

"Do you believe in prayer, Robbie?"

"Aw, come on, Fitz, you call that realistic?"

"I'm serious, Robbie, I think we ought to pray to God to save us." He pursed his mouth, the lower lip projecting defiantly and stared at Hayman meaningfully. "Really I do, Robbie."

Hayman was vaguely embarrassed, then irritated. He was not religious, though he had been brought up as a Protestant. He had never given spiritual belief much thought. He accepted the church, God, and the power of prayer as part of the world that was supposed to be good, or beneficial; but it didn't apply to him. Though Hayman had never recognized it, he was an atheist by osmosis. His military identification card carried the letter "P" for religion, which to Hayman was like a blood type. He was impatient with Fitzgibbons, who was regarding him fixedly.

"You'd better call on someone closer than that, Fitz."
Then, trying to relieve the moment, he added facetiously,
"Anyway, praying is probably like radio waves; won't
transmit through the water."

"You don't mean that, Robbie. Don't talk like that.
I'm going to ask the Exec if I can lead all hands in silent
meditation, so that each man can talk to his Maker."

Praying! Why did Fitzgibbons anger him so? Maybe it
was because of the suggestion that there was no other hope.
Hayman got up irritably. He wanted to get away from Fitzgibbons.

"Frankly, I don't feel it's as good as the underwater telephone, but have at it, Fitz, say one for me."

Hayman left the stateroom and went to the torpedo
room to inspect the signal ejector again. He would rather
have that vital link with the world operating than the
prayers of fifty Popes.

Because it was Sunday, Crawford gave Fitzgibbons his
approval to conduct services in the torpedo room, for those
that wanted to participate. Fitzgibbons had positioned himself between the tubes and faced his congregation of sailors
in dungarees. Only a few men turned up in response to the
announcement over the loudspeaker system; the remainder
were men that normally berthed in the torpedo room. He
kept checking his watch, and when it was apparent no one
else was coming, he launched into a brief sermon that was
more of a speech. Once during the meeting Hayman paused
at the watertight door leading into the compartment. He
saw the broad shoulders of Tom Evers in the front row,
dutifully setting an example for his men. Some of the men
were perched on bunks over the torpedo racks and some sat
on deck hugging their knees, obediently pious. They were
mostly the crew members that Hayman would have expected to be there, except one, Dirksen. Now why would he

be there, Hayman thought, the most foul-mouthed member of the crew?

Fitzgibbons' voice took on a deeper timbre as he implored, "Almighty God, listen to the prayers of our men." A silence fell over the compartment and the men bowed their heads. One sound could be heard, superimposed upon the occasional shifting of a man—the trickle of water from the signal ejector running into the bilges. It was a melodic sound, and one could almost imagine a hidden stream in a deep forest.

The movie was shown that night in the dinette, with the audience limited to thirty men, to minimize the accumulation of carbon dioxide pockets in one compartment. Even so, only half that number showed up.

At 0730 on Monday morning the crew's berthing compartment was still dark and the air had a quiet thickness about it. Seaman Cruthers awoke from a fitful sleep and lay curled in a fetal position. His body felt sweaty and chilled. The stillness of the compartment accentuated sounds of others breathing or moving restlessly in their bunks. A pair of voices whispered in conversation behind him, and in the distance Cruthers could hear Bartolla and the messcooks stirring in the galley.

Like the day before when he awoke, Cruthers adjusted his thoughts to the sinister predicament and wondered if anything had changed while he slept. He looked across the narrow passage between the bunks and saw Dirksen in the dim light, sleeping fully dressed. He crawled from his bunk and stood shivering in his baggy underwear. Electrician's Mate Lombard came through the compartment with his clipboard and flashlight, making his security inspection.

"Hey, Howie," Cruthers whispered loudly, "what's up? Any contacts?"

The electrician lit Cruthers' face with the flashlight and paused over the log sheet.

"Nope, haven't heard anything. We're lining up to blow some oil, but nothing's changed. How about you and Rowboat getting a move on; you guys have got the next watch." He prodded the sleeping man with the flashlight. "Heave out and trice up, Rowboat. Come on, you tub of lard, you've got the next watch. 'Leggo yer cock and grab a sock.'"

A whisper, then a long sigh answered him. Cruthers pulled on his clothes hurriedly, arranged his blankets, and zippered the bunk cover. Dirksen sat on the edge of his bunk, braced against the tilt of the compartment. He stared blankly into space, tousled with sleep. Cruthers regarded him for a moment.

"Don't worry, Rowboat, we're gettin' out of here. I'm so sure, I'll make you a bet. I'll bet a thousand bucks we make it. If we don't, I'll owe you a thousand, okay?" He moved toward the dinette and Dirksen followed without comment.

"What do you say, Rowboat, is it a bet?" He looked over his shoulder, smiling sweetly at his friend.

"Up yours, Mouse."

Because the *Lancerfish* had been enroute to port before the accident, nearly all of her fresh stores had been expended. The last of the eggs and milk were used for Monday's breakfast. Except for about a hundred pounds of frozen pork chops and some butter, that was the end of fresh provisions. From then on they would be on canned or dried food. Crawford thought about the time they had been on the bottom, and it seemed much longer than it was. That morning he had studied his face in the mirror over the stainless steel washstand. He stared at the hollow-eyed visage that gaped back at him. He had not shaved for three days and was surprised at the amount of small white hairs in his beard.

Crawford kept the crew busy during the morning. A

bucket brigade was formed to bail out the torpedo room bilges. The water was passed to the back of the compartment and dumped in the officers' head. When the tank was filled, it was secured and blown to sea. Even though the sanitary tank had been vented through a charcoal filter after blowing, the septic stench was powerful. Crawford decided to release only a small portion of the diesel oil from number one auxiliary tank. He would save some in case they had to do it again. He doubted that such measures would have significant results, unless a surface ship should pass in the vicinity when the oil spread on the surface. More than fifty hours had passed since the collision and they were going into their third day. If it had not been for the scrubbers and oxygen generator, they would all have expired by this time. Their atmosphere had deteriorated somewhat after the breakdown of number one scrubber. Crawford remembered being awakened in the middle of the night by Langworthy, who reported the unit had been repaired, though it still functioned sporadically.

There was a very high relative humidity, which could not be reduced, and the analyzers showed traces of foreign gases and hydrocarbons in the air. Since Saturday, smoking had been forbidden, which had been an ordeal for some of the men. Some pressure had built up in the compartments, due to very small leaks in the high-pressure air manifold. To correct this, and possibly reduce some of the noxious odors that were becoming unpleasant, number one compressor was started. The manometers in each compartment slowly turned counter-clockwise as the pressure came off, until they showed a slight suction in the submarine. Air was then bled into the boat from the banks until the hands moved back to the pressure indicated at the time of diving. Because there had been an increase of carbon dioxide during Sunday night, each compartment was ventilated by portable blowers. This would help prevent concentrations of the gas in lower flats and bilges. Crawford knew that even

70

small quantities of carbon dioxide had a physiological effect that produced fatigue and mental depression. He ordered that extra oxygen be released from the reserve flasks in the torpedo room. Maybe this would improve spirits, he thought.

After the noon meal the men were again required to remain in one location or turn in to their bunks. Hayman had the afternoon watch in the control room. He sat in the helmsman's bucket seat and thought how strange it was in the command center of the *Lancerfish*. It was like being in port when there is no need for a helmsman or for an auxiliaryman at the trim control panel. The brass still gleamed on the manifolds, and the gauges indicated pressures, temperatures, and conditions of machinery. He wondered how long it all would remain in this state of preservation. What would it look like a year from now, or a hundred years? Most likely a sea valve would slowly corrode away, failing eventually, and the rest of the boat would flood up.

The watch consisted of only three men, but Hayman noted there were fifteen or twenty others lounging around. Some talked quietly, and others seemed almost asleep. He understood why the control room was so popular. It was here that any contact would be made with the surface by the underwater telephone. He turned the gain up a notch, increasing the background level from the speaker, and several men looked up from their thoughts. Hayman told himself the Navy would never give up the search, no matter how pessimistic they might feel about rescue. The *Scorpion* sinking was an instance of that. A whole fleet combed the Atlantic from Norfolk to the Azores for weeks before locating her. And the loss of *Thresher* before that was another example. In that case it had been known that the submarine had gone down in extremely deep water, nearly seven times as deep as the *Lancerfish*. The Navy knew there could be no survivors, yet they went to great lengths to find her crushed hull.

For most of Hayman's watch Crawford had been sitting on the chart desk, his customary position in the control room. They had talked perfunctorily in the beginning, but now all conversation was burned out. The Exec looked up when the engineering officer swung into the compartment. Before Crawford could ask, Ritter reported.

"The temperature on the pump is normal again. I don't know why; maybe the constant overboard discharge has jetted a hole through the mud." He stood in front of the bubbling carbon dioxide analyzer wiping his hands with a rag. "Not bad, the CO_2 is still coming down. We've got purer air to breathe than the people in New York City." He tapped the gauge with a knuckle. "We should be thankful; think of those poor bastards in Times Square."

Shortly before 1600 the watch in the control room was changed without ceremony. Hayman had given up his seat to Langworthy and now stood in front of the underwater telephone to write his remarks in the log. He paused— something had changed, some piece of equipment had altered in its monotonous operation. The underwater telephone had been on continuously, the speaker giving out a steady muted roar. The accustomed sound went unnoticed. They were inured to its constant presence until it stopped momentarily, then resumed as before. Only one thing would cause this—an outside transmission! Crawford had heard it too and jumped to the control panel, turning up the gain even louder. He grabbed the microphone.

"Hello, any station . . . any station, this is *Lancerfish* . . . *Lancerfish*. Come in, over." He waited, staring fiercely at the speaker. He started to transmit again, but a loud voice boomed in the compartment, making everyone jump. "*Lancerfish*, this is *Barnett*. I read you weak but clear, how me? Over."

Crawford's hand shook as he brought the microphone to his lips to transmit again. His knees felt weak and he was surprised by the emotional relief that made him momentarily inarticulate. The others in the control room pressed about him, struck dumb by the voice that had issued from the speaker, the words still ringing in the hull. He heard someone in the after compartment shout, "Topside contact, we've been found!" Crawford cleared his throat and finally spoke.

"*Barnett,* this is *Lancerfish,* you are loud and clear. After torpedo room and engineroom flooded. Main ballast tanks five and six ruptured. Deep gauge reads twelve hundred and thirty-five feet to keel. Do you hold our messenger buoy? Over."

Ritter in the meantime looked over the heads crowded about him, toward the chief standing by the hydraulic manifold, and ordered him to vent negative tank. This would release a large volume of air, which would boil up to the surface, marking their exact position to the *Barnett.* The *Barnett* requested a repeat, and Crawford transmitted his message again, looking around the compartment that was now packed with men. The speaker crackled again. "Negative your last, we are commencing a search for your buoy in the immediate area."

It was possible that it was rough topside and locating the buoy would be difficult, but Crawford was disappointed. A few moments later the *Barnett* reported that they had not seen the bubble released from *Lancerfish.* The sub was too deep. Crawford identified himself, explaining that Captain Hascomb had been left on the bridge. He asked if the captain had been picked up. The *Barnett* answered with a dispassionate negative. Several more transmissions established the situation in the submarine, and Crawford read off the names of those who had been in the torpedo room and engineroom.

Relief and joy ran through the survivors, most of whom were crammed into the control room or the close proximity of the after compartment. The fact that the messenger buoy had not reached the surface failed to dull their spirits. At least they had been found and the horror of being forever lost to the world was over.

A quarter of an hour after the initial contact, the *Barnett* telephoned that they had sonar contact on the buoy from *Lancerfish*. The submarine rescue vessel *Kingfisher* joined the destroyer, and the sound of her powerful propellers was heard in the *Lancerfish*. Divers from the *Kingfisher* went over the side an hour before sunset and located the buoy. It was nearly eighty feet underwater, its cable angling into the darkness of the depths.

ENDURANCE

5 – DOWNHAUL

MAY 19-22

I<small>T WAS</small> W<small>EDNESDAY</small>, May nineteenth, before the rescue vessel *Kingfisher* was positioned over the *Lancerfish* in a seven-point moor. Because of the water depth, additional steel cable and two four-ton anchors had to be brought to the site from the Philadelphia Naval Shipyard. The crew of the *Kingfisher* had worked throughout Tuesday night faking great loops of cable along the sides in preparation for dropping the anchors. Then each mooring buoy with its separate ground tackle had to be exactly placed, making certain the anchors had a good bite in the bottom. Twice the moors had to be retrieved and replanted, because the anchors had dragged too far before they held. The *Kingfisher* now rode easily to the seven long strands of manila which held her in the center of the buoys, as though caught in a gigantic web.

Commodore Holmes had moved from the *Barnett* to the rescue vessel soon after the *Lancerfish* had been found. This would be his headquarters until the rescue operation terminated. He chose to make his quarters in the sea cabin, where he would have quick access to the radio and underwater telephone. The Commodore had detached those ships of the search force not needed for rescue. The *Barnett* and one other destroyer, *Frobisher*, were detailed to remain with the group. They would serve as picket ships to keep stray vessels from plowing through the site and would provide high speed transportation between the rescue area and shore points. In addition to these units, the ocean-going tug *Hiawatha* had been sent to assist *Kingfisher* in the mooring operations. But, even with these preparations, rescue could not commence. The downhaul cable from the *Lancerfish* had to be passed through a spooling device and secured to the winch drum in the rescue bell. Even if this could be accomplished underwater, the bell would not reach the surface after each trip.

When the submerged buoy had been found on Monday, divers had shackled additional cable to it and buoyed it off on the surface. This provided visible location of the messenger buoy with its vital link to the submarine below. In his report to Rear Admiral Calhoun, Holmes had defined the predicament in detail. It was absolutely necessary to have a clear scope of cable from the decks of the rescue vessel to the hatch of the *Lancerfish*, in order to deploy the bell. He also requested information about the new rescue system that for so many years had been under development.

Holmes knew that for the moment the survivors were secure. They had the reactor and associated life support machinery in operation, which would purchase the needed time. If rescue was to be successfully carried out, sound planning and preparation would have to go into it.

A conference was held in the wardroom of the *Kingfisher* that morning. The commanding officer of the submarine *Striker*, the skipper of the *Kingfisher*, and his diving officer and Chief Master Diver Petrosky were there. The meeting had begun in a disjointed manner with several theories and methods for saving the *Lancerfish* survivors expounded. The captain of the *Striker* felt that if the bell could be attached to the cable underwater, sorties could commence in a few hours. Although the bell would not reach the surface, it would bring the men up to within one hundred feet of it. From there the men could make free ascents, after first pressurizing the bell. Holmes did not like the idea, but he turned to Lt. Morgan, the grey-haired diving officer.

"What do you think, Ben?"

"We need slack in the cable first off, Commodore." He paused as he thought the procedure out to himself, his head bowed. "We'd have to buoy the cable some distance below the messenger buoy, then remove the upper buoy while the bell is being attached. When the rescue chamber has the cable, the support buoy would have to be removed." Morgan shook his head, frowning; he was dubious about such jury-rigging. "It would be taking a big chance of losing the downhaul, Commodore, and I haven't got any divers that can go after it."

This confirmed Holmes's reaction to the idea, but he wanted Morgan, an old "hardhat" diver, to spell it out. During these discussions Chief Petrosky had been doodling on the scratch pad in front of him. He was a skinny, leathery looking man with faded tattoos on his forearms. He spoke suddenly, his loud baritone dominating the wardroom.

"Commodore, can I stick my oar in?"

Holmes nodded and Petrosky, whose hearing had suffered after many years of deep-sea diving, thundered out his plan.

"We can long splice the downhaul. First, we take a purchase on the cable at a hundred and fifty feet with 'come-alongs' and a buoy. Then cast off the sub's messenger buoy and make a splice into the bitter end from a stage. Once we have the wire on deck we'll take off the support buoy and we're in business."

Holmes thought for a moment, rolling a newly lit cigar

79

in his fingertips. The chief knew what he could do underwater, and this might be the answer, though it would take time.

"How about it, Ben? Think the bell will take the splice through the winch?"

"Maybe, sir. Horse has a good idea and we can test the winch in the meantime. The manual says the downhaul is not to be spliced, but I think it will work. In any case another buoy on that downhaul would be good insurance until something is rigged. We'll need some seven-sixteenth-inch steel cable and a buoy we can flood and drain." He jotted on the pad, "And a splicing vise secured to a work stage."

Details of the plan were refined. The cable would come from the *Striker*'s own messenger buoy. A radio message would be sent to procure a new splicing vise and airlift it to the site. In the meantime shipfitters would start construction of a work platform under Petrosky's supervision.

When the meeting broke up Holmes went up to the pilot house, where the underwater phone console was located. He was relieved to be able to start something in the way of rescue, but he was still apprehensive. It seemed a little too easy and pat. The two reporters, Wright and Lewis, were on the signal bridge talking with the watch. They had moved with Holmes the previous day and were berthed in the crew's quarters of the *Kingfisher*. Leonard Wright had his portable tape recorder with him and a movie camera. Edgar Lewis had two still cameras slung about his short neck along with light meters and a strobe flash unit. Both men wore the foul-weather jackets the bo'sun had provided them. Wright broke off his conversation with the signalman when he saw the Commodore through the door leading into the pilot house. Holmes motioned to the two civilians to come in.

"This will be of interest to you. I'll give you specifics after I've talked to Commander Crawford on the bottom."

A voice from the sunken submarine answered immediately when Holmes called. Wright started his recorder, holding the microphone near the UQC speaker. Holmes asked for the executive officer and then waited for him to answer. How strange this was, thought Holmes. It was like calling someone to an ordinary telephone about some minor matter. The message he wanted to give Crawford concerned the preparations necessary before rescue could start. The sub's exec and all those survivors were just below them, twelve hundred feet away. But they were in a different element, a strange world as remote as the mountains of the moon. If only they could get started soon, and the bell were able to work over the splice and seat on the escape hatch of the *Lancerfish*. What would he do if he lost that cable? What would he say to Crawford then? The speaker clicked— "Crawford here."

Holmes gave the plan of action to the sub's exec and predicted it would take two days before the splice was made and the rescue bell was operating. Diving to work on the splice would be done during daylight hours, and they had to wait for the splicing vise to be brought out. He ended his transmission with: "Think you people can sit it out awhile longer?" He spoke with as much optimism and cheer as he could muster. There was a moment of silence, and then Crawford's voice came over the speaker. "Ah . . . yessir. Understand it may be two days before you're rigged. Yessir, we're secure, should be no problems."

The tension and disappointment Crawford was feeling could be detected in his transmission. Lewis was taking photographs, scuttling around the Commodore to get close-up shots of him at the UQC.

On the afterdecks of the *Kingfisher*, men were busy coiling down hose lines and checking over diving equipment. The huge rescue chamber had been lifted out of its cradle and was suspended just above the deck. It looked like a giant top or steel balloon towering over the men. The upper hatch was open and a sailor was wiping the gasket and testing the handwheel. At the tapered bottom, which was a few feet off the deck, a man's legs could be seen as he worked on some inner portion of the lower skirt. Earlier, Lewis had photographed the rescue bell and would send the film off with his next story captioned: "The rescue diving bell that the Navy hopes to use to save the men in the *Lancerfish*."

Holmes went to the wing of the bridge and was joined by Wright and Lewis. It was a calm day with only a low swell running. The sun shined thinly through a wispy layer of cirrus clouds. They would need this good weather for the underwater splicing, and Holmes hoped it would hold. On the horizon the two destroyers circled about the *Kingfisher*. The crisp sound of a single-engined airplane passed over them. Holmes looked up and watched it bank steeply about them. More newsmen. Since the *Lancerfish* had been found and it was now known that men were trapped in her, even more attention would be focused on them. That morning a message had come from the Commandant of the Third Naval District in New York. The Public Affairs Officer was being harassed for information about the rescue operations. The Commandant wanted to know if any more news representatives could be accommodated on the rescue vessel. Holmes had answered with a negative, but suggested that the Navy furnish an information officer and service photographers to cover the on-board operations. Their news releases and photos could be sent to ComThree for distribution. The Commandant concurred and soon a Navy information team would be aboard.

The message-board had been thick with traffic that morning. There were orders and instructions from the Chief of Naval Operations and ComSubLant. Situation reports had to be made twice daily, or as significant changes occurred. The Chief of Naval Material was sending Captain Shepherd, head of the Deep Submergence Systems Project, to inspect the rescue preparations. The naval shipyard at Portsmouth, N. H., as well as the Electric Boat Company in

Groton, Connecticut, were alerted to provide top priority for any services or material that might be ordered by the Commodore.

Holmes knew he had the Navy and the whole industrial complex of the United States behind him. It was all under his control, and he was to use it with his experience and knowledge. He was the one best fitted for the job, and he was expected to take the correct steps to save sixty-one men from a sunken submarine. He knew, too, that his decision to splice in extra cable would take time. Time in which the anxieties of the trapped men, their families, and the nation would grow. It was feasible to attach the bell underwater and bring the men up to a shallow depth from where they could swim up the last eighty or ninety feet with escape hoods. But it would be taking too big a risk with the downhaul cable when transferring it from the messenger buoy to the bell. A mistake by a diver or the operator of the bell could lose the downhaul. First, he had to secure this tenuous connection with the submarine. Holmes explained the procedure to the reporters. Later, he described the plan in a "sitrep" message to Admiral Calhoun.

Edgar Lewis went down to the main deck and made his way aft, to the port diving station. He was beginning to know his way about the ship. He knew some of the sailors by their first names, and they called him "Ed." Wright, on the other hand, was aloof and was more often found in the wardroom or on the bridge.

Lt. Morgan was sitting astride the gunwale supervising the preparations for diving. Two sailors were connecting an air hose to the manifold, which would be used to blow the water from the buoy after it was attached. Another man coiled down the line that would lower the clamp and bridle to the divers. Two divers in black exposure suits and self-contained lungs were helped over the side to an outboard platform. When Morgan saw Lewis picking his way toward him, he called out, "Sir, if you want to cover this dive, you can sit behind me to be clear of the rigging." Lewis waved acknowledgment. When he took his position, Lewis said, "Call me Ed, I'm not used to that 'sir' business." He fished out his light meter and took a reading on the diving officer. Morgan leaned over the side and gave directions to the first diver.

"Okay, Murf, when you guys get to a hundred and fifty feet, bolt the clamp to the cable from the submarine. When it's secured we'll lower the support buoy to you."

The diver nodded and turned to his mate, gesturing toward the water. They tumbled into the sea and treaded water while the clamp was passed to them, then swam out to the big orange buoy which marked the location of the messenger buoy underwater. When they dove Morgan noted the time and watched the divers' bubbles boil up to the surface. The minutes passed and Lewis snapped pictures of the activity on deck and the diving officer.

A black head broke out of the water and a diver raised a clenched fist to indicate the clamp was bolted to the cable. Morgan signaled, and the boom lifted the big yellow buoy, swung it outboard, and lowered it to the water. The diver swam to it and opened the flood and vent valves, allowing it to sink. In a few moments both the buoy and the diver had disappeared. It grew quiet on deck except for the rumble of the big winch drum and squeak from the payout block. "One hundred and fifty feet," sang out the boom operator as he braked the winch. More time passed and Lewis found himself checking his own watch. The divers had been in the water nearly twenty minutes, and then suddenly they surfaced alongside the platform. One held up his hand, making a circle with thumb and forefinger. The buoy had the weight of the downhaul cable from the submarine. The divers came aboard and shrugged off their heavy gear, and the one called Murf reported to the diving officer. He was breathing heavily and the back of one hand was bleeding where it had been scraped between the buoy and the cable.

"Pretty tough, Mr. Morgan," he said between gasps. "There's a current running and we had a time rassling that monster in place, but it's secured now."

Lewis squatted and shot some views of the diver, then put his camera away. That night he filed another story:

May 19, at the rescue site for the submarine *Lancerfish.* The Navy's submarine rescue ship *USS Kingfisher* moored today over the sunken nuclear powered submarine *Lancerfish.* Rescue of the trapped men cannot be started until vital equipment is provided from shore. The submarine, which was sunk after collision Saturday with a merchant ship, is resting on the bottom more than 1200 feet below the *Kingfisher.* Communications between the rescue vessel and the sub have established that there are sixty-one men out of the original crew of eighty-three alive in the forward compartments. Twenty-two crewmen died at their stations trying to save the 2500-ton undersea warship.

Captain Barnaby C. Holmes, USN, the officer in command of rescue operations, said today that certain material would have to be brought to the scene before making further rescue attempts. It is expected that it will require two days to make the necessary preparations for using the rescue bell. The problem that is slowing the Navy in reaching the submarine's crew is that the steel cable that was floated up with the distress buoy is not long enough. The cable and its messenger buoy are nearly one hundred feet underwater. It is hoped by the rescuers to lengthen the cable so that rescue can start.

Lieutenant Commander Robert Crawford, USN, of Niantic, Connecticut, is in command aboard the ill-fated submarine. The search for the captain of the submarine, Commander Joseph Hascomb of Gales Ferry, Connecticut, who was lost overboard at the time of collision, has been called off.

Commander Crawford's telephone message to the surface today said that the survivors are in good condition and holding up well under the circumstances. The atomic reactor in the submarine is working satisfactorily. This power source makes it possible for the survivors to operate the oxygen generation machinery and

85

the carbon dioxide absorbers, providing a living atmosphere for the men. Without this equipment, which conventional diesel powered submarines do not have, the men would have perished by Tuesday morning.

Newspapers throughout the world headlined the finding of the sunken *Lancerfish*. The dramatic news had even more impact than the first reports of her collision and sinking. Other international news stories were pushed aside in order to tell the public of the appalling situation. Sixty-one men trapped on the bottom of the sea, with perhaps no way to get out, was horrendous and at the same time spectacular. With morbid fascination, readers devoured the accounts written by imaginative reporters.

A New York City taxi driver guides his cab through crosstown traffic and remarks to his solitary fare, "How about them guys in the submarine?" He glances up at the rear view mirror. "They say the sub is thousands of feet down and the Navy is having trouble gettin' the crew out. Chris', they must be going ape down there. You couldn't get me in one of them things. No, sir."

A housewife pauses in her ironing as a television newscaster earnestly describes the rescue preparations. A still photograph of the Lancerfish *flashes on the screen and his voice continues: "Naval sources, while not overly optimistic about such deep rescue operations, state that the only operational device that can save the men is on the scene. The rescue chamber, known as the McCann Rescue Bell, was originally designed in 1929 and used on only one occasion. In 1939 the bell saved thirty-three men from the sunken submarine* Squalus, *which went down in 240 feet of water off New England. Since then the bell has been modified for deeper dives, but its current design limit is less than a thousand feet. The* Lancerfish *is at a depth of over 1200 feet." The housewife shakes her head sadly and mutters, "How awful for their families."*

In another part of the country the customers at a tavern are turned toward the television set for the same news program. The bartender listens, too, with arms folded over a towel. ". . . The survivors are reported in good condition and have an almost unlimited air reserve. Since the previous submarine disaster, the loss of the Scorpion *in which ninety-nine men perished in 1968, the Navy has pursued a crash program for development of rescue methods for submarine crews in deep water. The program, called the Deep Submergence Systems Project, does not have, as yet, a workable device. The Navy has been working on a special midget submarine which will be able to locate and retrieve submariners stranded in deep water, as in the case of the* Lancerfish. *However, there is little hope this new device will be ready in time, since the concept requires modifications to the submarine itself."*

The bartender comments over his shoulder to the other viewers, "If we can put astronauts on the moon and take pictures of Mars, I can't understand why they can't go a few hundred feet underwater to pull those guys out." A man at the end of the bar sips his beer and adds, "We've got the know-how to put men on the moon and cruise submarines under the North Pole, but if anything happens in either case there's no way to rescue the crews. Even commercial jets aren't the safest thing in the world. How often do you hear about one of them crashing, wiping out a hundred or so passengers? Maybe the safety record of submarines is not so bad. Anyway, those guys get paid for taking the chance. You know what they used to say during the war when someone complained about pilots getting all that extra dough: 'They don't get paid more, just faster.' Same thing."

For the families of the crewmen in *Lancerfish* the news of her discovery was at first a relief. A new fear overwhelmed them when it was learned that immediate deliverance was not possible. The Navy representatives who called on the dependents and relatives assured them that everything within the power of the country would be done to save their men. The first rescue attempt would be made before the weekend if the weather held fair. For the families of the men who died in the flooded section of the sub, the waiting was over. The tragedy was upon them, and the saving of the remaining crewmen was anticlimactic.

An aura of grief and tension hung over the submarine base at New London, Connecticut. In the squadron offices, the workshops along the waterfront, and in the submarine school classrooms, personnel felt the ominous reality of the disaster. They spoke of the men that were gone and the relative chances of saving those still alive. Almost everyone knew at least one member of the *Lancerfish* crew, whose home port had been New London. On Tuesday the sub base chaplain held special services for the dead crewmen and prayers for the survival of the others. The ones to feel the disaster most poignantly, besides the relatives of the lost men, were the crews of other submarines, particularly those of the sister class.

With the second buoy now holding the downhaul cable, Holmes was tempted to try the method suggested by the *Striker*'s captain. The weather was exceptionally calm and diving conditions were excellent. The bell could probably be attached by a diver. But, at least seven trips would be necessary to bring up all sixty-one men. This would mean that seven times the cable would have to be buoyed and removed to bring the bell all the way to the surface. Or, at the end of each trip the bell would have to be pressurized and the passengers would have to swim up a hundred feet with escape hoods. Too complicated, Holmes thought, and it would take too much rigging time. He did not trust these brief periods of good weather; he knew how fast the wind could come up and the seas start mounting. If that happened and they were unable to bring the bell aboard, all could be lost. They just had to wait.

Holmes had set up a schedule of communications check-out on the underwater telephone. Every four hours the man standing by the UQC would call the *Lancerfish*, get his "loud and clear," and enter it in the log. Leonard Wright had witnessed this routine while visiting the pilot house on Thursday. There was little traffic between the rescue vessel and the submarine, and Wright wondered if he might get Holmes's authority to interview one of the survivors. That would make a great human interest telecast. A photo of the man could be shown while the interview was in progress; maybe even show some footage of the man's family. Wright looked over the roster of *Lancerfish* crewmen that had been provided by the Commodore. Johnson, the first class sonarman, looked like a possibility; his wife and two sons lived in New London.

Wright speculated on how to get Holmes's permission. He felt the Commodore would not be amenable to the idea. First, he would make up an interview questionnaire, he decided, then when an opportunity arose put it to the Commodore.

Wright waited until later in the morning when Holmes went to the wardroom with Captain Jenkins. Coffee was passed around and he sat down with the two naval officers. Holmes slumped in his chair with his legs stretched before him. He looked tired as he massaged his wide face with the palms of his hands. Jenkins gave Wright the opening to broach his request by asking, "Well, Mr. Wright, how are you making out with us? Sorry we couldn't give you better sleeping arrangements."

"No complaints, Captain, cooperation from you and the crew has been great. I can appreciate the inconvenience of having a couple of reporters underfoot at a time like this." He tasted his coffee thoughtfully. "Naturally the public has a great interest in this disaster. It touches them personally in a way. Those are Americans down there; the kid from next door, or it could have been a husband or son. My network is on my back for all the material I can provide on the scene." Wright hesitated a moment then directed his words to the Commodore. "Sir, I'd like to ask your permission to use the underwater telephone for a few minutes to interview one of the men on the *Lancerfish*." Holmes said nothing for a moment, and Wright knew by his look he had rejected the idea and was forming his negative answer.

Holmes scooted around in his chair and looked the reporter in the eyes. "I can appreciate your desire to do this, Mr. Wright. As a journalist, it is a logical request. I'm sure you understand what those people are going through down there. Every one of them knows that if they get out it will be a record achievement in submarine rescue." He picked his cigar out of the ashtray, puffed it going again, and continued. "I must turn you down on this. It would be too hard on the man's family." He tightened his wide mouth in a determined line. "I'm sorry."

Wright nodded understandingly, but he was not going to let it go that easily. "Commodore, I don't intend to ask the man questions that would cause anyone a greater worry. I've worked out a questionnaire to give you an idea of the interview. All I want is some human interest background."

"I have to say no again, Mr. Wright. There will be no unofficial transmissions on the UQC."

What a tough old bastard, Wright thought. He would have to bring some pressure on him, which he did not want to do; he would rather have his cooperation than risk any antagonism.

"Commodore, please understand that I sympathize with you and the Navy, about wanting to minimize the publicity that this tragedy is generating. A lot of people are asking questions, such as why is there no rescue equipment for deep-diving submarines. Or, why is it taking so long to get going with the gear on hand? My job is to explain the problems to the public, and I can't do this without the complete cooperation of the officers on the scene. To satisfy the public thirst for information I need more than just bare facts."

"What does that have to do with interviewing a survivor?" Holmes looked bleak. "Dammit, talking to some sailor scared half out of his wits won't give you the insight you want. You're damned right I don't want to fan adverse public opinion by putting out a sob-sister story." He closed the discussion with finality by clapping on his cap and leaving the wardroom.

Wright sighed and glanced at the noncommittal captain. "The Navy's mighty touchy, and I can understand why."

Jenkins had the mature composure that usually marks

the officers the Navy selects for command at sea. His face, which looked surprisingly older than his thirty-three years, was friendly, though it suggested it could be stern as well.

"You're right," he said, "but so is the Commodore. We're not at all sure we can bring this off, and if we can't, your interview would be pretty rough on the man's family."

Wright smoothed the back of his head and said nothing.

The fair weather stayed with them, and on Friday morning the after deck of the *Kingfisher* was like a stage before the curtain goes up. The big orange messenger buoy from the *Lancerfish* had been removed from the downhaul and was lashed to the starboard bulwarks. A large angle iron platform had been welded together the day before. Rising on each end of it were supporting bails from which it would be suspended. A framework in the middle of the platform held the splicing vise, which had been delivered that morning.

Chief Petrosky, in dungarees and sweater, inspected the preparations. He greased the vise and worked the threads back and forth. The chief would make the splice, and he wanted everything in readiness when he went to work under water. On the platform he had secured his tools by lengths of tarred marlin; hammer, pliers, wire cutters, and a roll of seizing wire. The steel cable from the *Striker* had already been prepared and was stopped off on the platform with one end free for splicing. The cable had been unlaid with the long strands seized at the ends. Petrosky looked over the equipment and was satisfied. In his loud voice he said, "Okay, let's have at it."

He kicked off his shoes and peeled off his dungarees, then joined another diver already in his canvas dress on a bench. The tenders held open the wide neck of the suit, which he pulled up over his legs. He slipped his arms into the sleeves and forced his hands through the snug rubber cuffs. They were making the dive in helmet rigs, because the work would take considerable time and they would need the leverage of their feet on the platform. Breastplates, lead-soled shoes, and weight harnesses were added. A sailor carefully fitted a helmet over each diver's head and twisted it in place. Telephone communications were checked out with the diving control panel. All was ready. Air flooded through the hoses and the faceplates were dogged in place. Lt. Morgan came over to look into the helmet window of each diver as they adjusted their air pressure and exhaust valves. "Okay, Horse? Jim?" They nodded, though deafened by the roar of air, and Morgan smacked his hand down on each helmet.

From atop the deck house a small gallery of spectators watched the activities at the diving station. Commodore Holmes and Captain Jenkins leaned over the railing, and the civilian reporters took seats on the ventilator. The Public Affairs Officer from ComThree, a young Lt(jg), and his two enlisted photographers had arrived that morning via the helicopter and were busy flashing off photos. Several sailors from the crew gathered respectfully behind the Commodore and their captain.

The boom swung the platform into the air with the two divers standing back to back, feet set solidly apart. From each end of the platform steadying lines were attached and tended by men on deck. The divers were quickly lowered alongside the marker buoy and submerged to just below the surface. The sound of their hissing exhaust air changed abruptly to a gay burble. Morgan checked the divers over the intercom, then signaled to the boom operator. The cable unrolled from the end of the boom when Morgan signaled, and he watched the divers disappear into the green depths. The nearly indistinguishable voice of Petrosky reported over the intercom when they reached a hundred feet. Morgan closed his fist with a jerk and the lowering stopped.

The spectators began to disperse and the after decks

became quiet. It would be a slow job; the divers would be down all morning. The tenders holding the lifelines relaxed against the gunwale. A bo'sun's mate sat on a coil of manila line and watched two seamen sweep down the after deck. Behind him the ensign flapped lazily in the light breeze. The *Kingfisher* rose and settled on a low, glassy swell and the sun intensified as traces of high thin clouds disappeared. The Commodore felt warm and so took off his windbreaker and cap as he looked at the sky. The latest weather advisory predicted continued fair weather until Saturday afternoon. That was a break. He climbed down the small ladder to the main deck and joined the diving officer, leaning on his forearms over the gunwale. Morgan acknowledged his presence by saying conversationally, "This good weather helps. Horse will be able to work faster with the platform steady. Should take him about two hours, I hope we can finish it off in one dive."

Holmes extracted a cigar from his shirt pocket. He stripped the cellophane and watched it bob down the side of the ship. "We may have more of a problem with the current than with the surface weather," he said, biting off the tip of the cigar and spitting it into the water. "Your bell all ready to go?"

"Yes, sir. I've got the best operator standing by, a first-class shipfitter named Crawford, no kin to the commander down there," he said nodding to the water, "and another man to back him up. I'd send Horse, except he will have a long decompression after this job."

The two hours passed slowly with Holmes frequently visiting the diving station. It was nearly noon and Holmes was getting impatient. He came down from the pilot house again and called to Morgan below the deck house.

"How they doing?"

"It's slow, sir. Horse says maybe another half hour, but they're fagging. Should bring them up for chow."

"What's the holdup?" Holmes demanded briskly. "I'd

like to get this splice done before you bring them up." He lowered himself to the deck and went to the intercom. "Petrosky, this is the Commodore. Can you hang on until the splice is completed?" The sound of air rushing in the diver's helmet came from the speaker, then Petrosky: "Yep . . . yes, sir. No need to come up, but might take a bit longer. I've got several tucks to make yet, then trim off. We'll stay on it."

At 1405 the divers completed the decompression and rose out of the sea like mythical deities. Water streamed from the helmets and canvas suits, sparkling in the sunlight. Morgan sent a man to report to the Captain and the Commodore that the splice was made. The activity on deck now was hurried and precise. Dressers assisted the divers back to their bench and quickly stripped them of the heavy gear. Other men unshackled the lift wire from the platform and transferred it to the bridle on the rescue bell. Lashings were thrown off and the big chamber was lifted from the cradle once more.

The next step was to remove the supporting buoy at 150 feet. Two divers went down with a light lifting wire from number two boom. This was shackled into the buoy, and after a slight strain was exerted by the winch, the buoy was flooded. When the buoy was negative in buoyancy, it was unclamped and hauled to the surface. Except for the splice at ninety feet, there was now a free scope of downhaul cable to the hatch of the *Lancerfish*.

At 1530 on May twenty-first the bell was in the water and ready to start the first descent. Holmes held a final briefing with the diving officer and rescue bell operators. He concentrated his attention on the man who would guide the bell to the hatch on the submarine, the first-class diver who would be in charge on this first attempt.

"Crawford, how deep have you taken the rescue bell before?"

"Six hundred feet, sir, on a test run near Bermuda."

"Did you make a seal?"

"Yessir, attached to a dummy hatch."

Holmes regarded the man for a moment. He was a stocky, well-built sailor with blue eyes set in a very tanned face. He looked more like a farm hand than a Navy diver who was going to plunge hundreds of feet in open ocean. Though young, his manner was sober and capable.

"Okay, Crawford, you're going twice that depth today; no need to tell you to be careful. Take your time and come up slowly on that hatch. You probably won't see it until you're almost there. Any questions?"

The diver looked at the Commodore matter-of-factly. "How many guys?"

Holmes had thought this out the day before. The bell could accommodate nine men besides the operators. That would mean at least seven dives with only seven passengers on the last run. "We'll start off with eight. If that goes well we may increase the number to nine. I'll talk to you after this first run."

The divers went aft to their station. They had put on heavy sweaters and foul weather jackets, as the water temperature on the bottom was forty-seven degrees. Crawford took a last puff on his cigarette, snapped it over the side, and followed the other man over the side to the top of the chamber. He disappeared through the hatch and dogged it shut. In a moment he reported over the intercom to Lt. Morgan at the diving control stand. The bell settled in the water heavily, and a sailor from the motor whaleboat scampered onto its yellow dome to disconnect the lift wire. Now the bell was attached to the *Kingfisher* by just the backhaul cable and hose with retrieving line. The ballast tanks were flooded and the bell sank deeper; then as the winch took hold on the cable, it pulled the bell down and it vanished.

As soon as the water closed over the bell, Holmes went to the pilot house with Captain Jenkins. He had some cheering news for the waiting survivors on the *Lancerfish*. But first he wanted to make certain the winch in the bell would take the splice at the ninety-foot level. He waited in front of the underwater telephone, rolling a short stub of cigar from side to side in his mouth. A telephone talker stood at his side, his hands pressed to the earphones, waiting for the report from the diving station on deck.

"Passed two-oh feet, descending slowly," he reported. The time seemed to hang in the air as Holmes waited, staring at the talker. Wright stood behind him and aimed his movie camera at the Commodore.

"One hundred feet," the talker said, "over the splice, no problems, continuing descent."

Holmes pressed the switch on the UQC. "Hello, *Lancerfish*, this is *Kingfisher*, over." He waited for the answering voice from the depths. There was no reply. He called again, growing more impatient, then apprehensive. What the hell, he thought, this is a lousy time to lose contact. Almost casually a voice finally came from the speaker; it sounded slightly garbled and weak. Holmes spoke again: "*Lancerfish*, this is Holmes. The bell is in the water and on its way. Have eight of your people ready for evacuation, over." The wavering, hollow voice from the submarine answered, "Roger topside, we're ready."

The talker next to Holmes reported 150 feet, and this figure was relayed to the submarine. The minutes dragged on. At 300 feet the bell reported a strong current was evidenced by the sharp angle at which the cable tended out of the lower skirt. The talker suddenly spoke: "Bell reports the downhaul is vibrating badly and the clutch keeps kicking out when they try to go deeper. They're holding at three hundred and seventy feet." Holmes handed the microphone to Jenkins.

"I'm going aft to see what's going on."

When Holmes approached the diving officer, he noticed deep concern in his manner as he turned to him. "They managed a few more feet, they're at four hundred. That safety clutch keeps slipping and it's adjusted to maximum pull."

"What do you recommend, Ben?" Holmes tried not to show his impatience.

"We might bring her up and add some lead ballast to make it easier on the downhaul winch. The lead can be left in the sub."

"All right, abort the dive and let's try that." Holmes returned to the pilot house disappointed and full of foreboding. If that current stays with us, he thought, it might be pretty hard to pull the bell onto the seat, even if they do get down. His message to the *Lancerfish* was short and vague: "We're recovering the bell to make an adjustment. Should be starting again within the hour."

But it was much longer than that. The bell was hoisted aboard and the winch inspected. There was no way additional power could be added. Five hundred pounds of lead pigs were secured to the deck inside the upper compartment. It was nearly 1800 before the bell was back in the water. The sun was low on the horizon, and the wind was picking up, creating sharp little waves that danced against the hull of the *Kingfisher*.

The rescue bell only got to 300 feet on the second attempt. It was closer to neutral buoyancy, and the metacentric height had been altered by the lead ballast, causing it to list sharply in the current. Crawford reported severe vibrations which caused the cable to romp violently in the fairlead. The winch clutch repeatedly kicked out, preventing the bell from going deeper.

Holmes ordered the bell to be brought aboard and secured in the cradle. No more efforts would be made that night, or until a diver inspected the cable. He explained the situation fully to Commander Crawford on the bottom; no use pulling any punches. Also, Holmes wanted to have the opinion of the design engineers about the winch before making another attempt. They were due to arrive in the morning.

It was obvious to Holmes now that they would not be able to save the men in *Lancerfish* right away. The environmental conditions were extremely poor. Strong currents, squally weather, and the very depth of the submarine had to be reckoned with. He hoped no serious damage had been caused to the downhaul cable. He had made his first sally naively and had been smartly repulsed. He realized his rescue efforts had to be based upon practical considerations and not influenced by his anxiety for the men waiting below.

Holmes and Captain Jenkins had a late meal in the wardroom. While he ate, Holmes formed his plans, writing from time to time in a small notebook next to his plate. Wright and Lewis had dined earlier with other members of the wardroom and now sat at the table over coffee. Wright was anxious to get a statement out of the Commodore for his story. He waited until Holmes dug into his apple pie before speaking.

"Commodore, I wonder if you can fill me in on a couple of items. I'm calling the marine operator in New York to file my release for the late news. I know Ed also has some questions for the morning editions."

"Fire away," Holmes answered without taking his eyes off his plate.

"If the cable is all right, will you make another attempt tomorrow?"

"Only if the current has let up, which I doubt like hell."

"Then, if there is a current, or if the cable has been damaged, what will be your next move?"

Holmes wiped his hands on the napkin. "We're having a conference on that in just a few minutes. At the moment I would rather hold off any statements until plans are firmed up." One thing that had to be done before any announcement to the press, Holmes decided, was his report to the Admiral on the failure of the bell and what he intended to do. Old Tom Calhoun would have a fit if he heard about it on the late TV news or read it in the paper at breakfast, before Holmes's official report had been received. The Admiral was probably being dogged by the press too.

Wright frowned at his notebook. The Commodore was making it tough for him by deciding when news was ready for release. He would have to push Holmes a little.

"This makes it sort of hard to wind up the events of the day. I would like to be able to say something hopeful, rather than just saying that the bell failed today."

Holmes signaled the steward for more coffee and said, "Mr. Wright, I would prefer no releases at all go out tonight." Wright was silent. This was so characteristic of the military—whenever anything sour happened to them they clammed up, but when they wanted air time for Armed Forces Day, or to promote the Navy Relief Society, they had a different attitude.

"But, Commodore, I can't hold up the news. The whole country is waiting to know if they are going to be saved or not. It's not as though security was involved."

"In a sense it is. I'm thinking about the dependents and people who have sons on the *Lancerfish*. If you must make a report, just say that the bell encountered difficulties with the current and operations will continue tomorrow."

A knock sounded on the wardroom door, and then Chief Petrosky entered. Holmes looked at Wright and Lewis.

"And now, gentlemen, will you excuse us. This will be a private conference. I'll have a statement for you in the morning after the inspection dive."

As the reporters departed Holmes noticed the young Public Affairs Officer sitting in the lounge area. Holmes

99

motioned for him to join the meeting at the table. "Wilkins, is it?" he asked.

"Watkins, sir."

"Well, Mr. Watkins, I hope you've had experience with these New York reporters before. They're a tough lot and will try anything to get something out of you. Be careful you don't become a 'Navy spokesman.' " Holmes regarded the officer as he pulled a chair to the table. He looked about twenty-four years old and seemed a bit hesitant in manner. Probably a reservist on a two-year tour of active duty.

"I had hoped ComThree would send someone with a little more seniority."

Watkins shifted uncomfortably, knowing the steady stare from those hooded eyes required an answer.

"I'm single, sir, and Captain Billings, the district information officer, thought this might turn into a long assignment."

Holmes made no reply and thought, the peacetime Navy! Their only concern was whether or not they would have to work after five o'clock.

"Well, you might sit in on this, Mr. Watkins, to learn what we're doing. Please clear your releases with me before sending them on to ComThree."

Holmes had half written his detailed report to ComSubLant. The second part of the message requested the services of an oceanographic vessel with current meters and a submersible with manipulators. He explained to the group about the table that the first objective in the morning would be a dive to inspect the downhaul cable. He needed to know if it had been damaged at the point where the powerful resonance had prevented the winch from pulling the bell deeper. It would be a deep dive and would require the use of the mixed gas rig, referred to as the "helium hat" by Petrosky.

"At the same time the diver can observe what kind of a

current is running," Holmes said. "If there is a significant decrease, I'll consider another bell attempt."

"If the current doesn't let up, what do you intend to do, Commodore?" Morgan asked.

"In my message I'm requesting that engineers be sent out to look over the winch. We need more pulling power and they might suggest how we can get it. If we can get the bell below the main catenary of the downhaul, I think the vibration caused by the vortex shedding will be minimized."

Saturday at 0900 Chief Petty Officer Whittier was swung out on his stage. He wore a deep-sea helmet for helium-oxygen diving, because of the deep depth he had to reach. Breathing compressed air would produce severe intoxication from the nitrogen. Whittier had been instructed to make an inspection of the cable, coming up from 450 to 350 feet. Lt. Morgan and Chief Petrosky were at the air manifold station.

Whittier was lowered away and the tenders paid out the canvas covered lifeline. In a moment Whittier's voice came over the intercom: "On the downhaul." At 100 feet the diver stopped and reported that he was ventilating. He descended again, and the air and lifeline snaked over the gunwale until he reached 200 feet. There he stopped and reported ready to receive the helium-oxygen mix. His voice had changed because of the pressure and had a nasal, effeminate quality. Petrosky cracked the valve on the manifold and watched the pressure build up, then secured the compressed air supply. "You're on the mix," he said to the speaker. The tenders unlaid more hose, passing it into the water and watching the diving officer attentively. Whittier reported at depth and commenced the slow inspection.

Commodore Holmes was on the deck house ventilator watching the operation. A light breeze ruffled the low swells moving from the west; the meteorological outlook was good through Sunday. The night before the helo from the *Frobisher* had been sent to New York to bring out the visitors that morning. Captain G. G. Shepherd, III, who headed the Deep Submergence Systems Projects, and two design engineers for the downhaul winch would be on hand to lend assistance. The party was expected at the rescue site by 1000, and the inspection of the cable would be completed by then. Holmes hoped the engineers could come up with a simple solution for modifying the winch clutch to take more pull. He had met Captain Shepherd once, while visiting Admiral Moran's office at the Navy Annex in Washington. He remembered Shepherd as a highly intelligent though somewhat pretentious officer. He was a naval engineering specialist in submarine systems and had been a prominent contributor to the symposium on deep submergence after the *Thresher* loss.

Morgan reported to Holmes's sea cabin after the dive. The diver had observed no damage to the cable, but there was less encouraging news about the current.

"Whittier says there was a good three to four knots running down there. It became more noticeable after he passed two hundred feet. He said the cable tended at a smart angle."

That canceled any hope for another bell attempt until the winch could be modified. Holmes directed the diving officer to have the bell hoisted out of the cradle and personnel stand by. "We'll have the experts look it over when they get here," he said.

Holmes went down on deck when he saw the motor whaleboat approaching with the visitors. Captain Shepherd came up the accommodation ladder first. He snapped a salute to the ensign fluttering from the fantail and went through the routine of requesting permission to come aboard. Jenkins stepped forward and introduced himself and the Commodore, then stood by as the two civilian engineers came over the side. Shepherd moved toward the Commodore.

"Ah, Captain Holmes, it's good to see you again."

He extended a long thin arm to shake hands. He was very tall and cadaverous. His manner of speaking had a quality of precision, marked by a faint, unidentifiable accent. He stood over Holmes with his gaunt face cocked slightly, peering through heavy, black-rimmed glasses. The thin face had a very short nose, giving it a skull-like appearance. "It's a ghastly business, eh?"

Shepherd turned to the engineers and presented them to Holmes. "And messieurs Porter and Cunningham from the Naval Material Command." He handed Holmes a bundle of newspapers he had been carrying under his arm. "I thought you might be interested in what the press has to say about your efforts."

Holmes led the group to the wardroom for a briefing on the operations. Afterward they would inspect the bell. Shepherd took a seat on Holmes's right and listened to the Commodore's dissertation without comment. A frown crossed his rather pale face once or twice. Holmes summed up his plan. "Knowing that the survivors are relatively secure for now, I intend to modify the winch in the bell, or maybe replace it." He turned to Shepherd. "I've requested some current meters and an oceanographer. You've probably seen the message. I want data on the current from the surface to the bottom, so I can try to establish if there are diurnal fluctuations."

Shepherd removed his glasses and polished them thoughtfully. He turned his gaze on Holmes. How different he looked without those strong lenses, Holmes observed; the eyes didn't look so unnaturally large. Shepherd said, "I appreciate these preparations, Commodore, but what will you do in the meantime?" He seemed to select each word, examine it, then add it to the sentence. Holmes was again aware of a vague accent.

"Those survivors are fortunate that their life support facilities are functioning," Shepherd continued, "but we must not be lulled into a false sense of security. One of those components can malfunction at any time. Then we are up against a very short deadline." He shook his head, "We must get on with what we have at hand with all speed." He looked at each man around the table and added superfluously, "Lives are at stake."

Holmes repressed a blunt reply and asked mildly, "What are your recommendations, Captain?" Shepherd looked around the table again, studying each man, then addressed himself to the commanding officer of the *Kingfisher*. "Captain Jenkins, what is your position over the *Lancerfish*? Are you exactly over the escape hatch?"

"As close as we can determine, sir."

"Well, it seems to me you possibly are not. Otherwise the downhaul cable would not be tending so sharply." He smiled as though he had revealed the answer to all the problems. Jenkins glanced at Holmes to see if he intended to answer the Captain and saw that he still had the floor.

"Sir, once the bell has the downhaul cable, it is pretty much independent of the ship, except for the backhaul. The action of the current is on the bell itself, which causes her to . . ."

"I know how the rescue bell operates, Captain Jenkins," Shepherd interrupted. "You do have the backhaul on deck, and by adjusting the *Kingfisher* in the mooring you might get the bell in a more perpendicular aspect. Do you follow me?"

"Yessir, I understand, but you see the tangent, or the angle that is causing the problem, is the cable in the fairlead. The current swings the bell out of line." Shepherd nodded in a slow, exaggerated show of patience and started to speak, but Holmes cut in quickly.

"Well, look, gentlemen, we're simply talking about the nuts and bolts of procedure. I suggest we take a look at the bell and then rejoin here before lunch." He got up and the rest of them clambered to their feet. Holmes was a little annoyed by the smug and superior attitude of Shepherd. He wondered how long the Captain planned to stay aboard.

When the conference resumed, Mr. Cunningham gave his analysis of the downhaul winch. He believed the motor which drove the winch was performing to full capacity, but the clutch plates were worn out. He recommended replacement of the entire winch assembly and estimated that it would require two to three days to get a new unit on board. The Commodore told him to go ahead with the procurement; in the meantime they would leave the old unit installed. Possibly the current would let up and they could make another attempt.

After lunch the discussion was mostly about the new rescue system known as the Deep Submergence Rescue Vehicle, (DSRV), which Shepherd had been working on for the DSSP. Shepherd gave a glowing account of the new concept, which was nearly operational, though it could not be employed to rescue the men in *Lancerfish*.

"However, the contractor tells us they may come up with a design alteration that would permit its use. They're working on it around the clock," Shepherd said, "and if all else fails, it may be ready for deployment in a few weeks."

Shepherd accompanied Holmes to the pilot house to communicate with the submarine and inform the survivors of the new delay. When Holmes finished talking with the Exec, Shepherd asked if he could say a few words.

"Commander, this is Captain Shepherd from the Naval Material Command. You are doing a splendid job down there in keeping your equipment going. As soon as the bell is repaired, we'll have you out of there. It may be another day or so, but keep the faith." He handed the microphone back to Holmes and said, "Captain, we've got to get on with this; you're not going to have this good weather forever."

105

"I wish to Christ I could get on with it," Holmes answered. "If that new winch doesn't do it, the next move will be up to you to get that rescue submersible operational."

Holmes went to his cabin. On the bunk were the newspapers brought out that morning by Shepherd. The story of the rescue efforts occupied the front pages of all editions. The lead story carried the headline "First Sub Rescue Attempt Fails," with a subhead "Mechanical Breakdown Blamed." In one story, on an inside page, was a photograph of the rescue bell with Lt. Morgan standing near it. Another account quoted Holmes as predicting all survivors would be rescued by Saturday, the twenty-second. Lewis and Wright must have sent their releases the night before by radio-telephone, Holmes surmised. The news stories were not inaccurate, but they were slanted to make them all look like fumbling idiots.

The more he read, the angrier Holmes became. Why do journalists have to color the facts with innuendo, he mused. Here was one: "Lack of vital equipment has delayed rescue of the trapped men in the *Lancerfish*. The submarine, which sank a week ago, lies on the edge of the continental shelf in 200 fathoms of water. The rescue vessel *Kingfisher* has been moored over the wreck since Wednesday, unable to go to the aid of the survivors. The cable from the hatch on the sub was not long enough to reach the surface. Navy divers could not lengthen the cable, which is used to guide the rescue bell down, until a special tool was flown to the site on Friday."

Holmes sent for Lt. Morgan and Captain Jenkins. He wanted to discuss the possibility of using a bell from another rescue vessel. "Jim," he said to the Captain when he and Morgan had joined Holmes in the small cabin, "I want you and Ben to give me your opinions about bringing in another bell. Do you think a different unit could work?" Morgan spoke up first: "No, sir, it would be a waste of time. Those air motors aren't all the same, but I feel none of them would

106

pull a chamber down in that current, with that scope of wire. This guy Cunningham says the winch he will send out will be much different from anything on rescue chambers in service." Jenkins nodded agreement, adding, "We wouldn't be gaining much. By the time another bell could be brought here, we'll be ready with the new winch."

"That's my feeling too," Holmes affirmed, "but I wanted your views to back it up." He handed the newspapers to Jenkins. "We're catching it from the press, of course. You want to read how we're flubbing around? I'll prepare a statement for our reporters." As the two men started to leave, Holmes said to the Captain, "Jim, I'd like to have all radio transmissions to the marine operator cleared through me. That way I can monitor some of the distortions our press boys are putting out."

That evening Captain Shepherd and one of the engineers were transferred back to *Frobisher*. They were airlifted from the destroyer's helo pad back to New York. Mr. Cunningham remained aboard to help install the new winch when it arrived.

6 – FAILURE

Monday, may twenty-fourth was a cold, rainy day in Washington, D. C. The weekend had been mostly fair until Sunday night when clouds had piled up on the horizon, bringing the balmy weather to an end. Admiral Foster Moran, Commander Naval Material, was in his office early, as he usually was on Monday mornings. Messages and mail that accumulated over the weekend required immediate attention and answers. The Admiral did not look like a naval officer in his dark brown civilian suit and tortoise shell glasses. His grey hair was combed straight back and clung tightly to his head except at the sides, where it sprang free in feather-like wisps. His large face with its generous features wore a permanent, good-natured scowl.

On the walls of his large office were reproductions of paintings, mostly of ships, and on the bookcase stood a model of a destroyer. Several folders had been arranged on his desk by his secretary. One was marked *"Lancerfish"* and held all the incoming and outgoing messages concerning the sinking. The Admiral had stayed in constant touch with the weekend duty officer at the Navy Yard Annex. When Holmes's long report arrived on Saturday, the Admiral left his gardening in Arlington and came in to his office. He spent the afternoon making personal telephone calls and composing messages. Wood's Hole Oceanographic Institute had been requested to furnish one of their research vessels and a scientist. The Navy's Experimental Diving Unit had been ordered to have divers experienced in the newly developed deep-sea lungs standing by in case they were needed. The Admiral had also telephoned the directors of three big industries which had deep diving submersibles either in existence or near completion. If one of them were needed, he wanted to ensure it would be ready and available. The U. S. Navy bathyscaph *Trieste II* was already underway in her tender, enroute to the rescue site.

The folder contained Holmes's last "sitrep" detailing the failure of the rescue bell on the first attempt. As the Admiral read the report he tapped his empty coffee cup on the edge of the saucer, the signal for the secretary to refill it. When she came in, she had a long message in her hand.

"This just came in on the *Lancerfish,* Admiral. It's from the Chief of Information to ComThree, and we're an info addressee."

He traded the cup and saucer for the dispatch without looking up. "Not so much sugar this time, Betty," he said and laid the message down. He was worried, not so much by the malfunction of the chamber as by the knowledge that survival of the crew depended on the continued operation of the reactor and life support system. Of course, one of the big boats, the *Triton,* had circumnavigated the world submerged, generating her own oxygen. But the *Lancerfish* was on the bottom, probably grooved deeply in the mud and sand, which could cause trouble at any moment. They were on borrowed time.

The Admiral believed the sub could be reached with current rescue methods. It might require some jury-rigging, or even building a new bell, but it could be done somehow. Time was pressing, however. Even now, Holmes reported the survivors were having difficulty with the air purifiers. He picked up the message his secretary had brought and scanned it:

All addressees take for action. Complaints have been received from media representatives stating they are not getting the cooperation desired regarding rescue operations on *Lancerfish*. Guidance for relations with all media is hereby promulgated. Commandant Third Naval District will be responsible for all releases concerning the *Lancerfish*. In that capacity, ComThree will work in close liaison with this command and the Commander of the rescue force. Requests for information, photographs, motion picture coverage, or statements shall be referred to ComThree. ComThree is directed to provide all possible assistance to accredited press and television news representatives. The only information to be withheld will be that which has security classification, or involving casualties to personnel. Commander, Rescue Force will provide communications facilities to media representatives at the site, on a not-to-interfere basis.

Admiral Moran called his secretary and dictated a memorandum to all departments in the Naval Material Command. It directed that inquiries concerning the sunken submarine be forwarded to the Chief of Information. When he had finished he called his Chief-of-Staff and instructed him to set up a conference which would include the Director of the Deep Submergence Systems Projects and the Supervisor of Salvage. If the rescue bell did not make the *Lancerfish*, they had better be ready with an alternative plan. The Admiral was not completely satisfied that ComSubLant had assigned Barney Holmes as the rescue force commander. Once the submarine had been found, Admiral Moran had wanted to give the job to Captain Shepherd, because of his involvement in the development of the new rescue system and the "Man in the Sea" program. But Admiral Calhoun had argued that Holmes was better suited for the job because of his experience in equipment and techniques that were "state of the art" in submarine rescue. The

110

new deep-diving system was still not certified, and the rescue submersible that had been under development since the *Thresher* disaster was not operational.

That morning at the rescue anchorage, Holmes read his copy of the message from the Chief of Information. There was no doubt in his mind that Leonard Wright had been the originator of the complaint, because he had refused him the interview with one of the survivors. Holmes was furious and considered calling Wright to his cabin to let him know his disgust with such tactics. The job was hard enough, Holmes thought, fighting the elements and equipment failures without having to be a public relations expert too. Why couldn't ComThree send a more experienced officer to be his liaison with the press? He went on deck and looked up at the sky. The *Kingfisher* pitched slowly in the mounting seas. The wind was increasing, spinning the anemometer high on the mast, and an occasional gust of rain swept across the weatherdecks. It was a dark day and the barometer was dropping. They could not have dived that day even if the bell had been ready.

Holmes climbed the ladder to the port wing of the bridge and saw the buoy marking the *Lancerfish* a hundred yards on the beam. The downhaul cable had been passed to it for security, and the rescue vessel had hauled to starboard in her moorings. He knew Wright would be after him again to use the UQC for his interview. In light of the message from Chinfo he was obliged to comply, but he felt sure that if the facts were explained to ComThree he would be backed up in his refusal. He read the message over again. "Commander, Rescue Force will provide communications facilities to media representatives at the site, on a not-to-interfere basis." There was no question in those explicit instructions. Holmes looked at his watch; nearly 1000. He decided to call the Public Information Officer at ComThree.

It took several minutes to bring Captain Billings up on

the circuit, and Holmes paced the small radio room. The radioman finally passed him the handset.

"Captain Billings on the other end, sir."

Holmes explained the request made by Wright and his reason for rejecting it. He referred to the message sent out by Chinfo and asked the captain, if he concurred. "It's a sensitive situation and will cause some repercussions when I deny his request again," Holmes explained, "so thought I had better clear with you. Over." There was a short pause before Billings came up again.

"Roger your message, Commodore. I believe this should be taken up with the Commandant. I'll call you back in half an hour. Out."

Holmes returned to the empty bridge, leaving instructions with the radioman to keep that circuit free. He waited only fifteen minutes before the radioman stuck his head out of the doorway to the pilot house.

"ComThree calling, sir."

Holmes was unprepared for the message from Billings. "The Admiral feels you should grant permission on the network request, Commodore, as long as it doesn't hamper your operations. Captain Shepherd is with the Admiral and also advises cooperation."

Holmes closed out the circuit. He certainly was not going to argue by radio. Anyway, they had heard his objections, which he felt were valid enough. And who the hell asked for Shepherd's advice?

When Holmes told the reporter that he would permit the use of the UQC for an interview, he had the feeling that Wright had been expecting it. Wright lost no time in setting his tape recorder and threading a new reel of tape. Lewis had come to the pilot house to get photographs of Wright at the underwater telephone. Several members of the crew had gathered in the pilot house as well.

"Okay, fellas," Wright admonished as he made final preparations, "I'm going to ask that you not talk while we're on the air." He then spoke into the microphone of the recorder, identifying and dating the tape. He started his machine when Holmes called the *Lancerfish* and explained what was desired.

While sonarman Johnson was being brought to the underwater telephone, Holmes gave a summation of the topside preparations for the next rescue attempt. The executive officer of the *Lancerfish* reported their machinery status: all equipment seemed to be operating normally. There was some difficulty again with the carbon dioxide scrubbers, but so far they were able to hold the level to a safe percentage. Holmes sensed the strain in Crawford's voice. The men had been on the bottom more than nine days, and the only rescue attempt had been a failure. They had two more days to wait before knowing if the new winch for the bell would work.

Crawford reported sonarman first class Johnson was standing by and added, "A final question, Commodore. In case the McCann chamber can't make us, are there any other solutions?"

Holmes answered as casually as possible. "There are several ideas being considered. The new rescue submersible is being worked on day and night. The DSSP boys think it might be modified to mate with your hatch. There's a lot of talent working on this, but personally I feel the chamber will make it Wednesday."

Wright, nodding to himself, was pleased with the exchange between Holmes and the sub's exec. He held up a thumb to indicate it had been well recorded. Then he took Holmes's place in front of the UQC, cleared his throat, and transmitted: "Hello, Johnson? This is Leonard Wright. I'm covering the television news on the rescue operations. A lot of people back home are naturally anxious about you and your shipmates. I think they will feel better by hearing something from one of the crew. Can you give me a few facts? Over." After a moment Johnson's voice came back:

113

"Yessir." The transmission was clear but had a strange echoing quality which Wright felt would lend a sense of drama. To Holmes the sound of the hollow voice was unsettling; it was eerie, like a supernatural communication from the grave.

"Johnson, what is your full name, how old are you, and where is your home?"

"C. Taylor Johnson; I'm twenty-five . . . will be twenty-six in a couple of months. My home is in Norwich, Connecticut."

"What does the 'C' stand for? Over."

"Claude, but I go by CeeTee."

"Well, CeeTee, how long have you been on the *Lancerfish*?"

"Too long, I reckon. About two years, and I'm ready for a transfer."

"I'll bet you are." Wright looked around at the men about him and smiled grimly. Then, with grave seriousness, he asked, "What is it like down there on the bottom of the ocean?"

"Well, we've got air and it's not too bad. It's cold in the torpedo room, but the rest of the boat is warm enough. We're getting a little tired of the food—CPO dogs, canned peaches, and tons of 'Aunt Jane's Homemade Pork and Rice Stew.' The bread is finished and we're on soda crackers, though most of them is busted up. We're in pretty good shape, I guess, though some of the guys got colds."

"How do you spend your time while waiting for the rescue bell?"

"We sit around and talk. Some sack out a lot. We've read everything aboard, even the instruction manuals. We had a poker game goin' but that's sorta petered out. There's watches to be stood on the oh-two generator and in the reactor compartment."

"Sounds like it's a bit quieter down there than up here. The sea is a bit rough today and the *Kingfisher* is rolling around. . . ." Holmes nudged Wright and shook his head from side to side pointedly. Wright continued, "Besides being rescued, what do you think about mostly?"

"Never setting foot on a submarine again," Johnson replied, a facetious quality in his voice. "Naw, I think mostly about my family, I guess. They must be worried, but we'll be out of here soon. I'd like to pass on to my wife to take it easy. It's not bad here, and we'll be home soon." Johnson paused but kept the transmitter open, then added, "We talk about a lot of things when just sitting around. Some of it would sound screwy if we weren't here. Like, everyone has his own idea what's important or what they'd like most to do again. Some guys talk about nothin' but food. When they get out they want to go to some big restaurant and have a really big feed. Johnny Mack comes from Arizona and wants more than anything to be in the middle of the desert. Saunders has a new car and he spends all his time figuring trips to Canada, Mexico, things like that."

"Do you have a special wish, CeeTee? Over."

"Yeah. Next to seeing my wife and kids, I'd like to get a suntan."

"Well, Johnson—CeeTee, you've got a lot of people working on getting you out. Commodore Holmes is doing everything possible. Thank you for this interview. We hope to be seeing you all soon, in another day or so."

Holmes closed out the underwater telephone circuit with Crawford. Wright had moved to the other side of the pilot house and was playing back the interview. Holmes felt particularly disturbed by the intimate exchange with the crewmember. What a hell of an ordeal for the survivors, waiting down there with no assurance they would ever get out. Yet they had hope and even confidence that in two or three days it would be over and they would be sunbathing somewhere. The human spirit must steel itself when faced with such grim prospects. The anxiety and strain of waiting for the next forty to fifty hours must be nearly unbearable.

Each time they awake from whatever sleep they can get, they must face the terror all over again. Holmes went out to the bridge and hoisted himself up in the captain's chair. The wind slapped the canvas bridge awning against the frame, and a fine rain speckled and runneled the windshield. Edgar Lewis made his way to Holmes's side, gingerly footing his way across the swaying, wet deck. His face, white and puffy, made him look old and weary. He fished out a last cigarette, crumpled the pack, and flung it toward the water, but the wind arrogantly sent it back.

"They say you can't do that, or spit to windward, until you've been around the Horn," Holmes told him matter-of-factly. "How long have you been a newspaperman, Ed?"

"About as long as you've been in the Navy, maybe longer. I started the old-fashioned way. Was a 'printer's devil' as a kid, swept the composing room, made the coffee, and ran errands. Then one day my editor sent me out to cover a firemen's ball, and he was pleased with my copy."

"Must have been a good story for such a routine assignment."

"Yeah, the ballroom burned down. Since then I've covered about every kind of news you can think of. Other fires, court blotters and trials, murders, near murders, riots, parades, and political speeches. But I've never had a job like this before." He was silent for a long moment, staring at the distant dark grey horizon. "Once I was sent to Pennsylvania to do a story on some trapped miners, but even that wasn't like this. I remember we stood around the shaft entrance with the company officials and the silent, grieving wives, and waited. When they had finally dug them out, the miners had had it. All they brought up was blackened corpses. Here we're talking to the men by telephone and know that for the moment they're not bad off. In a few days they can be dead too, but they're relatively cheerful, hopeful. We don't know really if they will make it or not."

Holmes listened without comment, watching the

marker buoy as it danced a crazy jig in the rough water. Lewis studied him a moment.

"Off the record, Commodore, what's their chances, if the bell can't make it?"

Holmes looked at him a moment before speaking. "It doesn't take a sailor to answer that one. Even a printer's devil can make a pretty good guess about that. The Navy has some other rescue gear which is still under development; maybe it can be put to use. I don't know, Ed, I don't want to think about that bell not making it."

By Tuesday morning the storm had passed and the seas were slowly subsiding. The order was given to start removing the winch in the chamber to make ready for the replacement. At 1100 the New York marine operator patched in a telephone call to Mr. Cunningham. It was from his assistant in Cincinnati. The new winch was on its way and would be at JFK International Airport by early afternoon. Holmes called ComThree on the harbor frequency and arranged for a Navy pick-up with a police escort, to transfer the winch to the Coast Guard landing in lower Manhatten. The *Frobisher* was dispatched for the job of bringing the winch to the site. Holmes did not want the helo to airlift it in case the weather closed in again.

Just after sunset the destroyer was seen on the horizon, a great bow wave testifying to her speed. Holmes watched the rapidly approaching vessel, which now winked a blinker light. The shutters on the big signal light over Holmes' head slammed receipt, and the signalman yelled to the bridge deck.

"Sir, from *Frobisher*. Winch aboard, request transfer instructions."

Holmes sent the *Hiawatha* to the outer buoy and instructed them to heave-to just outside the moorings. Then he signaled the *Frobisher* to have the tug come alongside to pick up the winch. It would be easier for the tug to maneuver alongside the rescue vessel, where caution had to be ob-

117

served to avoid the mooring lines. It would soon be dark and Holmes wanted the new unit aboard that night. When the destroyer slowed near the mooring buoy, a great plume of steam billowed from her stack as the safety valves lifted, releasing the excess boiler pressure. She must have had the super-heaters on most of the way, Holmes thought.

Even with the still turbulent seas, the transfer was quickly made to the *Kingfisher*. Captain Jenkins joined Holmes and Morgan on the fantail, where the wooden crate was being pried apart. Cunningham squatted alongside the two men working on the box. He looked up as the ship's captain approached. "We'll have this baby mounted before midnight, I think."

But some difficulties were encountered. The brackets in the chamber skirt did not match up with the fittings on the new winch. Holes had to be drilled and tapped on the winch before it was shimmed and bolted into place.

Looking back on that Wednesday, Holmes remembered it as a day crowded with events, people, and frequent communications with ComSubLant. Early in the day two press boats arrived on the scene. They were small private vessels chartered by media representatives in hopes of capturing some exclusive aspect of the rescue. The oceanographic ship from Wood's Hole had reported to the rescue force the night before and had already provided some information on bottom current conditions. The scientist in charge had lowered his strange devices after the ship had anchored just outside the moorings. Current readings were not encouraging. From the surface to 300 feet a fluctuating velocity was reported moving in a northeasterly direction. Its force was between 1.5 and 2 knots and would not affect the rescue chamber too severely. But near the bottom much stronger currents were encountered. They varied from 2.5 to a little over 3 knots, like streams on the ocean floor, spilling from the continental shelf into the great ocean depths. A bottom sample was brought up bearing loose sand and mud.

Other arrivals in the near proximity of the rescue site were private boats from New Jersey. Cabin cruisers, some forty to fifty feet in length, idled about. The brightly hued hulls and chrome plated fittings contrasted sharply with the dowdy grey warships and workboats of the Navy. The owners of these yachts were permitted to steer with a hundred yards of the moorings to take photographs and satisfy curiosity. Some of the spectators waved from their cockpits and pilot houses. Another visitor to the rescue area was a large, mysterious looking stranger. The ship remained much further out, prowling the perimeter. When the destroyer *Barnett* investigated, she reported back to the Commodore that it was a Soviet ship—either a large fishing mother-ship or some sort of research vessel. As long as the ship remained at a safe distance, it was of no concern to Holmes. After all, they were in international waters.

Holmes briefed the bell operators again, feeling less optimistic than on the earlier attempts. The information concerning the erratic and strong bottom currents was uppermost in his mind. If such currents were sweeping over the hull of the *Lancerfish,* the divers would have a hell of a time making the attachment and seal. Chief Petrosky dogged the hatch and reported ready, and again the huge orange bell was hoisted into the air and swung over the side. Petrosky reported they had passed the splice. At 200 feet the report came that there was a definite current felt in the bell, but the winch continued to haul them down. It looked like they would make the *Lancerfish* this time. Holmes telephoned the submarine before the dive and informed the survivors the dive was experimental. If the bell was able to reach the hatch and make a seal, the rescue would continue. He did not want them to be too hopeful.

The bell passed the previous depth record and stopped at 700 feet. Petrosky reported over the intercom: "The clutch is not tripping out, but there is a lot of vibration. We're leaning almost fifteen degrees; seems to increase with

119

depth." The strong bottom currents were beginning to be felt. Holmes was standing at Morgan's shoulder near the diving control stand. "Tell him to continue to seven fifty and report back," he said. Petrosky reported the new depth, saying that the vibration had increased. The order was given for 800 feet.

Holmes was tense and he paced a few steps forward and aft, stopping defiantly behind Morgan again with his arms akimbo, fingers gripping his waist. The time dragged. Four minutes after his last order, Petrosky's gruff voice boomed from the speaker. "We're putting a helluva strain on the downhaul, topside, sounds like a bass fiddle in here."

Wright and Lewis were at their customary vantage point on the deck house ventilator. From there they could watch the diving officer near the air manifold and the activity on the after deck.

Petrosky's excited voice burst again from the intercom. It was indistinguishable to the newsmen, but something serious had happened below. Lt. Morgan yelled to the motor whaleboat drifting off the port side. "Clear out of there! The bell is broaching! Downhaul parted and the chamber is coming up out of control!" The boat gunned away, heading in a direction away from the position where the backhaul entered the water. If the rescue bell came up under the *Kingfisher,* the momentum would carry it crashing through the hull, sinking her. Moments later the bell surged out of the water, well astern of the ship, then settled back into a gentle rocking motion. The whaleboat went alongside the bell, and a line was secured to the top to tow it back to the ship.

Holmes slowly climbed the ladder to the pilot house, his broad mouth set in a thin line. He watched the bell being lifted clear of the water. The now slack downhaul cable was brought aboard and coiled down; it had parted at the fitting on the *Lancerfish.*

Holmes reported first to the survivors in the submarine,

telling them that as soon as it was decided what the next step would be, he would inform them. The downhaul cable would be reattached somehow, and the rescue bell would have to be modified further.

Holmes went to his cabin with a pad and pencil to prepare the long report to ComSubLant. He wrote the first two sentences: "Shortly before noon the rescue chamber was deployed for the third time and reached a depth of 800 feet. At this depth the downhaul cable parted at the hatch of the *Lancerfish.*" He sat for some moments staring at his words before continuing.

7 – CONFERENCE

AFTER RECEIVING THE disheartening message that the downhaul cable had parted, Admiral Moran had called together a review group to determine what could be done to save the men in *Lancerfish*. Department heads, design engineers, and submarine specialists under his command were ordered to be on hand. Industry too would be represented. Electric Boat division of General Dynamics, builders of the *Lancerfish*, had three engineers from their Deep Submergence department present. Rear Admiral Calhoun, the submarine commander of the Atlantic fleet; Captain B. C. Holmes, Submarine Squadron Two Commodore, and now officer-in-charge of rescue operations; and the DSSP head, Captain G. G. Shepherd, III, also attended. From this meeting Admiral Moran hoped to establish a *modus operandi* for the rescue mission.

A sizable number of research ships and deep-diving submersibles had been assigned to the operations. The *Aluminaut* of Reynolds Aluminum Company was being brought up from Miami. Westinghouse Corporation was flying the *Deepstar 4000* to New York from its project in the Bering Straits. Already on hand was the newest deep-sea vehicle,

122

the *Seasearch,* under contract to the Navy from Oceanics International, Inc. One of these sophisticated new vehicles might be able to attach another cable to the stricken submarine.

It was nearly 1000 before the attendees settled into their seats at the long conference table and the extra chairs arranged along the walls. Admiral Moran stood at the head of the room on a small dais and greeted acquaintances with a brief nod of recognition as they entered the room. Behind him was a wheeled blackboard that had a rudimentary diagram chalked on it depicting the ocean surface and the bottom where *Lancerfish* was sunk. The Admiral, as well as other naval officers in the room, was in uniform. Holmes, who had flown in that morning, sat nearby on the rostrum with a lecturer's pointer across his knees. After introductions and a short address by the Admiral, Holmes was to give a briefing.

"Gentlemen . . ."

Admiral Moran paused to let the room become quiet. "Gentlemen, thank you for coming. I know many of you came a long distance and your personal plans have been disrupted. However, I know you understand the emergency nature of this meeting, which concerns the *Lancerfish* tragedy. The Navy is faced with a grave situation. A submarine has been sunk in deep water—over twelve hundred feet— and sixty-one men are trapped in the forward compartments. Yesterday, during the third attempt to get down to her with the McCann Rescue Bell, the cable attached to the sub's hatch carried away. The *Lancerfish* is now completely cut off from the surface." He paused to give emphasis to his statement. "I've asked you here to lend your expertise, and the resources of your activities, to our rescue efforts. Captain Holmes, the 'on scene' commander of the rescue force, will give you a background briefing. This will be followed by a short question and answer period. After lunch we will rejoin here for reports from those involved in the Deep Submergence Systems Projects. Captain Holmes, will you proceed?"

As Holmes faced his audience he was struck by a profound sense of familiarity in the proceedings, almost a psychic feeling of *déjà vu*. But, he knew he *had* participated in just such a meeting three years previously. That occasion was for the nuclear powered submarine *Scorpion*, lost with all hands. And, even before that, in 1963, he had been a member of the Deep Submergence Systems Review Group, called after the *Thresher* disaster. Many of the faces that confronted him now had attended that first conference and the subsequent meetings. What had been the outcome of all that effort? In both of the previous accidents the submarines had gone to depths far exceeding the crush limit of their hulls, and the Navy had not been confronted with the problem of personnel rescue. But they had all perceived that someday such an event might happen. The new generation of deep attack boats was increasing in numbers, and thus increasing the possibility of what they now faced. Study groups had been commissioned, funds allocated, and the acronyms assigned. The Deep Submergence Systems Project was established, and the Large Objects Salvage Systems report was published. As the years went by, names like DSSP and LOSS were familiar terms. It was to be an era of ocean exploitation. The schemes were enthusiastically pursued and illustrated by imaginative artists' concepts showing men living at the bottom of the sea, crews being rescued from disabled submarines, and huge industrial complexes extracting the mineral wealth of the ocean floor. The legislators, particularly those from coastal states, were the most ardent of the evangelists for exploitation of the sea. "Hydrospace" became a popular term, and grand phrases like "the great cornucopia of the sea" were often repeated.

Then the budget cuts came, brought about by the Viet Nam "commitment," an inflationary economy, and the necessity of continuing a quixotic strategic arms race. When the spending had to be reduced in the Defense Department, the first to suffer were the scientific research and development programs that had no tactical military applications. The submarine rescue vehicle, which was to have been operational in five years, slipped a year, then another. The concept was tremendously complicated, requiring vast expenditures for development of components that were not "state of the art." The vehicle had finally been launched, but the submersible was plagued by equipment failures, late deliveries from subcontractors, and exorbitant cost overruns. Fate had caught up with them. The *Lancerfish* was down with men stranded in the intact compartments and Holmes had to rely on a technique that was outdated and totally inadequate.

Holmes's presentation was short; there was little to tell. He dealt with the environmental conditions, the strong bottom currents, and the unpredictable weather at the site. He felt that if the downhaul cable had not parted, he would have had the men up by now. The cable itself had not failed, but rather the steel attachment terminal on the sub had torn loose. When the cable had been brought aboard the *Kingfisher,* the bitter end had a piece of the fixture still dangling where it had been connected. The next step was to send the small research submersible *Seasearch* down to inspect the hatch. Another cable had to be attached somehow.

When he had finished the briefing, Holmes asked for questions. He surveyed the group and recognized the slim, uniformed arm of Captain Shepherd rise at the far end of the table. "Yessir," he acknowledged and Shepherd stood up, identifying himself to the assemblage.

"Captain Holmes, what alternatives have you considered if the rescue bell can't be used?"

"None at the moment. I've got to have a look at the *Lancerfish* from the *Seasearch*."

Shepherd remained standing with his head bowed and his fingers arched on the table as though it were a piano. Holmes knew he was using the question to introduce some comment or idea of his own. "I'm hoping our representatives of industry with us today will have some suggestions," Holmes said, adding with a trace of a smile, "or perhaps even something that is operational from your shop, Captain."

"The *Seasearch*, yes . . ." Shepherd paused portentously and resumed in his studied, pseudo-Oxford accent. "It will be interesting to learn just how deeply the submarine has settled in the bottom. We might consider trying to lift the *Lancerfish* at the stern. If slings can be placed under the tail fins, the new salvage barges might be able to raise her. After all, the sub has buoyancy forward." He turned his head sideways to look down the long table at Holmes through his thick glasses.

Holmes was incredulous. "Your lift cable could be tied in knots by the current, Captain, and the slings, I doubt that . . ."

"But it is worth considering," Shepherd cut in. "It *is* an alternative, don't you agree?"

"We'll consider anything, of course, if the most practical methods fail, but rigging slings in two hundred fathoms . . . getting your barges in a secure mooring . . ." Holmes for a moment was speechless. "Why it would take weeks, if not months."

Shepherd smiled patiently and added, "if at all," and sat down. He commented in general to the group, "I don't think rescue by salvage should be rejected too quickly."

The exchange annoyed Holmes. There was no time to be wasted on useless harangue. Shepherd would like to get his department involved in the rescue operation, and Holmes would gladly have accepted this help, if they had a

126

realistic system that could be deployed. Shepherd was no doubt a brilliant theoretical engineer, but he was no seaman, Holmes concluded. He didn't know the elements.

A few technical questions from other members of the group followed. Most were concerned with the *Seasearch* and the inspection dive Holmes would make. When the meeting adjourned for lunch, Holmes left for the airport and his shuttle flight back to New York. At JFK International airport a helicopter waited to airlift him out to the rescue site. Holmes was anxious to be back on the *Kingfisher*.

During the afternoon session the group heard from several speakers representing industry. They described advances in technology that had been realized and which permitted deep-diving vehicles to perform impressive functions underwater. None of these, however, could accomplish the one feat Admiral Moran was looking for: a means to deliver sixty-one men from what would otherwise be their grave.

Captain Jenkins was on deck when Holmes returned that afternoon. He was hatless and a light breeze ruffled his thin grey hair as he waited for the Commodore to come up the accommodation ladder. When Holmes faced him questioningly, he announced without preamble, "Their number one scrubber is out and there have been some problems with the other one too." He followed Holmes up to the bridge, continuing his report. "Crawford feels they can correct the one on the line now, but number one air purifier is gone for good. He doesn't seem too worried."

"Yeah, but I am, Jim. I don't know how long it's going to take to get another cable attached." Holmes looked at the ships moored around them. There were more than when he had left. The tender for the *Seasearch*, a converted minesweeper grandly named *Marine Explorer*, was anchored a half mile to starboard. "Can I dive their gadget now?" Holmes asked, indicating the tender by a nod. "There's more than four hours of daylight left."

"They reported ready in all respects when they arrived this morning, Commodore. I didn't think you would be back this early." Jenkins moved quickly into the radio room to call the tender. Holmes did not expect to accomplish much in such a dive, except survey the *Lancerfish*. Even if the hatch was clear, he had no idea how the cable would be replaced, but he had to do something and do it soon.

The *Seasearch* looked incredibly small to Holmes when, a half hour later, he climbed the short ladder to the stern of the *Marine Explorer*. It was less than thirty feet long and shaped like a giant ocarina, painted orange. The hemispherical front had two large portholes that canted down and slightly to each side, giving the vehicle a wall-eyed appearance. A mechanical arm, drawn up like an elephant's trunk, was poised in the center below the viewports. Mounted on the bulbous brow were four pressure-proof mercury vapor floodlights and a deep-sea camera. A man in sky blue coveralls emerged from a group of men at the stern where the shrouded propeller was being tested. He approached Holmes, extending a hand. "I'm Tom Parsons, Commodore, pilot of the Seasearch," he said, adding as a tall thin man came up behind him, "and this is Bob Hoffman, our project engineer."

Holmes nodded and explained the situation. "The bottom gradient is steep here, with some outcroppings. The oceanographer reports currents of two knots or more. Do you think your minisub can handle that?"

The pilot, who appeared surprisingly young to Holmes, described the small submersible with familiarity and pride. "This baby has a working depth of ten thousand feet and a life support system good for forty-eight hours. Cruising speed is more than five knots, with a full power capability of eight knots. She's the latest model of our deep workboat series developed at Oceanics International." Holmes walked around the cradled sub. The boom of the hydraulic crane

128

was already positioned over it. They would dive to the west of *Lancerfish*, then home on her by sonar.

Holmes lowered himself into the spherical cabin of the *Seasearch*. The interior was crowded with instrument panels and controls; it looked more like the cockpit of a jet aircraft than a research submersible. Parsons slid into the pilot's seat and pulled the hatch shut, spinning the dogs home. He deftly flipped down a row of toggle switches, energizing the life support blower and interior lighting. The speaker over Holmes' head hummed, and the small TV screen on the control console came to life with little figures of the men on deck.

When the check-off list was completed, they were swung out and lowered to the water. As soon as the lift bridle was disconnected, the little craft began to roll in a giddy motion, even though the sea had looked quite calm from the tender. Aquamarine light from the submerged viewports flickered on the bulkhead and faces of the two men. The pilot checked the underwater telephone: *"Marine Explorer,* this is *Seasearch;* diving." He reached behind him and opened the valve that would flood the ballast, then started a timer on the console. "We're on our way, Commodore," he said confidently and turned his attention to the echo sounder.

The swaying sensation subsided and soon stopped. The blue light from the viewports darkened and Holmes watched their descent on the illuminated depth gauge. Propulsion and attitude controls were tested and then shut down while they settled. The pilot adjusted the rate of dive once, slowing it as they approached the bottom. The depth gauge showed they were dropping past 400 feet; the water outside had deepened to a crepuscular twilight. The underwater telephone was again tested, this time with the *Lancerfish*. The voice from the sunken sub sounded garbled, the words clipped off due to the disparity in frequencies between the two sound equipments. It made little difference,

Holmes thought; there was no real need to communicate with them. Perhaps it gave the trapped men some comfort to know the little sub was just outside their hull, trying to do something for them.

At 600 feet the pilot reported to the tender, giving the outside water temperature: forty-eight degrees. The pilot maneuvered the submersible into a position facing the upward slope of the bottom and turned on the exterior floodlights. Holmes crouched by one of the observation ports but could see only a great circle of brilliant light. A few particles in suspension in the water seemed to move upward as they sank; but it looked relatively clear. At a depth of 1100 feet Holmes suddenly saw the sea floor angling up in front of them. It seemed to be moving, rather than the *Seasearch*. The hard mud and sand was eroded and carved by the scour of the current. Slender tube worms grew out of the bottom, all bent in the same direction as though blown by a mute wind. The terrain was bleak and foreboding, and Holmes felt an almost despairing apprehension for the men in *Lancerfish*.

The *Seasearch* turned and followed the sloping bottom into the depths. The sonar radiated circles of light on the scope as it scanned ahead. A bright pulse indicated a target; it had to be the submarine. The pilot adjusted course and slowed the propulsion thruster. Combined with the current they were doing more than six knots over the seabed. When the range closed to fifty yards, the pilot stopped the motor; the bottom gliding under them slowed. As the range shrank to thirty yards, reverse power was applied, which reduced the forward movement to a slow creep. Holmes was cramped and numbed with cold. He pressed intently against the viewport, wiping it from time to time as it became fogged. The mercury vapor floodlights cast a disc of light that crept over the surrealistic landscape. There was a swelling of the bottom and in the gloom beyond the pall of light rose the blunt bow of the *Lancerfish*.

The pilot corrected their angle as they came up on the wreck. They were drifting down the port side and Holmes could easily see details of the fore deck heeled toward them. The circular main ballast vents recessed in the superstructure, the deck cleats, and the great, empty socket where the messenger buoy had been before it was released were clearly visible. Then he saw the torpedo room hatch. All was so still, it was difficult to believe that just beyond that pressure hull were living, breathing men.

They moved slowly down the pitched deck, and the pilot triggered the exterior camera. The strobe flashed like summer lightning. In a moment the high pulpit of the conning tower leaned toward them. The diving planes protruding from each side gave the impression of an aircraft, banking endlessly. The plexiglass windshield on the bridge caught and reflected their floodlights.

"Move in closer, Tom. I think I see something adrift on the bridge." Holmes's voice was muffled by its closeness to the viewport. "That's it . . . a little more." Horror filled him. There was a man motioning to him. He was kneeling with head bowed and arms floating up, as though he were conducting an orchestra in slow motion. The force of the current rippled the duffle coat and turned the body toward Holmes. "Oh God, it's Joe!"

"What?" the pilot tried to peer over Holmes's shoulder.

"That was Commander Hascomb, skipper of the *Lancerfish*. Something must have trapped him on deck and he went down with the boat." A fearful dread welled in Holmes; he wanted to be away from there, away from that specter of death, away from the whole damned, pitiful tragedy of the *Lancerfish*. The scene was gone now, but he was left limp, with an icy sweat standing on his body.

At the stern of the *Lancerfish* they saw a small stream of bubbles rising on the far side of the hull. It came from the ragged gash caused by the collision. Probably an air line still leaking into the water, Holmes guessed. The stern fins were clear of the bottom, though from bow to just forward of this the hull was deeply grooved in the mud. They took more photographs; Holmes knew Shepherd would be particularly interested in this area. Even if slings could be swept under the tail fins, Holmes was doubtful that a lift could be made. There was as much as fifteen feet of the sub's hull buried in the bottom, which would present a colossal suction. The breakout force would be measured in thousands of tons.

Holmes dreaded the return inspection up the starboard side. He did not want to see that macabre apparition again, bowing and swaying in the current. It seemed they had been down for hours, yet the timer on the console indicated only thirty-seven minutes. As the *Seasearch* rounded the stern of the submarine, Holmes noted their depth; 1270 feet.

The collision damage was formidable. A vertical area of about twelve feet testified to the tremendous impact of the bow of *Ocean Belle*. From there for about twenty-five feet a horizontal rip in the steel plates opened the main ballast tanks and breached the pressure hull. As they moved up the side, more power had to be used against the head-on current. They passed the bridge again and Holmes was relieved to see that the body was not visible.

The forward hatch area was completely clear. No fragments of the downhaul connector were to be seen. When the pilot tried to hover the *Seasearch* near the hatch, he found that the current caused them to crab from side to side or slowly twist. They could not hold a definite attitude or position. Holmes tried to communicate with the survivors inside the *Lancerfish,* but he could not understand the chopped and fragmented words that blasted from the speaker.

"All right, Tom, let's get out of here," Holmes said, taking one last look at the black hull outside his viewport. "I think we pretty well covered everything photographically." He thought for a moment.

"Did you take any shots around the bridge? I mean, did you photograph . . ."

"No, sir," the pilot cut in, "I didn't shoot that."

Nearly a full minute passed with Holmes lost in thought. Then he said grimly, "I'm glad of that."

It seemed to take less time to surface than it did to dive. But it was because the Commodore was deep in thought. Seeing the *Lancerfish* nearly half buried in the ocean floor, the powerful current that made it nearly impossible to remain in one position, the darkness and cold, the very remoteness of the depth, all this depressed him. They could not even retrieve Hascomb's body. It would have been too dangerous maneuvering in the bridge area. In spite of his feelings, Holmes knew what the next step would be. Another deep-diving submersible would be needed to assist the *Seasearch*, or even clear it if it got fouled while working on the bottom. Then they would install padeyes and rig a means to hold a work sub over the hatch while a new cable was attached.

When Holmes returned to the *Kingfisher*, he found Leonard Wright waiting for him. He could tell the correspondent was annoyed and Holmes surmised the reason. Neither Wright nor Lewis had been informed of the inspection dive in the *Seasearch*. They were expecting that event the next day. Holmes apologized briefly, promising some of the photos which were being developed aboard the *Marine Explorer*. Before the evening meal Holmes held a debriefing in his cabin for Jenkins and Morgan. He expressly invited the two reporters to attend, to make up for his thoughtlessness.

At 2000 Holmes went with Captain Jenkins to the pilot house to communicate with the *Lancerfish*. Commander Crawford sounded weary and was having difficulty in speaking. His cold infection had obviously progressed. Nearly half of the survivors in the stricken sub were down with respiratory infections.

133

Number two carbon dioxide scrubber had been repaired to some extent, though it still functioned erratically. The carbon dioxide level was up to two percent but was not increasing. The contaminated atmosphere and the debilitating effect of twelve days on the bottom was no doubt responsible. Crawford reported that two of his men were seriously ill.

"It looks like pneumonia, Commodore. Our chief corpsman gives a very pessimistic prognosis if we don't get them out of here in another day or so." There was a long pause before Crawford could continue, sounding hoarse and breathless. "We've got them in an oxygen tent rigged out of blankets, but they seem to be getting worse."

"I hope it won't be much longer," Holmes transmitted. "We'll try to attach your cable in the morning, Commander. We're doing everything we can." His assurances to Crawford sounded lame. Holmes was getting to hate these communications with the sub.

Long afterward Holmes would look back on this day and realize that it represented an end to a phase in the rescue operations on *Lancerfish*. Until that day there had been no post-collision fatalities or other terrible episodes. It was the last time he would entertain any optimistic hope. It was the last time he would ever speak with Lieutenant Commander Crawford.

8 – DESPAIR

Hopes rose in the survivors when the rescue bell made the last attempt to reach them on Wednesday, only to be cruelly dashed when the cable tore loose. This was followed by the ominous failure of the carbon dioxide scrubber the next morning. The polluted air caused the men to pant with the slightest physical effort. To go from one compartment to another, or even to speak, left them breathless and exhausted. All hands were again ordered to their bunks, to reduce the increase of carbon dioxide, and a deserted quiet settled throughout the submarine.

Hayman lay in his bunk thinking about the men working on the air purification system in the machinery compartment. The suspense of not knowing whether or not it would be repaired pushed aside all other considerations. Even progress in the surface rescue efforts seemed unimportant, compared to the immediate danger of a contaminated atmosphere. With both systems out, Hayman calculated they would survive less than twelve hours. It was obvious that under the most favorable circumstances it would take much longer to install another downhaul cable and commence evacuations by bell.

Maybe this would be their end, Hayman thought, simply this mechanical failure which would allow all life in the submarine to slowly expire. Other machinery components would continue operating for a time. The reactor and generator would furnish the electrical power for ventilation blowers, lighting, and even the underwater telephone. All would go on functioning, senselessly and unsupervised. Long after they had all perished, the rescuers might finally reach them, only to be greeted by the stillness of unoccupied compartments. He dozed for some moments, fitfully, with half-conscious thoughts merging into absurd dreams.

Presently Hayman awoke and focused his eyes on the chair opposite his bunk. He had been talking with a stranger, a naval officer who sat in the chair discussing the rescue operations. In his dream the officer had told him he would be allowed to leave the *Lancerfish* only on the recommendation of the Exec, and if he had the proper qualifications as a lieutenant. Silly dream, but a terrible loneliness swept over him. It was too silent. No voices or sounds of movement could be detected to reassure him he was not alone.

Hayman got up and made his way aft to see if there was any progress on the air purifier. As he passed the wardroom he saw Fitzgibbons slumped over the table, his head cradled on his plump arms. By the time he got to the control room he was struggling for breath. Crawford was sitting on the chart desk, his head bowed and his arms propping hunched shoulders. He looked up as Hayman approached; the red-rimmed eyes were glassy, and the flushed face testified to a raging fever. When he spoke his voice was a husky whisper.

"Ritter says scrubber on line . . . not up to par . . . should hold CO_2 level." Hayman noted the CO_2 analyzer indicated 2.8 percent relative accumulation. Crawford continued with effort, his chest heaving.

"We're spreading more absorbent in after compartment to speed up . . . purification." He paused several moments, trying to catch his breath. "I gave orders to stay in your bunk, Hayman."

"I got up to make sure you hadn't left without me."

By noon the air had improved and the men were permitted to circulate so they could get their lunch of pork and beans and canned pears. Hayman found only Fitzgibbons, Roche, and Ritter in the wardroom. No one was interested in the simple meal Rumford had prepared. The Exec had turned in to his bunk, and Chief Ryan was with him.

The officers sat about the table with little to say, their gaunt, bearded faces pensive. Roche stared at his plate, his fork poised uncertainly, and announced to the group: "We've got two more down with lung infections." His eyes swept the table. "Ryan thinks it's the bad air that is irritating lungs and creating symptoms similar to pneumonia." Ritter, starting to eat, replied with a full mouth, "Yeah, we've got at least another two days down here, maybe longer. Only one scrubber now for sixty-one pairs of lungs." He looked up to see Chief Ryan standing in the doorway. "Yeah, Chief?"

"The Exec is pretty sick, sir. Temperature over a hundred and three. I gave him a shot, but I'm not sure antibiotics help much."

Ritter stroked his nose. "And the others, how are they?"

Ryan shook his head. "Looks bad. Sorensen's temperature is up again, and Chief Evans is having trouble breathing. Each case starts as an upper respiratory irritation, then digresses into the lungs. After a few hours the exudation—fluid—accumulates rapidly, like pneumonia."

Fitzgibbons stopped eating and opened a notebook on his lap. "How many are sick now, Chief?" he asked.

"Four, sir, with the Exec it's five." Fitzgibbons made an entry in his notebook. "What's the purpose of that, Fitz?" Roche asked with interest.

"A journal, sort of a chronicle of our ordeal. If the Lord sees fit to deliver us, I'll have it published."

"Suppose your friend screws up and we gotta stay here," Hayman interjected. "What'll you do then, Fitz, put it in a bottle and float it up?"

"Don't be blasphemous, Robbie." Fitzgibbons looked hurt. "We'ah in no position for that kind of talk. It wasn't amusing."

"Come off it. You weren't so holy before we got into this jam," Hayman sneered. "I remember your activities during our last Med cruise. Talk about raunchy . . ."

"I don't deny it, but I've changed. I've seen the truth. Maybe it takes something like this to show a man he has been wrong, sinned thoughtlessly. Discovering my faith again has been a revelation for me, and I thank God for it. You might turn to Him, Robbie, and ask Him for salvation."

"Balls."

"I know you profess to have no belief, but you do, you do, and whether you like it or not, my prayers are for you as well as myself."

"Fitz, you're a pain in the ass. Goddammit, just let us get out of here and I'll bet all your piety will go right out the window!"

Fitzgibbons straightened in his seat and tilted his head back, as though searching for inspiration, and quoted: "In Thee, O Lord, do ah put my trust; let me never be ashamed; deliver me in thy righteousness."

Hayman slid out of his seat, taking his plate with him to deposit it in the pantry sink. He couldn't take any more of the conversation. Fitzgibbons had always annoyed him, but this rabid holiness was intolerable. He had to get away from him.

In spite of his weakened condition, Crawford insisted on being in the control room during Commodore Holmes's

138

inspection dive in the *Seasearch*. Several men crowded about the control stand to listen to the operation as it was described over the underwater telephone from *Kingfisher*. Even the unsuccessful attempt at communications with the small submersible was interesting. It was impossible to distinguish the fragments of words that squawked from the speaker. Yet it was a comfort to know that this emissary from the rescue force was so close, even though nothing could be done. Later, when Holmes was again on the rescue vessel, they learned that the hatch area was clear. Hope began replacing the despair that had hung over them since Wednesday. Holmes did not report the fate of their captain; it seemed pointless at this time.

Hayman observed that this lighter mood was not reflected in the Exec. He appeared distracted, as though some inner thought absorbed him. After signing off on the underwater telephone, Crawford made his way feebly to his quarters. Ryan visited the Exec's stateroom several times that night. There was little he could do except record Crawford's deteriorating condition. The chief's other patients in the after compartment also were not responding to treatment.

Hayman awoke to hear someone calling his name. It was Fitzgibbons.

"Come on, Robbie, you'd better get up. There's bad news."

Hayman massaged his face, then propped himself on his elbows. "How's the Exec?"

"The same, or worse maybe. Ryan is rigging an oxygen tent for him." Fitzgibbons was silent for a moment and then said abruptly, "Sorensen died last night." His flat statement sounded like an indictment, as though Hayman was somehow responsible. "Ryan says he went back to check on him about two this morning and he was gone. Dead. That's the first one, Robbie, now it starts. One by one each of us will go." Fitzgibbons' melancholy eyes searched Hayman's face to see his reaction to the tidings. Hayman, noncommittal, dressed.

Ritter entered the stateroom looking very haggard. He had taken most of the night watch in the machinery compartment. He was still concerned about the scrubber and wanted to be on hand in case it failed again. "You heard?" he said to Hayman. "In a way it was a surprise. I expected Evans to go. Ryan is talking to the force doctor on the underwater telephone now. Doesn't seem much can be done for the others." He sprawled on the bunk. "We'll have to do something with the body. Have a couple of your seamen make up a bag out of a mattress cover and we'll trice him up in his bunk."

"We can't leave the body in the sleeping compartment," Hayman declared thoughtfully. "It would be bad psychologically for the others. We don't know how much longer we'll be down here. Four of the tubes are empty in the torpedo room. We'll load him in one of those."

"I'll perform the service," Fitzgibbons announced importantly. "We'll hold it in the torpedo room." He left to make his preparations.

Chief Harris stuck his head in the wardroom where Hayman was finishing a lukewarm cup of coffee. "Where's Mr. Ritter?" he demanded.

"Turned in, I think. He was up most of the night," Hayman said. "What's up?"

"I've got to give him a message from the rescue ship." Harris turned to go.

"Hold on, Chief," Hayman called out querulously. "What's the message?"

Harris stepped back into the wardroom. "*Kingfisher* says Commodore Holmes is making another inspection dive with a Captain Shepherd, director of the DSSP. They should be on us about ten hundred."

140

"Very well, don't bother to wake Lt. Ritter."

"But he left instructions to keep him informed of all new developments." The chief's gaze was vaguely contemptuous, "I figure Mr. Ritter is in command while the Exec is incapacitated."

"Lieutenant Ritter will get the message when he wakes up, Harris. "Anyway, that's hardly a new development." Hayman turned away, dismissing the chief.

Hayman went to the torpedo room to instruct McGovern to make number four tube ready. The compartment seemed crowded. No doubt the extra men were from the after compartment, where they normally berthed; they now wanted to be away from the solemn preparations of Sorensen's body. Several men were grouped about the breech doors talking. How different they looked, Hayman mused as he made his customary check of the signal ejector. Some were so disheveled he barely recognized them. Bartolla, the cook, had a thick black mat of a beard. A baggy khaki sweater, stained dark at the elbows and down the front, completed a repulsive sight. Others, like Cruthers or young Lombard, had only a trace of fine whiskers etching their white faces. One man, with his back to Hayman, was talking. He was called "Harpo," for his thick curly hair and reputation as the ship's clown.

"They say we're going to run out of food if we have to stay down here much longer."

"Who says?" Bartolla demanded.

"Mr. Roche. He said we got lots of air and water, but the chow can't last forever."

Bartolla picked his nose. "There's enough for another month, especially if Mr. Roche starts rationing."

"Man, imagine if we began starving," Harpo said. "D'you suppose we'd become cannibals? Jesus, can y'imagine eatin' Bartolla? Just looking at him turns my stomach."

Bartolla clasped his bicep and thrust up a phallic forearm. "Rotate, Harpo. Maybe you ought to take first dibs on Sorensen."

"You're rotten, Guinea Wop," said a voice in the group, adding in wonderment, "I saw them take him down from his bunk. Hell, he didn't look dead, only sort of white, like he'd passed out. It'll seem funny without Seapig around."

McGovern looked over the heads of the group toward Hayman. "Yes, sir. You want me?"

Hayman checked the tube with his torpedoman and found it dry. The water in it had been blown to sea after the collision, when they were trying to recover buoyancy. Now all that was necessary was to vent it off. Hayman ordered the bunks in the forward section of the compartment rigged up, explaining to the men that the operations officer would be holding burial services there. To Hayman, these ritualistic preparations were too much. Fitzgibbons was making a big production out of it. Soon they would be repeating the performance for Chief Evans and maybe for others later. When it got near 1000, Hayman went to the control room to learn how the inspection dive was going. Lt(jg) Langworthy had the watch. As soon as the submersible completed the survey, they would go ahead with depositing Sorensen's remains in the torpedo tube.

At 1120 word came down from the *Kingfisher* that the *Seasearch* had completed her dive. Work would commence as soon as the new parts were fabricated and a second submersible was on hand to assist. It was expected the two submersibles would attempt the replacement of the downhaul cable the following evening. The constant force of the current made it impossible for the little sub to remain in a fixed position over the hatch while it welded a new fixture in place. A trapeze-like device had been devised, which was to be attached to the hull forward of the hatch by explosive bolts. The submersible, with a specially designed mooring hook, would latch into the trapeze frame facing the current. Once attached, the vehicle would lower to the deck of the *Lancerfish*. In effect, the submersible would be moored to the sunken submarine and able to work. All of this required considerable time. The apparatus had to be made and tested on the surface. Adaptations to the submersible had to be made and 1500 feet of cable faked out on the after deck of the rescue vessel.

All the lights were on in the berthing quarters of the after compartment. Sorensen's body had been encased in a green leatherette bunk cover and rested on a litter in the passageway. Hayman found Fitzgibbons had changed into his service dress blue uniform. He looked very solemn and official as he gave the order to remove the body to the torpedo room. The procession moved awkwardly along the canted deck, shifting the burden carefully as they passed through the watertight opening into the control room. Hayman followed the grim party and as he passed the radio room he saw Schoenberg sitting behind his typewriter, staring straight ahead. The radioman had always been a curiously quiet type, Hayman observed, but this complete withdrawal from the rest of the ship's company bothered him. There was certainly no need for a radio watch, yet the man was always in there.

The litter bearers put their load down in the torpedo room. They were breathing heavily from the exertion. Though the atmosphere had improved, there was still a relatively high percentage of carbon dioxide. The word was passed from the control room that the service was about to begin, although a majority of the survivors were already crowding into the torpedo room. Fitzgibbons had positioned himself by the starboard breech doors and faced number four tube. The heavy brass door had been opened and the dark sepulchral tunnel was ready for the interment. To Hayman this was no longer a torpedo tube, a piece of ordnance, but a tomb. It occurred to him that this was not just

143

the temporary stowage of a body, but Sorensen's final resting place, just as the engineroom contained the bodies of the other crewmen. Eventually, the *Lancerfish* would be only for the dead. A fitting sarcophagus for a submariner.

Hayman made his way to Fitzgibbons' side, a vague amusement welling in him as he looked at the pompous officer. His dress blue uniform and immaculate shirt contrasted sharply with his two-week-old beard.

"Fitz, get this over with as quickly as you can. The carbon dioxide will build up fast with so many men in one compartment."

"I'm using the burial guide, it isn't long. A few minutes will hurt no one." He turned away, opened a small volume and began quoting:

"Blessed be God, even the Father of our Lord Jesus Christ, the Father of mercies, and the God of all comfort; Who comforteth us in all our tribulation, that we may be able to comfort them which are in any trouble, by the comfort wherewith we ourselves are comforted of God." Fitzgibbons then read the service from the manual for burial at sea. As he finished he nodded toward four men, who lifted the body and gingerly placed it in the tube. The heavy breech door was swung shut and McGovern looked to Hayman. "Shall I flood it, sir?"

"No, just dog it," Hayman said, "and shut the vents." Flood it, Hayman thought impatiently—Christ, we're not going to fire him to sea.

As he turned to go, Hayman saw Ritter at the after bulkhead motioning to him. Chief Harris must have awakened him in spite of his orders. As he drew alongside Ritter said, "The Exec wants to see all officers right away in his quarters. Chief Harris will take the watch in the control room."

The executive officer's stateroom, which Ritter shared, was too small to accommodate them all. Evers and Roche stood outside the doorway, allowing Hayman to squeeze between them. The blanket that had been serving as an oxy-gen tent had been pulled aside. Hayman was astonished by the transformation of Crawford. The face was pale and the eyelids drawn over the sunken eyes, and the lips had a bluish cast. His labored breathing came in short exhalations and long struggling intakes of air. Ritter bent over him. "All here, Bob. Make it short so we can get you back under the oxygen tent." For a moment there was no response, then Crawford nodded almost imperceptibly but did not open his eyes.

"Del, you . . . take charge . . . next in chain of com-mand, can't . . ." For a painfully long minute the only sound was the wheezing respirations. ". . . make it. Bell should make us in a couple of days. Keep morale up in crew."

The eyelids flew open and he seemed to be looking about the room, but he was slipping into a coma again. Chief Ryan stepped forward and tucked the blanket into place and opened the valve on the oxygen tank. He placed a stethoscope under the covers and listened intently.

"Heart rate up—acute anoxia is setting in. I don't know how long he can hang on."

Crawford lasted nearly thirty hours more. The news of his death came from Fitzgibbons, who had been with him during the late afternoon on Saturday. He came into the control room where Ritter was waiting for word from the surface concerning the operations of the submersibles.

"The executive offisuh has just passed away," Fitzgib-bons announced to the men in the compartment. "Com-mander Crawford is gone," he repeated.

A few minutes later the voice of Commodore Holmes came from the underwater telephone to tell Ritter that it was necessary to postpone diving the submersible that day. The sea conditions on the surface had become too rough for launching. When Ritter told the Commodore that Crawford was dead, there was a long hesitation, then Holmes's gruff voice said, "I'm sorry, Mr. Ritter. As soon as we get a break in these seas we'll get down to you."

That night the burial service was repeated in the torpedo room, but this time it was shorter, and Fitzgibbons did not put on his dress blue uniform.

Sunday morning the underwater telephone failed and the *Lancerfish* was completely cut off from the surface. It was assumed by the survivors that the submersibles would begin work sometime during the day. Not until late afternoon, when the UQC was again operational, did they learn their rescuers had been unable to dive, because of the storm blowing topside.

The atmosphere in the submarine had been cleared of excess carbon dioxide, revitalizing the men and bringing with it renewed optimisim. Ritter kept the men busy bailing water from the torpedo room bilges. A long bucket brigade passed the buckets to the machinery compartment to be dumped in the copious bilges. Ritter did not want to use the dwindling high-pressure air that was required to blow the sanitary tank. Trash and garbage were also becoming a problem, because there were no means for disposal. The empty tins were flattened and put in cardboard boxes along with other refuse. As the cartons collected they were stowed in the useless refrigerator room. When that space became filled, they would have to pile the boxes in the passageways.

Chief Ryan reported to Ritter that his patients were resting more comfortably. Chief Evans was still under the oxygen tent and was considered the only critical case. All of the sick men had been moved to one corner of the berthing space, where it would be easier to keep them under observation. They would be the first to go up when the rescue chamber started operations. The remainder of the crew had been given numbers corresponding alphabetically with their surnames and would leave the boat in that order.

When the bailing had been completed, Fitzgibbons conducted Sunday lay services in the torpedo room. Hayman observed that these functions were growing longer as Fitzgibbons improved upon his liturgical style. His sermon was delivered firmly, reflecting his preparation the night before. He seemed to enjoy his role as spiritual leader of the men, not caring that his Fundamentalist preaching fell upon Jewish and Catholic ears alike.

All morning the crew waited to hear some exterior sound that would tell them the submersibles were at work on the hatch. Johnson, the sonarman, concentrated on the circuitry of the underwater telephone. He probed the maze of electronic elements with an ampmeter, finally locating and replacing the faulty part. Shortly before 1700 Johnson put down his screwdriver and snapped the power switch on. The dials lit and after a moment the sound of the carrier frequency hissed on the speaker. Ritter called the rescue vessel, and Holmes himself answered, obviously relieved to be in communication with the submarine again. He told the survivors that a force-5 storm had prevented their dive that day. The *Kingfisher* was having trouble staying in the moorings, and if the seas continued to mount they would have to take in the lines and clear the area. It was difficult for Ritter to think of the rescue vessel rolling and pitching above them. In the submarine it was quiet and there was a cryptal immobility to the listing deck.

The *Kingfisher* held on and the seas began subsiding on Monday. By Tuesday morning it was possible to deploy the little subs, and a large number of the survivors gathered in the torpedo room. Most of them faced forward, waiting expectantly for some sound indicating the efforts of their rescuers. The anticipation of these operations had roused them out of their soporific weariness, and there was a murmur of voices. A metallic scraping above their heads suspended the talk; like entranced spectators, they looked up at the hull. A series of sharp reports were heard throughout the subma-

147

rine, signaling the firing of the explosive bolts. The first phase of the job was complete; now the submersible could work on the hatch. There was a three-hour interval in the operations while the *Seasearch* returned to the surface to be fitted with the welding apparatus.

Step by step the crew in *Lancerfish* followed the progress of the work, relayed to them over the underwater telephone. The most difficult and longest part of the work involved rigging the new downhaul cable. To avoid fouling the long scope of cable in the current, and to permit the *Seasearch* to handle the attachment end, a special procedure was used. A reel containing 1500 feet of cable was mounted in a steel frame. The end that was to be attached to the hatch was passed through a drag brake and a 200-foot leader unreeled. The *Kingfisher* lowered the spooled cable to a position near the port side of the *Lancerfish*. The *Seasearch* then maneuvered the end of the leader to the sub's hatch, where it was attached by the other submersible. It required extreme care by the submersibles to avoid becoming entangled in the lift cable. When the downhaul had been secured, the submersibles cleared the vicinity and the rescue vessel lifted the reel in its frame, the cable paying out as it was brought to the surface.

When the word came over the underwater telephone that the downhaul was on the *Kingfisher,* a chorus of cheers resounded in the control room. Ritter grinned with satisfaction and announced over the speaker system that they were once more connected to their rescue vessel. He looked at his watch, 2130, and happily noted the event in the log. The men pressed about the control stand, their faces jubilant, everyone trying to talk at once. Ritter held his arms over his head.

"All right, sailors, hold it down. Quiet . . ."

A voice was coming over the underwater telephone, but Ritter could not understand the transmission. He asked for a repeat, turning up the gain. The voice from the surface

148

told them the rescue chamber was being readied for the first descent. Fitzgibbons, who had squeezed into the control room from the forward compartment, said, "Our prayers have been answered," looking from side to side at the crew members, his face beaming. Then becoming fervent he clasped his hands, tilted his head back, and intoned, "Thank Thee, O Lord, thank Thee for hearing our prayers."

The relief and joy was evident in the after compartment. All the lights were on in the berthing space, and Chief Ryan checked his patients. Two of them sat on the edge of their bunks, their wan faces smiling feebly. They would go up in the first chamber load and were waiting for Ryan to take them to the torpedo room. Chief Evans was the only one who did not know that perhaps their rescue was at hand. He was in a deep coma, barely alive.

In the dinette Cruthers tossed the remains of his coffee into the sink and said to Dirksen, "Jesus, I think we're gonna make it, Rowboat." Then to Harpo, "What'll you give to trade places with me for the first trip?" The other man didn't reply, knowing Cruthers was not serious. There would be about seven chamber runs to account for all of them. It would take fourteen to sixteen hours to complete the rescue. The general announcing speaker interrupted the bustle of voices: "Let me have your attention, this is Lt. Ritter. When the rescue operations commence tonight, dress warmly and stand by in the after compartment or control room until your group is called away. When you go to the torpedo room, keep the noise down, stay in numerical order, and pay attention to instructions from Mr. Hayman."

Hayman stood under the hatch which led up into the escape trunk and the upper, exterior hatch. If the bell was able to make a seal around that hatch, they might be on their way soon. He felt relieved that a cable had been installed, but at the same time he was fearful of being too hopeful. That bell had to work its way down 1200 feet. It seemed impossible that the nightmare was almost over. His apprehension stemmed from the possibility that this attempt would end in failure, revealing their plight to be completely hopeless. How would he face such a fact? To know they were irrecoverable, lost forever, would be an insufferable ordeal. It would be better if the reactor failed and cut the time shorter. In a few hours they would suffocate in their own exhalations, and it would be finished. No, that would be horrible too, he thought. For a while the batteries would furnish some lighting; then, as the power was used up, the light would grow dim and finally would disappear altogether. To die in total darkness would be terrifying. Unthinkable.

Hayman cautiously opened the drain valve on the escape trunk. Any accumulation of water in that space would run into the torpedo room. It was dry, so he opened the lower hatch and climbed up into the small cylindrical compartment. On the side there was a circular hatch, used for making escapes in shallower water; in port it provided access to the forward part of the submarine. Many times he had used this hatch to the topside deck when they were moored alongside a pier in New London. If now he could just swing that hatch open and step up into the sunlight of a spring day in Connecticut, what a relief that would be. To feel a cool wind against his face, see a limitless sky, God, to hear birds again! He lowered himself back into the torpedo room and shut the hatch. Soon they would know, and perhaps in a few hours they would be free.

Time passed slowly as they waited. Perhaps there was some problem connecting the downhaul to the bell, or maybe the sea was too rough and it would be hours before the first run. At 2225 the *Kingfisher* telephoned that the chamber was in the water and slowly winching its way down the cable. A sound powered telephone talker was stationed next to Hayman to relay progress of the rescue bell.

The first group came into the compartment and assembled on the starboard side. The two pneumonia cases were wrapped in blankets. Chief Evans was to be moved when the bell had made its seal.

The phone talker grasped the transmitter on his chest: "Torpedo room, aye." He reported to Hayman, "Sir, main control says the chamber is at five hundred feet and descending." A smile spread over his face. Hayman acknowledged and said to the group, "almost half way," thinking to himself that if all went well his turn to leave would come in about eight hours. Ritter would be the last officer out, after returning to the reactor room for the last time to shut down the pile. Lt(jg) Evers was scheduled to make the second trip up and would be the first officer rescued. Earlier he had volunteered to remain until the last group, but Ritter had rejected the idea, remarking lightly that he had no need for a navigator.

Another report from main control: the bell was encountering a strong current but was having no difficulty in continued descent. Depth 700 feet. The report cheered Hayman considerably, and an overwhelming optimism pervaded his thoughts. If the rescue bell could operate despite the current, it would surely be able to seal to the escape trunk. They were going to get out.

This feeling was fortified when the chamber reported at 1000 feet that the current had diminished a little. Even the weather topside was improving. The waves had abated and Commodore Holmes told Ritter it was a starry night on the surface. Then the chamber was reported at 1100 feet. They must be just over them, Hayman thought. The mood of the men in the torpedo room was one of relief, but there was little talking. They were waiting almost breathlessly, hoping to hear some evidence that the chamber had settled around the hatch.

The minutes passed and they all stared at the phone talker. To relax the tension a little, Hayman said to the as-

151

semblage, "They'll approach the hatch very slowly; probably take a few minutes." The suspense in the compartment mounted. More time passed and Hayman had the talker inquire about the progress.

"Still about eleven hundred feet, sir," the talker reported automatically. A chilling foreboding passed over Hayman. Why had they stopped there? Were they having problems? More than five minutes had passed since the last report.

"Mr. Hayman," the talker suddenly broke the silence that had settled in the torpedo room, "Mr. Ritter wants you in main control."

Ritter was standing in front of the underwater telephone, the microphone in his hand. "They've got a jammed winch," he said to Hayman bleakly. "At the moment the rescue chamber can't go up or down." He put a foot on a rung of the ladder to the bridge, resting his forearms on a knee, and continued. "There's more than fourteen hundred feet of cable on the winch drum because of the catenary. Too much, sounds like a turn of cable slipped over the drum cheek. At any rate, if they do clear it, the dive will be aborted."

Fifteen minutes had elapsed since the rescue chamber had come to a stop at 1120 feet. The tired, resigned voice of Commodore Holmes came from the speaker: "*Lancerfish*, the bell is stuck at depth with a fouled winch. We must cut the downhaul cable to retrieve the chamber." After a long moment he repeated, "We're cutting the downhaul to bring up the chamber, there's no other solution. We'll re-rig as soon as possible and modify the winch."

The crew of the *Lancerfish* were stunned with disappointment. Slowly the men of the first and second chamber groups drifted back to their spaces. The two pneumonia cases returned to their bunks. Chief Ryan planted thermometers under their tongues and looked across the narrow aisle to the blanket that hid Chief Evans. He was oblivious to the whole event of the rescue attempt, Ryan thought, reaching for Evans' wrist to take his pulse. But Evans was dead.

9 – FIRE

It was shortly after midnight when the body of Evans was put in the torpedo tube. There was little ceremony except a quick service performed by Fitzgibbons. The condition of one pneumonia victim had declined and Ryan had him transferred to the bunk vacated by Evans. The blanket serving as an oxygen tent was still rigged and might relieve the labored respirations of the sick man. Most of the crew turned in, emotionally exhausted by the events of the day. Each phase of the rescue attempt had progressed so favorably throughout those long hours that they had begun to feel almost confident that their ordeal was over. When the vital downhaul cable was cut, the mood changed to one of frustration and disappointment, but not hopelessness. After all, Hayman reasoned, the rescuers had been able to attach the new cable, and the bell had come within feet of the hatch. If it could be done once, it could be done again, and the next time the winch would be adapted to hold the extra length of downhaul wire.

Hayman went aft to inspect the other compartments before going to his stateroom to turn in. Chief Harris had the watch in main control with seaman Cruthers, his messenger. Harris addressed Hayman as he passed through the control room.

"You'd better have a talk with Schoenberg. He refused to take the watch on the underwater telephone."

Hayman stopped and looked at the chief, who faced him with his hands plunged in the pockets of his foul-weather jacket. He still looked very much the chief-of-the-boat, wearing his gold master-at-arms badge and chief's hat. "He's holed up in the radio shack and hardly ever leaves there," Harris said, his mouth gyrating slowly over his chewing gum.

"Do you really need him? I doubt if the rescue ship will be calling us tonight, and if they did, you could answer."

"That's the way I set up the watch and the . . . Exec approved it."

Hayman moved on, murmuring, "All right, Chief, I'll talk to him, but I don't think you need him for the watch."

Some routine had to be observed, Hayman conceded, though the chief's insistence seemed ridiculous. He doesn't like his authority flouted, even under these circumstances, Hayman thought as he stepped into the radio room. He saw Schoenberg lying on a mattress that he had brought into the tiny compartment. By the light over the typewriter he saw that the radioman was awake. He did not speak as Hayman straddled the desk chair, crossing his arms over the back.

"You have a run-in with the chief-of-the-boat?" Hayman asked casually. Schoenberg had not moved, but only stared into the overhead gloom. When he got no response, Hayman continued: "Everyone's a little tired of this waiting, and the disappointment today was a ball breaker. Looks like it might be another day or so, too." He looked to see if his words made any impression, observing only a slow blink of the eyes. "We should be out of here in a couple of days—seventy-two hours at the longest."

155

Schoenberg's deep voice almost startled him. "I don't care if we do or don't. We all cop it sometime. I'd just as soon have mine now."

The remark and the man's resignation made Hayman uneasy. The despair seemed unwarranted. Did Schoenberg have some overpowering premonition of doom?

"You want to see your family again, don't you? See your wife, who as I remember is a real doll. You're the envy of every guy on here." Hayman lapsed into silence, thinking about the vivacious little blonde he had seen with Schoenberg at the last ship's party. "Imagine how worried she is and how relieved she'll be to have you home."

"Bull."

Schoenberg pulled himself into an upright position. His unkempt hair hung in his eyes; he was a sharp contrast to the well-groomed sailor Hayman had known in the past.

"Look, Lieutenant, it's more than just being stuck down here. I hope all you guys make it out, but for me I just don't give a damn."

"What is it then? What could be more important than getting back to safety? To your family again?"

Schoenberg took a deep breath. "Okay, Lieutenant, I'll tell you a sweet story." He hugged his knees and was silent for a long time, as though searching for the words. "There's this guy, a car dealer who sold me the tee-bird last January. Big operator—bleached hair, long sideburns, deep tan, the whole bit. One night I get home and this dream-boat is with Val—tells me he just happened to be in the neighborhood and dropped in to see how the car is running. What a jerk I was." He reflected a moment before continuing. "Then, that afternoon the Old Man gave us early liberty before we got underway. I went home and found this Carl has his car parked in front. I guess I knew what I'd find, but they were pretty fast. I didn't actually see them doing it, but when I got inside this bastard was stuffing him-

156

self back together." Schoenberg's voice became tight, packed with emotion.

"I went ape, really out of my tree. I accused them, but this bastard says I got no evidence, and I didn't, but I wanted to kill him. I tried to fight him, but he kicked the crap out of me. Just kept calling me 'junior' and kicked the crap out of me."

Hayman could think of nothing to say. He sat there letting Schoenberg recover. After some moments the sailor went on.

"That wasn't the worst part, Lieutenant. You see, the kid was there. He's only four, but he understands things. He watched this guy whip me and he cried. He'll never forget seeing me getting beat up. A couple of days afterwards I tell Val I want a divorce, and I want the kid. She just laughed, really laughed; she'd been drinking. Then she tells me the kid isn't mine anyway. The more I think about it, the more I know it's true. I don't want to see either of them again."

"But that's not the end of everything," Hayman said. "You've got to get back to straighten your life out, maybe start over again."

"Screw it."

Hayman got up. He was tired and the story Schoenberg had told depressed him immeasurably. He had to get out of that gloomy little cubicle. Why did people marry in the first place, he thought, what was the purpose? He continued aft through the dinette. There were only two men sitting at a table talking. He moved on cautiously through the darkened berthing space. Nearly all of the bunks were filled with men seeking the escape of sleep. The air was fetid and disgusting. For more than two weeks no one had been permitted to bathe. They could not afford to fill the sanitary tank too often. He hurried into the reactor compartment and then down the short ladder and through another watertight door into the machinery room. Dirksen was making the hourly inspection of the bilges from the lower flats. At the rear of the compartment an auxiliaryman and electrician sat wordlessly, waiting for the long watch to pass. Hayman welcomed the smells of oil and grease after the pungency of the sleeping compartment. There was a comfort in the humming machinery and muted howl of the ventilation blower.

When Hayman passed through the control room again, he avoided speaking with Harris, who was busy looking over the security check-off. Hayman was extremely tired, but before dropping into his bunk he pulled out the writing folder and looked at the girl's photograph. More than ever she appeared as a stranger. She looked impersonal now, and so damned clean and lighthearted.

Shortly before 0400 Dirksen shuffled into the control room to report that the next watch had been awakened. He told Chief Harris that he had also roused Chief Ryan, because the pneumonia case under the tent sounded bad. "Breathing like he was gargling," Dirksen said descriptively. He squatted next to Cruthers, who sat huddled on the deck to wait for their reliefs.

A dull concussion resounded through the submarine, and the decks quivered. Cruthers bounded up, like a puppet yanked to its feet. Harris stumbled around the chart desk, yelling that it had come from the after part of the boat. Cruthers leaped through the watertight hatch and got as far as the dinette, then saw the orange glow on the bulkheads of the berthing space. Thick gobs of smoke boiled over him. He turned back to the control room. "Fire!" he shouted between choking coughs. "Fire in the after compartment!" As he swung through the opening, he heard what sounded like a whistle behind him; then it descended into a man's scream. The fire alarm blotted out the horrible sound, and Harris was shouting at him to shut the watertight door. A plume of smoke poured into the control room. Cruthers looked around wildly.

"But Chief, those guys in there . . ."

"Shut that goddamn hatch!" Harris bellowed again, simultaneously closing the bulkhead flappers of the ventilation line. Cruthers brought the massive door shut, winding the dogs home. Harris grabbed the microphone of the general announcing system, and his voice filled the compartments.

"Fire in the berthing space."

Dirksen had manned the sound powered phones and got a report that the reactor room was secure; the watertight door leading to the berthing space was shut. Men from the forward compartments piled into the control room, dazed and confused. Lt. Ritter prodded his way into the compartment and quickly surveyed the situation. He ordered the damage control team to get two men ready in emergency breathing appliances. "Have them stand by with CO_2 extinguishers," he said to Hayman. Then he went to the watertight door and looked through the glass peephole. The whole after compartment was dense with smoke. When he undogged the door, a curl of acrid yellow smoke seeped around the gasket.

Hayman gave instructions to the two men who were struggling with the harnesses of their breathing gear. They were to locate the fire and determine if it was electrical or from some other source. As soon as it could be brought under control, they were to get the men out. The watertight door could be opened for only an instant; it was too dangerous to allow more smoke into their already heavily contaminated atmosphere. The men climbed through the opening quickly and were handed the extinguishers. The fumes stung the eyes of the men in the control room and set off a chorus of coughing. To Hayman, the smoke smelled like burning mattresses rather than electrical insulation or oil.

Reports came in from the reactor compartment and machinery room. There was less smoke there, and only the two watch standers were in those spaces. They were ordered to put on emergency breathing units and stand by the air compressor. As soon as the fire was under control, the exhaust ventilation line would be opened and the compressor started. Ritter would then release air from the emergency bank into the control room. In this manner the smoke-laden air would be carried back to the machinery compartment, compressed, and discharged into a low air bank.

The firefighters fumbled back to the control room and reported the fire was out. It had been on the port side of the berthing area and apparently had been caused by the oxygen exploding over the sick man. The smoldering remains of blankets, mattresses, and bunk covers were wetted down and thrown into the refrigerator room under the deck. Personnel in the berthing space were either unconscious or dead. They had to be brought out as soon as possible. Two more men from the damage control party were rigged out in emergency breathing gear and sent in to relieve the exhausted firefighters.

The circulating air began to clear the after compartment, and the limp forms of the men who had been in the berthing area were pulled into the control room. Only one man showed any sign of life, writhing and gagging on deck. Chief Ryan and all the men on the port side of the compartment had died almost instantly from the blast of the exploding oxygen. Later, when Ryan's corpse was being removed from the debris, a small cigarette lighter was found clutched in his hand. The chief had unthinkingly used it to check his patient because a flashlight was not available. And that had flashed the raw oxygen-soaked blanket into a ball of flame.

Out of the thirty-six men who had been in the berthing space, five survived. Others hung on for a short time, then one after the other they slipped away in spite of the efforts to resuscitate them. The men who had been in the control room during the fire had inhaled considerable smoke. They could barely function and were sent to the torpedo room where the atmosphere was clearer.

160

For Hayman, every inhalation sent a spasm of pain into his throat, spreading into his bronchial passages and lungs. His head swam as he moved about with Langworthy dragging bodies out of the passageway. His mind and body seemed to react automatically, and he had the sensation that he was standing apart, observing a dim nightmare. Then slowly he made for the torpedo room, exhaustion coming on rapidly. Each step was a leaden effort and he felt the strength draining from his body. At the watertight door leading to the forward compartment he stopped. The high coaming was an insurmountable barrier, and he would not have made it except for Evers, who practically lifted him through the opening.

When the surviving crew members had sufficiently recuperated, they faced a grim task. The bodies were moved back into the sleeping compartment; there was no other place to put them. Each was zippered into a mattress cover and placed on a bunk, which was then partly folded up. Chief Harris supervised the work, noting the name of each casualty on a pad of paper. Lt. Ritter was going to raise the *Kingfisher* on the underwater telephone to tell the Commodore the tragic news. There were only twenty-seven of them now. More than half of the original survivors were dead.

Members of the after compartment that escaped the fire moved to the torpedo room. Later that day Cruthers ticked off the names of his shipmates who had died.

"Jesus, Rowboat, they're all gone. Howie, Lewis, Harpo, Saunders . . . just like that." Then suddenly remembering, "and Saunders owed me twenty bucks, not that it's important. I'd give a lot more than that to be out of here."

After Ritter read the names of the new casualties to Commodore Holmes he learned that progress was slow on reestablishing a downhaul cable. Also, the winch in the rescue bell had to be replaced with a special type, and it was

161

doubtful that one existed. The winch would have to be made up, and that would require additional time. The situation in *Lancerfish* was not desperate at the moment, but Ritter felt dubious about the life support system. The air purifier was holding the carbon dioxide to two percent relative. They could last if that critical piece of equipment held up. But other vital auxiliaries were showing signs of possible failure. The overboard discharge pumps were again overheating and could fail anytime. Even the underwater telephone was erratic. Ritter had to have the Commodore repeat some of his transmission.

All of the remaining men in *Lancerfish* had suffered smoke inhalation to some degree. Of the twenty-seven survivors, twelve were so seriously affected that they were totally incapacitated. Most of these cases had been in the berthing compartment or the damage control party in the control room. Except for the watch in the machinery room and Chief Benson in the control room, all hands were in their bunks. Ritter was reluctant to use any more of the remaining air in the emergency bank in case the life support system went out altogether. But if the atmosphere did not improve by the end of the day, he would use some of this vital reserve to ventilate the compartments.

Late in the afternoon Hayman went to the wardroom. He felt stronger and able to move about, though a throbbing headache persisted. He dropped into a seat at the deserted table and poured a cup of warm orange juice from one of the cans left out by Rumford. Hayman wondered if anything had taken place since that morning, so he called the control room. Fitzgibbons had the watch and told him one of the submersibles had made a dive, but no work had been accomplished. Two of the men from the torpedo room were in the galley preparing an evening meal for the survivors. The rescue vessel had called to inform them that Sunday was the soonest they could expect another attempt. The best news was that the carbon dioxide percentage was still decreasing. The reason for this, Fitzgibbons pointed out, was that there were fewer of them left alive.

Roche came into the wardroom and took a seat opposite Hayman. "Feeling better?" he inquired as he poured some of the canned juice.

"Yeah, but I've got a headache that won't quit. The air's clearing, so it should go. How are you hacking it?" Hayman noticed the dark circles under Roche's eyes seemed more pronounced.

"I was in the torpedo room and didn't get much of the smoke. Some of the others are in pretty bad shape. I don't know if they can make it until Sunday." He tasted the orange juice and made a face. "Sure doesn't improve with age. Robbie, Fitz told me he plans to hold another of his pray-ins tonight." Roche looked across the rim of the cup. "What do you make of Fitz—I mean, all this religious fervor? I don't mind him praying for me, but the fanatical way he goes about it is weird."

"The *Lancerfish*'s first casualty," Hayman answered. "I mean it. I think something snapped in him after we were sunk. He just can't cope."

"And he's so damned officious about it," Roche continued. "He wants to know each man's religious beliefs and if they've been baptized, or 'saved.' That journal he keeps has all our names in it, with remarks. He's probably tabulating our sins; sort of acting as God's scribe. He'll most likely be on hand at the Pearly Gates to muster us out."

Hayman smiled. The image of Fitzgibbons importantly calling out names and citing those who could or could not enter the Kingdom of Heaven was droll. "Maybe he's doing some good; if it brings the men a little comfort, you can't knock it. Maybe they need it." Hayman shrugged tolerantly.

"And how about you, Robbie? Do you need it?"

"I've thought about it. We may buy it down here and it would help if there was something to hang onto. But Fitz's

163

approach is not it. Religion for me—God in capital letters, the Bible, the whole thing—seems to belong to this world and not the next. I don't believe it, I can't, and yet I also find it hard to accept that Crawford and all those guys in the berthing compartment don't exist anymore." Hayman fell silent, lost in thought, then said, "We all die sometime. If this isn't it, there will be another day. We can't escape that event."

" 'A man can die but once; we owe God a death,' " Roche quoted. "I think that's Shakespeare." Then, attempting to change the mood, he added, "Well, it isn't hopeless, not yet, just a hellish wait until Sunday, or whenever it is they finally get to us."

No progress had been made by Saturday, the end of their third week on the bottom. The little research submersibles had made several dives, scraping and bumping over the torpedo room, but had not been able to remove the fitting on the hatch. The day before one of the smoke cases had died, a third-class sonarman named Miller who was hardly known to Hayman; he had reported to the *Lancerfish* just before they sailed.

Worse still was the news that the rescue bell could not be adapted with a new winch. Instead, another chamber at the Portsmouth Naval Shipyard was being redesigned for the task. It needed considerable modification to the lower skirt and would require additional time. In spite of these setbacks, Commodore Holmes was optimistic. He told the survivors that he believed the cable could be replaced and the new bell would make the rescue. He also told Ritter of the large fleet of ships that were participating in the operations. A new submarine tender was on hand, destroyers, ocean-going tugs, and even an additional rescue vessel. Of the civilian ships assigned to the rescue force, there were three industrial research vessels with their submersible workboats; a special catamaran ship with a new deep-div-

164

ing system on board, and oceanographic ships. To make it complete, there was even a large Russian ship seen from time to time on the outskirts of the rescue area. The previous day the civilian divers on the catamaran had tested their capsule by pressurizing it to a comparable depth of 900 feet. With this unique diving apparatus, which had previously been used in offshore petroleum exploration, they could technically achieve a depth of 1200 feet. If the submersibles were unable to reattach a downhaul cable, Holmes intended to use the divers. If the divers were able to take the pressure, it would be an open sea depth record, and it would certainly be risky.

The tragedy of the fire and subsequent loss of so many shipmates had drastically altered the mood of the survivors. The crew's dinette was now deserted except at meal times. The men avoided this area of the submarine, which was adjacent to the berthing space containing the bodies in tiered bunks. Miller's remains had been added to this space, which Cruthers called the "peanut gallery." When the men gathered to eat whatever dish could be concocted from their dwindling stores, they ate quickly and silently. It was as though all those still forms were reminding them of their own ultimate fate. Death had carelessly cut a swath through their ranks, missing them, but would return to reap them all eventually. The torpedo room was now their gathering place; a refuge for the living.

Late Sunday night the rescue vessel reported to the *Lancerfish* that the remaining cable had been cut away. The attachment fixture now had to be removed before rigging the new downhaul.

Monday morning Langworthy came to the wardroom where Ritter was eating breakfast to tell him that the underwater telephone had failed again. "Can't transmit or receive. Johnson is working on it now," he said as he sat down next to Hayman. "And, oh yeah," Langworthy said, remembering, "the *Kingfisher* called before the UQC crapped out. They had a message from the shipyard saying the new chamber will be ready Wednesday if they get the new winch on time." Another forty-eight to fifty hours of waiting, Hayman calculated, and another two nights to get through. That was the worst part now, trying to sleep away those hours. And lately he had been having fearful dreams.

Hayman went to the control room for the morning watch and found Johnson going over the operating manual for the underwater telephone. The console was open and his tool chest was on the chart desk, to protect it from the moisture on deck. From time to time the sonarman would hold a finger on the page, marking his place, and peer at the exposed circuitry. "I don't know where the trouble is," he answered to Hayman's query on progress. "There's a lot of condensate in the air, maybe something shorted out."

When Hayman remembered the accident later, it seemed to have taken an incredibly long time and was burned indelibly in his mind. Ritter had come to the control room and was standing behind Johnson as he worked. After each adjustment, Johnson would turn on the power and key the microphone to see if the transmit light would come on. Ritter watched the sweating sonarman impatiently, his thin body poised like a whippet, ready to dash off at any moment. He made involuntary movements, as though he would snatch the screwdriver from Johnson's hand and complete the repair himself. His whole being vibrated concentration. He spoke suddenly.

"There you are, Johnson, see that capacitor? It's burned, shorting the whole circuit." He had leaned up close behind the man's shoulder to point. "Here, give me the screwdriver." Johnson resignedly moved aside.

Then it happened. At first there was just a sizzling sound in the air that seemed to last some moments. Ritter turned slowly to the right, as though executing a difficult dance step. His blank eyes swept the unperceiving men in the compartment. He was already dead. As his body dropped away from the panel, a sharp crack rang against the steel hull. Lt. Ritter's face reflected the blue flash.

DETERIORATION

10 – THE PROPOSAL

COMMODORE HOLMES TOOK a turn around the main deck of the *Kingfisher* before going to the wardroom for breakfast. It had been three days since the last communication with the *Lancerfish,* and he wondered what their situation was now. This was their twenty-sixth day on the bottom. Though he had no voice communications with the submarine, Holmes knew there were crewmen alive down there. Near the beginning of every watch someone pounded on the hull. They had heard other evidence too. It had been reported by the *Kingfisher*'s sonar watch that he heard what sounded like a group of men singing. Holmes knew the submariners could neither receive nor transmit on their underwater telephone. He had called them and asked for acknowledgment by pounding on the hull three times if they were able to hear him, and there had been no response. It was just as well they had no communications; there was nothing to report. The night before, a long message had come from the shipyard which described unforeseen problems in the modification of the bell. Also, he had not been able to connect a new downhaul cable. Holmes thought of the sub's crew and could imagine them sitting under the torpedo room hatch, waiting and hoping that momentarily they would hear some evidence of the rescue chamber over them, and then at last the hatch would open and they would be free.

On the fantail Holmes encountered Chief Petrosky, who with a cup of coffee supervised the morning washdown. Holmes returned his casual salute and looked about the wet decks. Everything was shipshape and ready for use. Fathoms of canvas-covered hose looped in figure eights hung from the after bulkhead of the deckhouse. The rescue chamber was in the cradle and griped down, no longer needed. The new downhaul cable on the large spool was mounted in the steel frame, ready for lowering to *Lancerfish* once the new securing device was attached. Holmes looked out across the water at the ships that either steamed slowly on the periphery of the rescue site or rode easily at anchor. It would be a fine day, with few clouds and a light breeze that had a hint of warmth, a softness that suggested summer was not far off.

From the side of the destroyer *Frobisher*, anchored less than a mile abeam, Holmes saw a motor whaleboat make for the *Kingfisher*. It would be bringing the mail and newspapers that had been picked up in New York. He leaned on the gunwale and watched the small grey boat knifing the water toward him. He was interested in what new articles and editorials might have been written about the operations to reach the *Lancerfish* crew. Since the first week, after the sunken submarine had been located, the public reaction had been one of increasing dissatisfaction with the Navy, as well as with his own efforts. An editorial in one paper had suggested that the Navy was concealing the fact that they were more interested in the atomic reactor than in the rescue of personnel. "Eventually," the article read in part, "these safeguards and fail-safe features of the nuclear reactor will be affected by the sea. Over a period of time, be it long or short, corrosion will expose the core of the reactor and thus permit nuclear contamination of our entire eastern seaboard. What effect will this have on the fishing industry? Indeed, what effect will it have on the whole ocean ecology?"

Well, at least he didn't have the press and television people aboard now, Holmes reflected. Wright and Lewis had left the *Kingfisher* after the near disaster with the chamber on Tuesday. They would no doubt return when and if another bell could be made ready. Holmes remembered that night and how close they had come to losing the bell and the two operators. In addition to the downhaul becoming fouled, there had been the problem with the power cable that provided the lighting. It had shorted, leaving the two-man crew with only a single emergency battle lantern when the winch jammed. The experience had convinced Holmes that the rescue bell would have to be extensively modified if it was to be sent to such great depths.

Captain Jenkins joined Holmes at the gunwale to inform him of a message that had just been received from the Naval Material Command. Admiral Moran and Captain Shepherd would be visiting them in the afternoon. This was curious, Holmes thought; no rescue attempt was being made. In fact, Shepherd had not been to the site since his inspection dive in *Seasearch* the previous week. It had been decided then that trying a salvage lift of the *Lancerfish* was out of the question. It was just too deep. What could be bringing them out, Holmes wondered.

The coxswain of the motor whaleboat handed up the newspapers and a mailbag, then headed his boat for the *Hiawatha* on the opposite side of the formation. Holmes glanced at each of the editions, noting that the rescue operations were still covered on page one, though each story was reduced to a single column. Subheadlines read: "No Progress In Sub Rescue," "Lancerfish Survivors In Fair Condition," "Navy Races Death To Save Sub Crew."

Later at the wardroom table Holmes discovered a solitary story on an inside page quoting the Tass News Agency concerning a Russian rescue device. The submarine force of the USSR had a bell that could operate to a depth of 500 meters. The release claimed that the rescue bell, called *Bentos V,* could have saved all of the crew in the American submarine. The Commodore smiled after reading the short account aloud to the few officers still at the table. "That just about takes care of everybody having a comment on our operations," he said. "Now all we need is for Red China to criticize us for not using a bamboo chamber."

"They don't miss a chance for turning any situation into propaganda," Jenkins said, looking up from the paper he was reading. "Ivan must be keeping the Red press up to date on our failures," he added, referring to the Soviet vessel that had been lurking about the rescue force.

Holmes thought about previous accidents to U. S. submarines where the rescue of personnel was involved. Back before World War II there had been a rash of accidents. In 1920 the USS *S-5* had gone down in 165 feet of water, but the crew had escaped. In 1925 the USS *S-51* was lost by a collision that flooded all compartments. In that case the crew had all perished immediately, except for a few that jumped clear before she went down. Then, two years later on December seventeenth, 1927, the USS *S-4* was accidentally rammed by a Coast Guard cutter near Provincetown, Massachusetts. Survivors in the torpedo room were trapped, though the water depth was only slightly over one hundred feet. There was no way to get them out, and the Navy could only listen to the men pounding on the hull. Mercifully, the doomed men had only hours to contend with. They didn't have the sophisticated life support system that existed in the *Lancerfish.* As a result of that tragedy the Navy conceived and developed innovations such as the Momsen Lung for escape and the McCann chamber for rescue in greater depths. It was twelve years before the chamber was ever used, except in training. That one occasion saved the lives of thirty-three men in the *Squalus.* From 1939 until now, there had been no necessity to rescue personnel. The McCann bell had been improved to dive deeper, but the technique and its limitations were the same. Essentially, Holmes had the same chamber for an operation five times as deep as the *Squalus* rescue.

Something in the attitude of Admiral Moran presaged the astounding announcement he was to make later. Holmes and the *Kingfisher*'s skipper met the Admiral and Captain Shepherd at the accommodation ladder when they arrived late in the afternoon. The Admiral ordered the coxswain to lay to, because he planned to return within the hour, further mystifying Holmes. This was obviously an errand of grave importance that brought him out to the site for such a short time. Holmes led them up to the chart room just off the pilot house. He would give the Admiral a summary of the situation and show him the position of the submarine plotted on the chart.

When Holmes's short briefing was completed, Admiral Moran stepped out on the bridge to look over the ships in the force. "Where's the Russian ship that's been hanging around?" he asked, following Holmes to the port wing.

"When in the area, she usually anchors about five miles to the west," Holmes said, looking over the water, shielding his eyes. "She must be underway again, I don't see her. We've observed them frequently steaming on north-south legs, conducting some sort of research with nets."

"And that's where the *Lancerfish* lies?" the Admiral said, pointing to the big conical buoy close aboard on the beam.

"Approximately," Shepherd answered for Holmes, taking a step closer to the Admiral and pointing with a long arm. "The submarine itself is about a hundred yards more to the right. The current pushes the buoy some distance off the exact location."

Admiral Moran sighed and gave a short awed shake of

175

his head. "Where can we talk privately? I've got some interesting information for you, Barney, but it is quite confidential."

Jenkins suggested his cabin, where there was more
room. When they were settled, the Admiral turned to
Holmes and said, "Well, Barney, ready for a jolt?" He
paused. "This morning the Soviet naval attaché, Admiral
Michaelovsky, invited me and Mr. Hirsch from the State
Department for a conference at the Russian Embassy. The
Soviets are offering to rescue the men in *Lancerfish*." A
suggestion of a smile played over the Admiral's face as he
studied Holmes's reaction.

"Damned decent of them," Holmes said, puzzled.
Surely this wasn't the reason for Admiral Moran to come to
the site. "Unless they have something we don't know about,
how are they going to do it? The rescue chamber used in the
Soviet Navy is a clumsy copy of the McCann bell."

"Except it goes deeper and has a winch that will take
all of the downhaul cable. We've checked dimensions and it
appears the sealing ring will fit around the *Lancerfish*
hatch."

"Maybe it can, but by the time the Reds get their bell
here, we'll have the one from the shipyard. I hope to God
we have the survivors up by then."

The Admiral shook his head. "No, Barney, it looks like
we're in trouble with that. There's been some slippage on
delivery of the drive motor for the winch. Anyway, their
chamber is here, supposedly ready to go. That Russian ship
nosing around here is the *Nikolai Trunov,* an oceanographic
ship commanded by a Captain Vasili Vashenko, and the
gear is on board."

Shepherd, who until now had been silent, explained.
"The situation has become terribly delicate. The U. S.
Navy has become the public whipping boy in this disaster.
The Communists are using this opportunity to the fullest
extent, inferring they have a superior submarine technol-

ogy." He removed his glasses and stroked his eyes, continuing with resignation. "Oh, it's possible their bell could accomplish the rescue, but whether it can or not is unimportant. What is, is that we may be forced by public opinion to let them try."

"And this will get to the press," the Admiral interjected. "The Russians will leak it or put out a story. When that happens we'll be under pressure from certain quarters to let them make an attempt, because it will be several days before the McCann bell is ready."

"Why have they waited so long to propose this?" Holmes asked. "Their ship has been here nearly two weeks. If they can reach the *Lancerfish,* they could have saved the men that died in the fire."

"Probably thought we could do it until your last unsuccessful attempt," the Admiral offered. "At any rate, we've got to put them off. We'll try to set it up for you and Shep to inspect their chamber, for appearances. Then we'll put together a statement saying why the *Bentos V* cannot be used."

Holmes was thoughtful for a moment. "Seems like an awful lot of trouble to go to, just to prevent the Russians from getting some good press. Whatever propaganda value it might be to them would be worth getting those sailors up."

"It isn't as simple as that," Shepherd said, frowning sagaciously. "They'll want to know some pretty intimate details about the *Lancerfish* class attack boat. We would probably have to show them the Ships Characteristics Manual for her class, which is classified."

"Well, declassify the topside plan. That's all they need to know; probably know it already." Holmes slid a cigar out of its wrapper. "Aren't we carrying this cold war attitude a bit far?" More than likely, he thought to himself, the Soviet bell could do it. They wouldn't risk a failure.

"There's another aspect to this, which you have overlooked, Barney," the Admiral said, his voice becoming softer and more confidential. "The *Lancerfish* has Top Secret publications and cryptographic documents on board, as well as highly classified equipment installed in her. We can't bring those publications up in a Soviet bell and we can't just leave them there. If the Russians do indeed have a capability for reaching the sub, you can be assured they'll return after we've left the area. Whatever happens to that crew down there will not mark the end of this operation. The *Lancerfish* must be completely destroyed."

Shepherd regarded Holmes with benign superiority, as though he forgave him for not having thought of this aspect before. "Also, Commodore, we may have some good news soon on the DSRV. The contractor now estimates two weeks for having the vehicle operational. You know the bad publicity the Navy has had on that; the cost overruns and the time it has taken to develop the system."

"Are you suggesting that I hold up the rescue in order to vindicate the DSRV? I'll be goddamned if I will!"

"No, Barney." The Admiral was conciliatory. "Take it easy. What Shep means is that if something happens to prevent the use of the McCann bell—if it gets delayed too long —you'll have the DSRV to fall back on. Most likely it will be used after your rescue operations to attempt salvage or demolition."

For some moments no one spoke. Holmes sat deep in thought with the other two staring at him. Then, changing the subject, he asked, "When do you want us to visit the Russians?"

"I'll try to clear it before the weekend."

"What if it's obvious their gear will work? How will you defend rejecting their proposal?" Holmes said in a quieter voice.

"That's going to be your job, Barney, yours and Shep's. You'll have to come up with something. Shouldn't be too hard to find some component that we could claim isn't adaptable to the *Lancerfish*. It can be anything, as long as we can gracefully decline their offer."

The Admiral looked at his watch. "We've got to get going. Generally, I think you have the picture. Monday there will be a meeting in my office to discuss the rescue and subsequent salvage procedures. I'd like you there, prepared to brief us on the new bell and the results of your visit to the *Nikolai Trunov*, if we are able to get the clearance." He rose and prepared to leave. "Of course, no need to tell you to keep this confidential," he said, looking from Holmes to Jenkins.

When the Admiral and Shepherd had returned to the *Frobisher*, Holmes contacted the project engineer on the *Marine Explorer* by radio. He was told that the new downhaul cable would be rigged by the end of the following day. Before turning in that night Holmes tried to raise the *Lancerfish* on the underwater telephone, just in case the survivors had been able to repair it. He was unsuccessful, but sonar reported the hourly signal of someone pounding on the hull. There was at least one man alive.

By noon the next day the new connector for the downhaul was attached to the submarine, and three hours later the cable itself linked the *Kingfisher* to the *Lancerfish* once more. No word had come from Admiral Moran on the visit to the *Nikolai Trunov*. A message came, however, from the commanding officer of the Portsmouth Naval Shipyard. It was short, estimating that the delivery of the new chamber would be the end of the following week. Holmes noted that Admiral Moran was one of the information addressees.

Holmes prepared an "operational immediate" dispatch to the Admiral, reporting the downhaul was attached and he was ready to proceed as soon as the chamber arrived from the shipyard. The radioman had the message typed up and brought to the wardroom for release. As Holmes returned the form after initialing it, he paused and read the

179

message over again thoughtfully. He crossed out the last part of the text and inserted, READY TO PROCEED AS SOON AS A CHAMBER IS AVAILABLE.

"And, Sparks," he said to the radioman, "have the radar watch see if our friend Ivan is on the scope. I'll be here when he's ready to report." Holmes wanted to hear the six o'clock newscast on the officer's receiver in the wardroom.

Most of the *Kingfisher*'s officers were on hand for the broadcast. At the end of the international coverage there was only a short mention made of the rescue operations. After "and now, a word from our sponsor," and the ensuing commercial, the sonorous voice continued.

"We have this late bulletin on the *Lancerfish* just in from Washington. The Navy Department has announced that the Soviet government has offered assistance in the rescue of the *Lancerfish* survivors. The Russian ship *Nikolai Trunov*, an oceanographic vessel that has shadowed the rescue force since the end of last month, has a special diving bell on board. According to a U. S. Navy spokesman, this device is similar to the one now being readied for a rescue attempt next week. Navy Department officials will not comment further until certain classification issues have been ironed out. Arrangements are being made at the rescue site to inspect the device on the Soviet ship tomorrow." The announcer then gave a review of the *Lancerfish* sinking and subsequent failures to reach the crew. Holmes smiled to himself. After all the cautioning about keeping this confidential, the Admiral went ahead and broke the news anyway. Probably wanted to upstage the Russians before they could announce it.

The half dozen junior officers lounging in the wardroom received the news with skepticism. A Lt(jg) gave his opinion that the Navy would not accept the help, particularly since the new McCann bell was nearly ready. "It's a grandstand play. You know their bell is no better than ours,

180

and most likely would need modification too. Isn't it strange that they just happen to have a submarine rescue chamber with them on an oceanographic ship?"

The sound powered phone whooped and was answered by Jenkins. "That was the OOD," he said after hanging up. "He reports that radar has three contacts but doesn't know if any of them is the Russian. Ivan was last known to be heading south."

Saturday morning Holmes was up early, pacing the bridge deck. He was a little piqued. He should have had some word from the Navy on his course of action with the Russians. After all, the news media had the word.

The radar operator reported on the bridge speaker that a "skunk" Foxtrot was closing their position. It was some minutes before Holmes could identify the small speck on the horizon through his binoculars. When the contact changed course to skirt the rescue force, he recognized the unique silhouette. The sweeping clipper bow and raked funnel told him it was the Soviet ship.

As he swept the area with the binoculars, Holmes's field of vision was suddenly filled with the buoy that held the downhaul cable. The cylindrical shape with the conical top leaned in the current, the water curling around the base as though the buoy was underway. No doubt it still held the cable to the *Lancerfish*. The frustration of not being able to do anything was acute. The cable had been rigged again, which in itself was quite an accomplishment at that depth, yet he was still thwarted because the new chamber was not ready. He would have to wait for at least five more days. He looked at the Russian ship again.

The Navy helicopter came out from New York and settled on the *Frobisher*. A short while later Holmes saw the boat heading across the water separating the two ships. As it drew alongside he saw the lanky figure of Captain Shepherd in the sternsheets. He was well turned out in freshly pressed dress blues. He waved an informal salute and greeted Holmes with a cheery cry from the bottom of the accommodation ladder. "It's a fine morning, Commodore, ready to go visiting?"

Shepherd towered over Holmes after he arrived on the quarterdeck. He grinned down on him. "Can we go to your quarters? I've got some instructions from the Admiral."

Holmes had coffee sent up to the sea cabin and after the steward had left turned to Shepherd. "I heard the news broadcast last night. The word is out, now what do we do?" Holmes pointed to the single chair and took a seat on the edge of the bunk. Shepherd's face grew serious as he stirred his coffee. "There were more conferences yesterday, at the Pentagon and at the State Department. Even the President was consulted. It's a touchy situation." The Oxford accent became more noticeable as he spoke. He probably had a tour of overseas duty somewhere that was connected with the English Navy, Holmes thought.

"As expected," Shepherd went on, "there is some congressional pressure being exerted on us to cooperate with the Soviets. Relatives of the trapped crewmen are demanding action through their representatives. What the politicians don't understand is that the Russians want to run the show. Admiral Michaelovsky has suggested that the *Nikolai Trunov* replace the *Kingfisher* in the moorings."

"Let's admit a fact," Holmes said in a clipped voice. "The U. S. Navy is trying to save face. If the Russian bell is suitable, it could save the men now. It could even bring up the classified pubs without compromising them."

Shepherd was silent a moment and then said flatly, "It has been decided that the men in *Lancerfish* will come out by a U. S. Navy method; either the McCann bell or, if that fails, the rescue submersible when it is operational. Our visit to the Russian ship is strictly for public relations and . . . intelligence."

Holmes drew a pad of paper to him and began composing a message to the Russian ship. "Then I want to do it as soon as possible, because tomorrow I plan to see the modified bell at Portsmouth." Shepherd nodded approvingly.

"Yes. The visit has been cleared and the Soviet Embassy has instructed their ship to expect us."

Shepherd leafed through a magazine while Holmes wrote out the message. Holmes paused once to ask the spelling of the commanding officer's name. When finished, he thrust the paper to Shepherd for comment, saying, "I assume they understand English." The dispatch read:

CAPTAIN VASILI VASHENKO. I HAVE BEEN INFORMED OF THE ASSISTANCE OFFERED BY THE USSR IN RESCUING SURVIVORS IN LANCERFISH. I WOULD APPRECIATE VISITING YOUR SHIP TODAY TO INSPECT BENTOS V. I WILL BE ACCOMPANIED BY THREE OTHER U. S. NAVAL OFFICERS. PLEASE LET ME KNOW WHAT TIME WOULD BE CONVENIENT TO YOU. CAPTAIN B. C. HOLMES, COMMANDER RESCUE FORCE.

Shepherd handed the message back hesitatingly. "May I suggest that just you and I make this call. There's no point in a group of us going aboard."

"I want to take along Ben Morgan, the diving officer, and Chief Master Diver Petrosky to have a look at their bell." Holmes noted Shepherd's disapproving arch of eyebrows and added, "Anyway, it will look more convincing when we refuse their help."

It was nearly an hour later when the signalman reported to the Commodore in the wardroom that the message had been sent. It had required slow and patient transmission on the big twenty-four-inch light before the Russians finally acknowledged receipt. Just before lunch the signalman returned with the succinct reply: YES COME 1400 HOURS PLEASE. V. V.

Well before 1400, Captain Jenkins' gig was ordered to the quarterdeck and Holmes with his party embarked. The trip to the *Nikolai Trunov*, anchored more than five miles to the west, would require nearly half an hour. Morgan and Petrosky had been briefed before departure concerning the visit. The boat churned toward the Soviet ship and Holmes watched the *Kingfisher* diminish astern. He had never met a Russian, as far as he could remember, and certainly had never been aboard one of their ships. He was becoming intrigued by the prospect of meeting this Captain Vashenko, and wondered what he would be like. The *Nikolai Trunov* was not a naval vessel, but classified as a merchant ship belonging to the Soviet state; an oceanographic ship, though some of the recent newspaper accounts of her presence termed her a "spy ship."

Holmes rose from his seat and looked around the canvas weather shelter toward their destination. The ship was much nearer than he had ever seen it before, and he was impressed by her size. The cream colored hull was broadside to their approach, and he could make out figures moving on the main deck. At the stern was a giant turreted crane that could surely lift twenty tons. Rather large, it seemed, for a ship that had only a scientific mission. Perhaps it doubled in other capacities, such as a submarine tender, Holmes speculated. After all, it did have a rescue chamber on board. But if this were so, why did the Russians offer to help, to let them see their ship, if it had some sort of clandestine purpose?

As the gig drew closer to the ship, Holmes ordered the coxswain to swing around the stern. There was no accommodation ladder to be seen, so it was probably on the opposite side. Shepherd had joined him at the opening of the weather cowl, and Holmes noticed he carried grey gloves in his left hand. Holmes caught himself adjusting his own coat and hat.

They came under the counter, and above them the big

red ensign with the gold hammer and sickle floated from the stern. From the yardarm the familiar stars and stripes of the U. S. colors fluttered in the light breeze. They were making the call more formal than he had anticipated. Figures appeared at the top of the accommodation ladder, and one hatless sailor leaning on the railing waved informally to the coxswain. A youthful, dark-haired man in horn-rimmed glasses leaned over the side and called to them.

"I say, do come alongside. Commodore Holmes, is it?"

Holmes was surprised at the British accent. As he came over the side, followed closely by Shepherd, Holmes nearly forgot to salute the Soviet ensign. The same man that had yelled down to them stepped forward with extended hand.

"Welcome, sir. My name is Alexei Gornin. Captain Vashenko asked me to greet you because I'm quite up on your language—four years at Cambridge." He smiled good-naturedly, revealing long, yellowed teeth that contained a gap in the center. "I am the chief scientist on board and will act as interpreter."

Holmes introduced the others and looked about at the men that stood at a respectful distance. Some were in civilian attire of one type or another. The sailors wore rumpled but very clean looking uniforms of light blue denim and boots that were nearly knee length. They regarded the Americans with sober curiosity, and Holmes wondered where their captain was. The after deck was spacious and well painted and contained several canvas-covered shapes. Probably winches, Holmes thought, but saw nothing resembling a diving bell.

"If you will follow me, gentlemen," their guide said and led off. As they proceeded in single file down the main deck, they encountered other men, mostly sailors, who visibly stiffened to attention as they passed. They were led up to the next deck, which was the top of the main superstructure, and then up another short ladder to an area just aft of the pilot house. Here they entered a quiet passageway, and

185

the Russian stopped at a polished mahogany door. He rapped twice and listened with turned head. A deep, indistinguishable voice replied. Alexei Gornin stepped in, holding the door open and announcing their arrival in Russian. A stocky man in his early fifties moved from behind a desk and first approached Captain Shepherd, mistaking the taller and more elegant officer for the Commodore. For a moment there was some confusion, which Gornin quickly corrected.

Captain Vashenko was not tall, perhaps less than six feet, but looked bigger because of a stocky build. His slightly receding hair was slate grey on top, changing abruptly to pure white on the closely cropped sides. The broad face was friendly, though unsmiling, and his blue eyes were steady on Holmes's face. There was an air of distinguished intelligence about him that was arresting. He was dressed in khaki slacks and a white turtleneck pullover.

"Please to excuse me, my English . . ." Vashenko searched for the word, ". . . *mal, en français.*" He turned inquiringly to Gornin, who said, "Bad."

"Yes, bod. *Peut-être, Commandant, nous parlons en français?*" He smiled questioningly.

"Forgive me, Captain," Holmes said. "I'm afraid my French is much worse than your English."

"Come to sit," Vashenko said, gesturing with a wide hand to chairs and a short leather covered couch. Petrosky remained standing, looking somewhat ill at ease, until Holmes caught the chief's eye and nodded toward a chair.

It was a spacious cabin, mostly paneled in dark wood. Behind the desk were two big oval portholes propped slightly ajar. Shelves of books hung over a chart table at the forward bulkhead. There was another door, most likely leading to the captain's sleeping quarters, Holmes surmised. It was a beautiful ship, and Holmes wondered if he would have an opportunity to inspect it later on.

Gornin completed the introductions quickly in Russian. When he finished, Captain Vashenko turned to Petrosky, smiling. "Ah, you are . . . Russian?" He pronounced it *roos-eye-in.*

"No, sir, Polish," the chief replied in his loud voice.

"Ah, 'tis same, 'tis same," Vashenko said, turning to the others. "You are Slavic."

A light knock sounded politely and a blond sailor entered with a tray of little glasses barely larger than thimbles. They were filled with a colorless liquid which Holmes thought was vodka but which turned out to be slivovitz. Gornin offered cigarettes from a little box. "They are Russian," he explained, but Holmes was the only smoker in his group, and he preferred his cigar.

These social amenities were pleasant and Holmes nearly forgot the purpose of their visit. Vashenko had an absorbing interest in the United States and questioned each of them about their home state. When Shepherd replied that he was from Oklahoma, Holmes could not keep from remarking aloud, "Oklahoma! I would never have thought you came from *that* part of the country, Captain." Vashenko, too, was impressed. He supposed the state to be still quite primitive, with a large Indian community.

Though he used Gornin very little for speaking, Vashenko did require translations when someone addressed him. It occurred to Holmes that the Russian captain was learning a great deal about them, either out of curiosity or perhaps to include in a report to his superiors. Holmes finally persuaded Vashenko to talk about himself and discovered he was a Ukrainian, born in Kiev. He was married and his wife and daughter lived in Odessa.

When at last they got to the reason for the visit, Holmes described the situation of the *Lancerfish.* He explained that the U. S. Navy wanted him to inspect the *Bentos V* to see if it could help in the rescue of the survivors.

"I am surprised, Commandant, your Navy is so great and yet powerless for making rescue." Vashenko's eyes

187

twinkled. "Bot, it is deep," he acknowledged. Then, slapping his knee, he rose quickly. "Come to see," he said, ushering them into the passageway.

Once more they were on the stern, and now in the center of the broad expanse there was the *Bentos V.* Evidently it had been stowed somewhere below decks and had been brought up since their arrival. Probably the reason for the long period of civilities in the cabin was to give the Russians time to have the bell brought up on deck, Holmes thought. Vashenko was not going to have the Americans see the inside of the ship. As they crossed the wide deck, Holmes observed a large red circle painted in the center. A helicopter landing zone. They must have a chopper hidden away too, he thought.

The bell, which was suspended from the huge crane, was the familiar bulb shape, but taller than the McCann bell. The hatch trunk was extended on one side, which differed from the U. S. chambers. Where the bell tapered toward the base, Holmes saw protrusions on both sides. They were thick deep-sea viewports with floodlights mounted over them. There was something crude and heavy about the appearance of the chamber. When Holmes drew closer he saw some small rust spots and areas of patchy paint where it had been quickly touched up. As the party circled the chamber, Gornin said, "You will have to excuse the untidy looks. It has been in use a great deal on this voyage."

"In use?" Holmes was surprised.

"Yes. Mostly for night observations. I have made more than a dozen dives during the cruise. We are studying the effects of pollution transmission to pelagic life in the Gulf Stream, and its effect on our fishing industry."

Holmes bent down and looked at the sealing gasket. There was no doubt, it was a rescue chamber. Of course, he thought, the economy-minded Russians were using a submarine rescue chamber for scientific work. That explained the large viewports and lights. When Holmes remarked on this fact, Gornin explained. "It is not often such a chamber is used for rescue, so why have it remain idle? There is no need to have two types of diving bells, don't you agree?"

A ladder was brought and they mounted to the domed top one by one, except for Captain Vashenko, who waited on deck. Chief Petrosky crouched to one side of the top and inspected the connectors for the high-pressure air hose and the power cable. Gornin slid into the chamber first and Holmes followed. The interior differed radically from that of a standard U. S. Navy rescue bell. The viewports were mounted in short, cylindrical barbettes that canted downward. Behind each was a swivel stool, separated by the hatch to the lower compartment. A shelf near each port contained books, a clipboard, empty film cassettes, and even a camera. It was cluttered and, with Shepherd and Morgan now in the compartment, very crowded. It certainly would not hold nine or ten men, as the McCann chamber could. The instrumentation and accessories appeared more primitive.

Gornin pointed out the various components, describing the function and operation. A simple blow and vent manifold regulated the amount of water in the ballast and trim tanks. The hatch to the lower compartment had a massive strongback clamping it shut. Gornin struggled with the securing wingbolts so the hatch could be opened. "We do not use the lower compartment, of course, for observation dives," he explained. "It has not been opened for a long time." He placed a spanner wrench on the wingbolt and hauled mightily until the threads creaked and finally began to turn. When the dogs had been laid off and the hatch cover lowered into the compartment, Holmes's first view was that of Petrosky. The chief was standing below in the open-bottomed skirt staring up at them.

The lower compartment was the part that would surround the hatch of the submarine. In operation, the winch would haul the bell down the cable to seat snugly against the flat deck area around the torpedo room hatch. The water would then be removed and the hatch could be opened, providing access to the interior of the submarine. Holmes inspected the winch, which was coated with thick grease. It was considerably larger than the McCann winch and would surely take the 1500 feet of cable. The remainder of the gear in the lower compartment was nearly identical to U. S. Navy equipment. The cable cutter, however, was fitted on the spooling device of the winch drum, and instead of a wire cable fairlead, they had a hinged bracket.

Lt. Morgan put several questions to Gornin, mostly concerning weight and handling techniques. Once, when the Russian was turned away, Holmes exchanged a glance with Petrosky which told him the chief was not impressed with the bell. Petrosky pointed critically at the electric motor drive of the winch, in silent disapproval.

Captain Shepherd was the last to rejoin the others on deck after the inspection. He wore a vaguely disdainful expression as he daintily wiped his hands with a cloth.

"May I ask, Captain, has the *Bentos V* ever been used as a rescue chamber?" He endowed Vashenko with a tolerant smile. It was necessary for Gornin to translate the question before Vashenko answered.

"Ah, no. Only for exercise, for to train. You understand? Russian Navy never lose a submarine with men inside."

They were escorted to the accommodation ladder, and Morgan hailed their boat, which was lying off about a hundred yards. Holmes thanked Vashenko for his hospitality and explained that he would communicate with him later if it was decided to make a rescue attempt with the *Bentos V*. First, he had to report to his superiors and evaluate the operation.

"I understand, Commandant," Vashenko said in his

deep accent. *"Bonne chance."* Holmes saluted and followed the others down to the boat.

On the way back to the *Kingfisher,* the men discussed their visit and the Russian chamber. The consensus was that it might be able to reach the *Lancerfish,* but it would be better to have the new chamber being fitted out at Portsmouth, because it could hold more men. Petrosky was dubious about the winch, the electric motor being his main objection. To him it looked too vulnerable and would probably leak at the depth where it was to be used, and short out. Shepherd delivered his opinion shortly before they reached the rescue vessel. "Obviously, totally inadequate; quite primitive."

Shortly after he was aboard, Holmes went to the sonar room. It was nearing 1600, and there should be the sound of hammering; the survivors usually signaled at the beginning of the watch. The operator turned up the speaker gain for the Commodore and listened to his earphones. They heard the familiar noises of the pumps and other machinery in the submarine, but no pounding. "It's been just like that since I came on watch, sir," the man said.

As the minute hand crept away from the hour, Holmes became worried. They could have just forgotten, he told himself as he stared into the eyes of the sonarman. Or had they at last all succumbed? Maybe they were too weak, or despair had overtaken them in their wretchedness. Maybe they just did not care any longer.

Then it came, resounding slowly, distantly, tolling a dirge of men lost in the sea. Holmes stood by for some moments after the pounding stopped. What must it be like down there after all this time? They had been on the bottom four weeks.

That evening Holmes left the *Kingfisher* with Shepherd, who was returning to Washington. Holmes was taking a commercial flight to Boston and the next day would visit the Portsmouth Naval Shipyard. After inspecting the new rescue chamber there, he would make a call on the civilian contractor who was to deliver the new downhaul winch. He would exert all the pressure he could to get that chamber out to the site, maybe even before Friday. Holmes felt very tired as he stepped into the boat in the gathering dusk.

11 – FUTILITY

JUNE 9–13

For Lt. Hayman, as well as the others in *Lancerfish*, the death of Lt. Ritter was a deep loss. As the chief engineer of the submarine, Ritter had sustained their belief in survival. His self-assured ability and experience gave them faith in the continued functioning of vital life support machinery. The failure of the underwater telephone, that comforting link to the surface, added to the deepening despair of the men. That very source of hope, by which they had been kept informed of the rescue preparations, had killed him—a penultimate event that seemed to prophesy a finale was at hand; possibly Wednesday, when the new chamber was due at the site.

Fitzgibbons held one of his prayer meetings in the torpedo room. Less than a dozen men showed up. At the end of his sermon, Fitzgibbons handed out sheets of paper on which he had copied the lyrics of a hymn. Then he led off the singing, beating the air with an arm and nodding encouragement. His tenor voice was surprisingly good, with no hint of the Southern accent. The men responded sporadically at first, then as the chorus was repeated, joined in unanimously.

Wednesday came at last and Hayman waited through the hours with growing apprehension, which was replaced by futility as the day ended. By Thursday, after the morning gave no hint of surface activity, he felt that they were all doomed and the time was near. Bitterness replaced fear; it was unfair, he thought angrily. Why must he suffer death so long? If only they could communicate with the *Kingfisher* to learn their fate; to know if there was any reason to hope. What had gone wrong with the chamber? Or perhaps it was the downhaul cable, hopelessly snarled about their hatch. If there was no way for them to escape from the submarine, no possibility at all, then he would cut short his agony. As the watches were rotated in the control room, several blows were struck on the bulkhead with a hammer. This would tell their rescuers that they still waited, they were alive, and perhaps give impetus to the preparations.

Then on Friday clanking sounds were heard in the torpedo room. Hayman was in the machinery compartment with Chief Benson, worrying over a salt-water pump that threatened to give out. He had not heard the commotion that the activities outside the hull had caused. Rumford, the steward's mate, brought him the news.

"They've come!" he shouted excitedly. "They're at the hatch, sir!"

Hayman, mistaking the announcement to mean the chamber had arrived, hurried to the torpedo room. Several men had gathered under the escape trunk, and he glanced up expectantly, but the hatch was closed. Cruthers gave him the details in a rush of words. First, there had been a noise, a clatter like something dropped on deck. This was followed by more rattling and a scraping sound.

Hayman quickly opened the lower escape trunk hatch, and the men bunched around him to stare up into the tiny compartment. Hayman climbed into the trunk, finding the air there considerably cooler. He listened and heard a remote metallic sound, then the muffled whine of an electric

194

motor. It was the submersible. Of course, he realized quickly—the downhaul cable. They had not heard them reattach that, and it had been cut ten days before.

In spite of this realization, Hayman continued to watch the handwheel of the hatch, hoping to see it move. Slowly he backed down into the torpedo room, his heart pounding from the burst of energy. As he lowered himself into the fetid compartment, he saw Tom Evers over the heads of the men that had gathered there. "The submersible is attaching the downhaul, I think," he said loudly to Evers, but meant it for the others as well.

For a while no one spoke, each listening for additional confirmation that something was just outside their hull. More crew members came through the watertight door from aft, searching faces inquisitively. Cruthers recited what they had heard again, for the benefit of the newcomers. Then, over the animated talk that had begun, Hayman heard the querulous voice of Fitzgibbons. "What's happening?" he demanded, pawing his way through the men to Hayman. "What is it, Hayman?" he asked again, shooting glances at the men under the hatch. Hayman explained tersely. Fitzgibbons, who was next in line of command since the death of Ritter, had become intolerably imperious.

"Ah'd appreciate it if someone had informed *me.*"

"God, it just happened, Fitz." Hayman was exasperated.

"Ah saw Rumford go rushing by the wardroom to tell you." He spun around, looking for the steward. "And I'll give the orders for opening any hatches," he said, looking up into the escape trunk. "Is that understood by everyone? The responsibility of the *Lancerfish* and our continued survival is mine."

Hayman made no reply, knowing it would be useless. He pulled the hatch shut and instructed Chief Harris to have all hands prepare for chamber operations. The chief hesitated an instant, looking at Fitzgibbons, then moved off.

195

The morale of the men brightened somewhat, but there was no joyous relief such as that felt on the last rescue attempt. The presence of the submersible and the attachment of the cable were cheering, but they had experienced that before. To have a rescue chamber reach them and make a seal was a different matter, and it seemed a long way off. There had been too many failures. Also, much had happened during these weeks on the bottom. Thirty-one of their number had perished suddenly in the fire, and the chief engineer had been snatched from them unexpectedly and brutally. Their physical and emotional state had deteriorated markedly because of constant anxiety and an atmosphere polluted by carbon dioxide and other extraneous gases. They had lost weight and many of them exhibited symptoms of neurasthenia. Even their sleep was no respite, providing only interludes of exhausted coma full of fantasy and terror.

Nine of the twenty-five survivors suffered with respiratory congestion and spent most of the time in their bunks. Lt. Langworthy had not eaten for two days and daily grew weaker. The most dramatic change was in Tom Evers. The young lieutenant who had been a strapping 200-pound athlete before the sinking now looked emaciated and old. Hayman, who all his life had been skinny, showed less the effects of the ordeal. He looked around at the men grouped in the torpedo room. It seemed that he had to remind himself continually who was still alive. Recently he had been having strange experiences. He would have startling encounters with dead crewmen, men that for some curious reason he had *thought* were dead. It was always unexpected, a fleeting notion, for often he had seen the man only hours before. Just as quickly, however, his mind would accept the fact that the man still lived. Conversely, in his hallucinatory dozings he would see the Exec walk past the door of his stateroom, or perhaps hear Ritter talking in his pragmatic manner in the wardroom. It became more and more dif-

196

ficult for Hayman to separate his dreams from the waking hours.

Some of the men began to disperse after several minutes had passed without further sounds from outside the hull. Fitzgibbons had returned to the wardroom, where he spent much of his time either making notes in his journal or poring through the Bible. Hayman went to Langworthy's stateroom to tell him about the work being done on the hatch. He found him awake and alert, though he did not speak. From there Hayman continued aft, inspecting the compartments. There had been equipment casualties too. In addition to the underwater telephone, the last operating CO_2 analyzer had failed, leaving them no means to determine the gas percentage in the atmosphere. He was sure it had increased, because physical effort was becoming more fatiguing and his respiration rate had gone up. The general announcing system had not worked for several days, but there was little need for it now that most of the men stayed near the torpedo room. As he stepped into the berthing space of the after compartment, Hayman smelled the acrid stench of burned out mattresses and blankets. The space was darkened, with only an emergency light over the passageway. The bunks, gruesome with the bodies swelling out the covers, were folded to a forty-five-degree angle. It was cold in the compartment, the heaters having all been secured, and Hayman moved on quickly to the machinery room. Chief Benson met him, shaking his head pessimistically.

"The pump is done for. That's the end of the distillation system. We can't make any more water."

"How much left in the tanks?"

"Maybe nine hundred gallons, more than enough to last until we get out, or whatever . . ." He shrugged. "A bigger problem is the air. I think the CO_2 is coming up." Hayman agreed, and turned back to the wardroom, the chief following him. "What do you think, Mr. Hayman, that bell going to get down here soon?"

"I don't know, I just don't know. If it *can* make us, it will be in the next few hours. A day at most." Hayman was puffing with the exertion of trying to speak and move through the compartments at the same time.

Fitzgibbons was sitting at the head of the wardroom table speaking when Hayman came in and flopped in a chair.

"All personnel will stand by in the torpedo room," Fitzgibbons said, casting a sidelong glance at Hayman. "Our rescuers will be here today, and I want to conduct a service of thanksgiving." Evers and Roche looked at him dully.

"What makes you so sure they're coming?" Hayman demanded. "Better save the gratitude until that bell makes a seal."

"I've been told."

"By whom, for Christ's sake?"

"Divine revelation. God spoke to me, not in words, but a feeling, a deep premonition that is more profound than words could ever be. It behooves you, all of us, to get down on your knees and give thanks."

"Look, Fitz, I'm not letting you tell the men the bell will be here until it's known for sure. They've had enough disappointments, and anyway your ranting will only create more carbon dioxide."

"Not *letting* me?" Fitzgibbons' voice rose to a squeal. "*I'm* in charge! I'm the senior officer and *I'm* ordering the service!"

Roche tapped Hayman's foot under the table to get his attention and almost imperceptibly shook his head. Hayman became gentle.

"Fitz, you're sick. Look, just take it easy. If we make it, we make it, and I'll shout all the hallelujahs you want."

"I'm in command!"

"Of what?" Hayman said, losing patience again. "If you keep up these holy-roly hysterics, I'll tie you up in your bunk." Fitzgibbons started to respond, but instead looked away furtively.

But no other evidence of outside activity was heard. As the hours passed, the quiet despair returned to the survivors. Whatever the reason for the chamber not coming, Hayman felt he could no longer think about it. He stayed in his bunk as long as possible, until an aching spine drove him to the wardroom, where he would slump over the table. Day and night could no longer be separated. Once he awoke with a terrible dread, looked at his watch, and read the meaningless time. Three twenty-five, when? Was it Saturday morning or afternoon? He shuffled into the torpedo room and asked a man slouched on deck, "Anything?" The man stared at Hayman uncomprehendingly at first, then shook his head slowly.

Hayman heard Fitzgibbons speaking somewhere in the forward compartment and got up to see what he was up to. He found him sitting at the small desk in his stateroom, his hands clasped tightly together and his eyes squeezed shut. Fitzgibbons rocked to and fro in fervent syncopation for a silent moment. Then he spoke again, the words tearing from his body in a plaintive cry.

" 'My God, my God, why hast thou forsaken me? Why art thou so far from helping me, and from the words of my roaring? O my God, I cry in the daytime, but thou hearest not; and I cry in the night, and thou dost not come.' "

Hayman was overwhelmed with unexpected compassion. The man's naked terror and loneliness touched him deeply.

"Fitz." He put a hand on his arm. "Hey, Fitz, take it easy."

The other man made no sign that he knew Hayman was there, and continued to rock for a moment. Then he

199

stopped, sagged into stillness, and said, "What do you want?"

"Take it easy, Fitz," Hayman said again. Slowly Fitzgibbons rotated his upturned face toward Hayman and opened his eyes. He stared at him malevolently, his look bleak with hatred. "You!" was all he said. Hayman was startled by Fitzgibbons' reaction. He had never seen him behave so violently.

"Look, Fitz, I'm sorry about blowing up at you, but—"

"You!" Fitzgibbons' voice was low and intense.

"This predicament has us all on edge, Fitz." Hayman realized Fitzgibbons was completely irrational, and he could think of nothing else to say. The two men stared fixedly at one another for a long moment.

"You! You dam-na-ble disbelievah. You are a devil. Because of you we'll nevah get out of here. Nevah!" He shot to his feet and brushed Hayman aside roughly as he left the stateroom. Hayman was surprised at the strength of his fury.

Hayman went to the wardroom and found Roche alone, eating stew from a can. "He's flipped out completely, Andy," he said sadly. "The poor bastard is a raving maniac."

"We'd better watch him. The state he's in could be dangerous," Roche said, pushing the can across the table. "Here, you want to finish this?"

Hayman ate some of the stew. It was cold and tasteless but would give him some nourishment; keep him going a little longer. "I think the best thing," he said between mouthfuls, "is to humor him. He's taking his responsibility as senior-officer-sunk pretty seriously. Play along with him, can't do any harm."

Hayman sat back, breathing deeply for a moment. Funny, he mused, the different types of men that made up a crew. Under normal conditions you see only a small part of their character. The Navy man, officer or white hat, reacts in a predictable manner in the ordinary state of affairs. You don't really know him until something like this occurs. Who would have thought Fitzgibbons would go off the deep end like this, and rather early in the predicament at that? He looked at Roche, who was lost in his own thoughts. He looked bad; the dark, yellowish circles under his eyes were like bruises. His brown beard had grown fast, and it curled out at the sides, giving him a monkish appearance. Hayman imagined that the Roche parents would be taking the disaster very hard.

"Why did you come in the Navy, Andy?"

Hayman's question seemed to catch Roche unawares. He frowned as he relinquished the deep reverie into which he had sunk.

"One has to have a goal, and nothing else appealed to me. I knew there would be the military, the draft, eventually, so decided to take the NROTC program. Submarines fascinated me. I thought I might even make it a career if nothing else turned up." He reflected a moment. "But I don't think I would have stayed in." His use of the past tense disturbed Hayman. Roche had given up hope they would be saved.

"We might still make it, you know, you have to hang on to that," Hayman said, almost imploringly. "I think what we heard yesterday was the cable being attached."

"Yes, I think so too, but then the chamber should have come down. Evidently there's something wrong with the gear."

"Or it could be weather again, Andy. You've got to have faith."

"Now you're sounding like Fitz." Roche smiled a bit sarcastically. "I just don't *feel* we will be rescued. It's been too long."

The acceptance of their fate by Roche almost angered Hayman, because it shook whatever hope he could sometimes muster. He did not want to give in to it—not yet. From the direction of the control room he heard the watch strike the hull several times. It was 1600.

McGovern was standing in the doorway of the ward-room. "Mr. Hayman, you'd better come have a look. I think Perkins is dead."

Hayman stood up but for a moment could not move. His head was swimming and he had to steady himself with the back of the chair. Then, with the torpedoman and Roche following, he made his way to the torpedo room. Perkins was a yeoman striker and had been one of the serious respiratory cases. His bunk was located high on the port side, and Hayman had to climb up to it by a short ladder.

"I noticed he hadn't moved," McGovern explained from the deck below. "Been laying the same way since yesterday, so I checked him and he doesn't seem to be breathing."

The young sailor had been dead several hours. The muscles were already stiffening. Hayman looked at the other bunks, noting those that appeared sleeping were definitely alive. The labored breathing attested to that. A few of the men had gotten up and were gathered around McGovern.

"Yes, he's gone, Mac," Hayman said quietly. "Have some men help you get him back to the after compartment." He swung to the deck and went to the control room, where Fitzgibbons had the watch. Hayman wondered how he would take the news of another death. Fitzgibbons sat in the bucket seat of the main control stand, his shoulders slumped and his hands limply folded in his lap. There was no change of expression when Hayman told him of the latest casualty.

Chief Benson came into the compartment from the machinery room. "That scrubber isn't staying ahead of the carbon dioxide," he said to Hayman. When told of Perkins' death, he said with simple callousness, "One thing about it, every guy that goes now makes it better for the survivors. I figure the CO_2 scrubber will now support only a few of us, maybe ten or twelve."

Hayman looked over the row of dials that indicated the pressure in the air banks. They were all empty except for the smoke-contaminated air that had been compressed into the low bank. "Have any idea how long we can last?" he asked the chief.

"It's hard to tell with no gas analyzers. The carbon dioxide is building up pretty slow, I think. I'd say two, maybe three days."

Hayman was disappointed. He would have supposed they could survive quite a bit longer. An oppressive quiet had settled in the control room, and on the far side of the compartment Hayman noticed Schoenberg observing them broodingly. Hayman had rarely seen him outside of the radio room and was surprised. They all turned when four men struggled by with the body of Perkins. How loud their heavy breathing sounded, Hayman thought. Fitzgibbons got up and followed the detail to the after berthing space.

The meals, which amounted to nothing more than canned provisions, were eaten in the torpedo room. The galley stove was no longer used for fear of fire, but the men had little appetite anyway. Though there was ample food for many days, the variety was reduced as time went on. The selection consisted mostly of vegetables or a prepared stew. Occasionally, whoever went aft to rummage through the cartons in the storeroom would find a few cans of pressed meat. Fortunately, there were several cases of canned juices, and the men could avoid drinking the brackish water. It now appeared that it would be the atmosphere that would be the limiting factor of survival after all, rather than food or water.

More than thirty-four hours had passed since they had heard the submersible working over them. It was Saturday night, the end of their fourth week on the bottom. Thinking back to the first day, Hayman wondered how they would have faced such an ordeal if they had known what was in store. They would have despaired at such a prospect. Most of the crew were dead, and those that still lived were not far from death. At any moment others could be expected to go.

Before going to his own bunk, Hayman visited each of the men. He instructed them to remain as still as possible, as the slightest physical activity generated carbon dioxide. He managed to get Langworthy to drink some juice, though he had refused it at first. As he went to his stateroom, Hayman wondered who would not make it for the next few hours.

Chief Harris had been standing by his bunk for a long time before Hayman realized he had been awakened. He heard himself say to the chief again, "What's up?"

"Lennie shot himself. Mr. Fitzgibbons told me to let you know."

"Lennie?" Hayman struggled to comprehend. He could not associate the name with the man.

"Yeah. Lennie Schoenberg. He used the forty-five kept in the radio shack for the in-port watch. I was in the control room and heard it. He's dead."

Hayman found only Fitzgibbons in the radio room, muttering something that sounded like a benediction; an extemporaneous last rite. The radioman was folded face down over the typewriter, and blood dripped from one end of the carriage. The scene was bizarre in its horror. Of all the deaths that had occurred in the *Lancerfish*, this was the first in which blood had flowed, the first that was not an accident. He let Fitzgibbons complete his ritual, then turned to Harris. "When did this happen? Anyone else hear, or see it?"

"Just a few minutes ago." The chief looked at his watch. "About two fifteen. I was alone in the control room and heard a loud bang. It sounded like it came from over-

204

head, outside the hull. Then I looked in the radio shack and there he was."

Hayman had the other two help him remove the body to the berthing space in the after compartment. "No point in telling the others," he said when they had returned to the control room. "At least, not now."

Hayman made his way back to his stateroom and collapsed on the bunk, breathing heavily. The exertion of moving Schoenberg's body had brought him to near exhaustion. He could not catch his breath and trembled from the lack of oxygen. Slowly he recuperated, and his thoughts turned to the dead radioman. Was their plight so hopeless and unendurable? He remembered how Schoenberg had withdrawn from the rest of the crew and preferred solitude to think about his unfaithful wife. Perhaps the crew knew about her. It seemed to Hayman that he had overheard a remark or two.

His thoughts took another tack—would others now seek escape in the same manner? The first would be the ones with less to live for. Was this the reason he had not wanted to let the other survivors know, for fear it would start a grisly exodus? No, when you get right down to it, Hayman reasoned, anything is preferable to such finality. His earlier thoughts about bringing his own fear to an end came back to him, and he knew such a step would be impossible for him. A man will not willingly give up when at any moment there could be a reprieve. Schoenberg's personal hell would not have been relieved through rescue alone. Most likely he would have taken this out if the sinking had never happened.

Hayman felt that sometime, someday, their rescuers would get to them. It was all a matter of being able to continue existing long enough. To wait hour by hour, breathing as little as possible, remaining motionless, and believing they would eventually come. Tomorrow he would talk to the men. They had to have faith.

Cruthers was awake, but he kept his eyes tightly shut. He had been dreaming he was home, and now he was reluctant to open his eyes to confirm that he was still in the torpedo room. But he did not have to. He could smell the hydraulic oil and the thick odor of the air. Below him he heard the dribble of water running into the bilge from the signal ejector. Since the fire Cruthers had been sleeping in one of the bunks left empty by a casualty. He rolled over and looked down upon Bartolla, who was also awake, lying on his back and staring up at the overhead.

"What time you got, Guinea Wop?"

"You goin' someplace?" Bartolla pulled his hands from behind his head and lifted his wrist to arm's length. "Ten past eight. It's Sunday, you're allowed to sleep in." After a moment he added, "Unless Mr. Fitzgibbons holds another of his services."

"Old John the Baptist, the frustrated preacher," Cruthers said, "if we get out of here he ought to go back to Texas and become a Bible pounder."

"He's better at that than being an officer," Bartolla agreed. "I wonder how a guy like that rates gold braid."

"Now he's playing skipper, since Mr. Ritter got it. Can you imagine him as a captain?" Cruthers asked wonderingly. Bartolla rolled onto his side. "Mr. Hayman doesn't take his shit; he's the one that ought to be in charge now."

"How about Mr. Roche?"

"Too hokey and stuck up. Remember the time he got on Rowboat's ass for using four-letter words?" Cruthers said. "He told him he could say 'copyoolate' just as well."

"Yeah, then for a couple of days Rowboat went around saying, 'copyoolate you,' until he forgot the word." Bartolla pushed himself upright wearily. "Well, I think we've all been 'copyoolated,' royally."

Their conversation had roused others, and there was a stirring in the compartment. McGovern stood between the torpedo racks and stretched, sucking in a great lungful of air. He sniffed for a moment and said, "Hey, I think the air is getting better again." Two or three other men sampled the atmosphere tentatively and concurred. Later in the morning Chief Benson confirmed that the life support system seemed to be catching up on the carbon dioxide. The equipment was still not functioning to his satisfaction, and what disturbed him most was that he did not know why. At any moment it could fail completely, as some of the other systems had, without warning. If it should, survival time could then be counted in hours.

Hayman made no objection when Fitzgibbons started his preparations for Sunday services. It would be a good opportunity to talk to the men beforehand. Benson's report that the air had improved was corroborated for Hayman by the fact that he felt no dizziness when he stood up that morning. He would have been actually cheered if the stark event of Schoenberg's suicide had not been with him. Hayman wondered if he should inform the men of this latest tragedy, then decided against it. Might as well let them have this respite while it lasted.

Though he was not hungry, Hayman managed to swallow a little of the stew followed by fruit cocktail. He then visited the sick crewmen and inspected the compartments. Tom Evers insisted on accompanying him, though he was nearly as bad off as some of the men. Hayman was relieved to find that they had lost no one else during the night, though three of the worst cases were steadily declining. They would surely succumb in the next twenty-four hours if help did not come. Another high concentration of carbon dioxide would be the end. Even if they were rescued now, Hayman was doubtful those cases would recover.

When they got to the control room, Hayman hurried Evers by the radio shack and through the gloomy berthing space. The water was high in the machinery room bilges, but there was still plenty of room for more, in case the torpedo room had to be bailed again. Hayman figured they could wait another day before starting that procedure again. It was an increasingly difficult job, because the available manpower was shrinking. They could probably forego the effort entirely for several days if they had to. The higher the water came in the torpedo room, the more volume was available, because of the hull curvature. It would mean that after a week or so they might be wading around. And Hayman knew that they did not have another week left to them, one way or another.

The improved condition had its effect on Fitzgibbons, bringing him out of his torpor and reviving his truculence toward Hayman. He kept the religious ceremony brief; no hymns were offered and he concentrated on silent meditation. When it was over Hayman gave a short briefing, referring to a list of points that he had written on a piece of paper. Mostly, it was a rationalization of the fact that their rescuers had not come. He felt certain that a new downhaul cable had been installed the previous Friday. He emphasized that the Navy would never abandon the effort to reach them, knowing that men were alive in the submarine. For this reason they had to continue the pounding on the hull during the period which was daytime on the surface. Attempts had been made to communicate by Morse Code, but he did not feel they were effective. The main point, he told them, was to survive as long as they could. The longer they could sustain themselves, the better the chance of being alive when the hatch finally opened. Summing up, he said, "Keep in mind it could be days yet or just five minutes from now. The important thing is to concentrate on reducing physical activity. Though our atmosphere has improved, we must give the scrubber a chance to catch up. No one is to be out of their rack. Hang on, sailors, we'll make it yet."

When Hayman returned to his stateroom, he was surprised to find Fitzgibbons waiting for him. He was sitting at the desk busily completing an entry in his journal. "Robbie, I wanted to talk to you," he said without looking up. It was the first time he had addressed Hayman with the diminutive in several days. Hayman sat on the edge of the bunk and waited for him to continue. Fitzgibbons, like the rest of them, had lost weight, and the pudginess had melted from his face. Hayman studied his profile and could see the changes that had been wrought by weeks of entrapment. The cheekbones and chin had become more prominent, there was a suggestion of hollows shadowing the jawline, and the temples were slightly sunken. It was curious, how much better he looked this way, Hayman thought. The features were finely drawn and missed being handsome only because of the sensitive, almost feminine mouth.

Fitzgibbons closed the book and hiked the chair around to face Hayman. "Robbie, this is the thirtieth day the *Lancerfish* has been down; we've been through a lot. Many of the crew are gone, and it may be that we will follow. But, whatever lies ahead I would like for us to work together." He paused, looking at his clasped hands between his knees. His manner was that of a father speaking with a recalcitrant son. "We have had our differences, Robbie," his voice became a trifle nostalgic and he glanced up earnestly, "and I know you've never particularly liked me."

"It's not dislike, Fitz. We just don't have anything in common." Fitzgibbons seemed to be more like his old self, but Hayman was wary. There was a tense aura of purpose in his bearing.

"Through circumstances," Fitzgibbons went on, "I find that I am the senior officer amongst us and as such must carry out my responsibilities. If anything happens to me, then the responsibility shifts to you, you being the next in the chain of command. I bring this up because lately you have been taking certain command initiatives without consulting me."

"Command initiatives?" Hayman was puzzled.

209

"Well, for example, opening the escape trunk lower hatch without permission; making decisions and giving orders, like in the case of Schoenberg, and now telling the men they are not to get out of their bunks. It isn't that I disagree with these measures, but you should clear with me. We must work together. You're giving the impression that you have taken over."

Hayman started to object, it was all so ridiculous. Command responsibility in a sunken submarine with just a handful of men left! Except for the reactor compartment, they were not even standing watches any more, and at that Chief Benson was running the auxiliary watch. Technically, Fitz was right, he thought, but what decisions could be made in the current situation? He was too tired to make an issue of Fitzgibbons' complaints. Better to have a little harmony through appeasement.

"I didn't mean it to look like I was taking over, Fitz. You're right, we've got to stick together." Hayman dropped back on his pillow. "If there are any more decisions to be made, Fitz, you make them."

He shut his eyes and after a moment heard Fitzgibbons say, "Someone much higher than me, or you, makes the decisions. He speaks through us, through me." Hayman heard Fitzgibbons draw the curtain as he left.

When Hayman opened his eyes again, he felt that several hours had passed, but it was actually less than two. He should eat something, which meant either kidney beans or soup. That was the only selection Rumford had left in the pantry. He might go to the storeroom and try to find some more fruit cocktail. Since Saturday the steward had ceased all efforts to prepare meals, even to the opening of cans. Hayman got up and noticed that Fitzgibbons' journal was still on the desk. He picked it up to return it on his way aft, then paused, taking a closer look. The book was a hardcover ledger type that was normally used by the quarter-masters as a rough log.

Hayman opened it, and riffled through the pages with mild curiosity. Nearly half of the book had been used up by daily entries describing events of the day, often in great detail. Some of the entries included lengthy quotations, mostly religious and probably copied from the Bible, Hayman decided. One read: "Thou wilt keep him in perfect peace, whose mind is stayed on thee: because he trusteth in thee." Hayman sat down, reading on with growing interest. He felt somewhat guilty in his prying. He turned to the front and saw a list of the crew, their names printed in pencil. Those that had died were dutifully noted and dated. One block of names was bracketed alone with a short "remarks" annotation describing those lost in the fire. The entire crew was alphabetically listed, with the officers on a separate page. After each man's name was a number which corre-sponded with his alphabetical listing. The numerical assignment was for rescue operations, Hayman realized. But after some of the names there was a second number, which at first mystified him. Then he noticed it pertained to those still living. They were new sequence numbers for the rescue chamber, but they were not in alphabetical order. He flipped back to the page for officers and was astonished to see after his name the figure one. He wondered what significance that priority had.

12 – FRUSTRATION

JUNE 13-15

Sunday morning Commodore
Holmes was picked up at his hotel in Boston by an official
sedan from the First Naval District Headquarters. The
early morning drive to Portsmouth, N. H., was a pleasant
change after weeks at the rescue site. A busy itinerary lay
before him. After looking over the modified rescue chamber
and conferring with the design engineer, he would fly back
to New York. Monday he would go to Hoboken, N. J., to
inspect the new winch, then on to Washington for the meeting with Admiral Moran at the Naval Material Command
headquarters. It would be Tuesday before he would return
to the *Kingfisher*.

They turned onto a secondary highway, leaving behind the smooth monotony of the turnpike. The road was
more familiar to Holmes, and he began recognizing features
of the little communities as they neared Portsmouth. The
driver slowed as they rounded a bend and entered a more
densely settled area. There were neat frame houses set back
from a tree-lined avenue. More automobiles and people
were evident now, mostly congregating at a white clap-
board church, its square steeple showing above the trees.

212

Holmes rolled the window down a few inches to let some of his cigar smoke out of the car. The crisp air was cooler than expected, reminding him they were farther north and spring was not so advanced in New England.

A sprawling, new shopping center on the outskirts of Portsmouth reminded Holmes that it had been several years since he had been to this special shipyard for the submarine force. That last occasion had involved another submarine disaster, the loss of *Thresher*. How quickly the years passed, almost unnoticed, he thought with chagrin. After all that time there was still no rescue device suitable for deep operations—at least not one that would get him down to the *Lancerfish*. The new DSRV system, an outgrowth of the Deep Submergence Review Group that had met after the *Thresher* sinking, was reportedly nearly operational. But it was doubtful this complicated device could be made ready in time to rescue the dwindling survivors. Instead, he would have to employ a technique that was last used before World War II; modified on a crash program to suit the depth. The amount of time it had taken to get going on the DSRV system was preposterous. It had required a shorter period to develop the fleet ballistics missile program. If the same proficiency for providing new weaponry had been applied to rescue technology, he would have had the men out of *Lancerfish* long before this.

Downtown Portsmouth seemed unchanged. They passed the public library and the old buildings with false fronts, the city diner, Elks lodge, all looked exactly as he had last seen them. As they rumbled over the drawbridge, Holmes could see the shipyard with its soot-grimed brick buildings. There were the main foundry, tall chimneys, the water tower, and the giant traveling cranes poised motionless over the graving docks. At the piers were barges, yard tugboats, and two submarines rigged with scaffolding. Because it was Sunday, the shipyard appeared deserted and quiet.

They rolled to a stop at the main gate, and a Marine in dress blues sprung a smart salute. Holmes received directions to the industrial manager's office, where he was to meet a Lt. Hagger. It was located in a one-storied prefabricated building near drydock number two. Except for two sailors heading for the main gate, they encountered no one in the yard, and it required some minutes of search before they found the building. Both doors were locked and to all appearances there was no one around. Damnit, Holmes thought, the shipyard commander had assured him all arrangements had been made for this visit. He pounded the door again with more force and looked about the empty expanse of pavement around the cavernous drydock.

Holmes was about to return to the main gate when a grey jeep barreled around a corner and headed for him. A tall Negro officer in work khakis jumped out, tossing him a careless salute.

"I'm Lt. Hagger, Captain. Sorry to have missed you, but I had to find the OOD to get the key to shop thirty-one. That's where the diving bell is."

"Where's the design engineer, this Mr. Edwards?" Holmes pushed the peak of his cap up. He was getting annoyed.

"Probably at home. We didn't expect you until this afternoon. Civilians here don't spend any more time than they have to at the yard," he answered affably.

Holmes's heavy lidded eyes rested on the lieutenant. "Get in touch with him and tell him to get here quickly as possible," he said firmly, prompting the junior officer to drop his casualness. Hagger led the way to his office, where he would telephone the design engineer. The call was brief and Holmes overheard the one end of the conversation.

"Mike? When you coming down?" A pause, and Hagger doodled on the telephone directory. "He's here now. . . . Yeah." Another pause. "Drove up this morning . . . yeah, I guess so." Hagger's eyes focused on Holmes's grim face. "And, Mike, hurry it up, okay?" He hung up and said, "It won't take him long, he lives near the base. Sorry, sir, for the delay."

It was approaching noon when Edwards, wearing slacks and a plaid shirt, arrived. He was a man in his late thirties, a trifle paunchy with very closely cropped hair. He seemed a little peeved at being hustled to the shipyard in such an unceremonious manner. They walked to the shop, which was nearby, Hagger preceding them to unlock the door with a large ring of jangling keys. He snapped on several switches, and overhead rows of phosphorescent lights faltered to life. They marched past the silent turret lathes, power drills, and hydraulic presses. At one side of the shop Holmes saw the rescue chamber resting in a wooden frame. Other pallets contained more current work. Giant valve bodies, manifolding, and shiny machined parts in boxes indicated that the chamber had been shunted aside for the moment.

To Holmes the bell looked quite unfinished. Most of the upper portion was painted in red lead primer. The new, modified lower skirt was still raw steel with chalked markings and a fine haze of rust already breaking out. He was more than disappointed. He had expected the chamber to be completed, except for the downhaul winch. Holmes turned to Edwards, who was standing with arms akimbo, petulantly silent.

"I understood that work was going on around the clock on this project," Holmes said tersely, "including Sundays."

"There's nothing else we can do until the winch comes."

"You mean it's completed except for that?" Holmes looked dubious.

Edwards strolled around the towering cylinder. "Well, there's some welding to be done—studs for the winch foundation—which is why we haven't primed the lower compartment yet." Edwards came up alongside Holmes and stood looking at the chamber. He reminded Holmes of a used car dealer who, after announcing a price, waits for the buyer to make the next offer. There was a "take it or leave it" attitude in his manner that aggravated Holmes's growing impatience.

"Can't the studs be welded now, so the chamber can be completed that much sooner when the winch arrives?" Holmes demanded.

"We only have sales drawings from the vendor, and those have no dimensions. I've called the company and was told the winch should be here next week. Then we'll know how to mount it. It won't take much time."

"Let's understand one fact," Holmes said, including Lt. Hagger in his gaze, "there *isn't* much time for anything. There are twenty some odd men sitting on the bottom of the ocean waiting for you people." His voice was hard. "Tomorrow I will visit the winch manufacturer in Hoboken and will have shop drawings sent immediately. If that chamber can be ready sooner, then by God I want it at the site sooner." He turned to Lt. Hagger. "Lieutenant, you're the project officer for the Navy on this, and I expect you to follow this job with the highest priority." Before Hagger could reply, Holmes had moved to the chamber to inspect the interior.

Before leaving, Holmes returned to the office with the two men. He wanted to check the arrangements for shipping the rescue chamber once it was ready. Lt. Hagger fished out a file folder and leafed through it for some time. "Yes, here it is," he said at last. "The rescue chamber is going by rail to New London."

"By *rail?* Like hell it is! The railroads have been threatening a strike for over a month. What'll you do if they go out?" Holmes fumed. The question hung in the air an interminable time. Holmes realized that this was not entirely Hagger's responsibility. In a milder voice he said, "Lieutenant, I want that chamber to be sent to New York by a flatbed truck. Clear the shipment through each state it will pass through so it will have unrestricted passage over the main highway system. State police escorts can be arranged to accompany the truck all the way to the Battery in lower Manhattan. I'll have the tug *Hiawatha* there to pick it up upon arrival. I plan to call the shipyard commander to request these arrangements, but make a note of it. I'd like you to follow this up."

It was curious, Holmes thought, that the longer the *Lancerfish* was down, the less everyone felt it was a pressing emergency. It seemed that everyone became inured to the tragedy. The immediacy of the first days of the accident was gone.

The visit to the shipyard had taken less time than anticipated, and Holmes was able to catch an earlier plane back to New York. A feeling of frustration settled over him during the return flight. He had not been able to meet with the shipyard commander, who was out of the area for the weekend. His sparse reception, the offhand manner of the design engineer, and the stalled progress on the chamber all seemed to thwart his efforts. He hoped his call on the winch manufacturer would be more fruitful. Then he thought of his wife, whom he had seen only once since the rescue operation started. She was coming down from Connecticut, to take advantage of his one night in New York. Separations were not new to her; she had been a Navy wife for more than twenty-five years. He felt a twinge of guilt at the prospect of dining in some luxurious restaurant that evening while the survivors in the *Lancerfish* waited for him to save them. But, for the time being, there was nothing he could do.

Monday morning was overcast and hazy as another official car took Holmes to his meeting with the president of

Oceanographic Instruments, Inc. They followed a semi-trailer along a bumpy, potholed street in the industrial section of Hoboken. Both Holmes and the driver peered intently at the drab buildings, looking for the address. When they found their destination, Holmes saw only a long, unprepossessing building with a newer addition at the far end. A sign proclaimed that Oceanographic Instruments, Inc., was in the vanguard of ocean engineering.

The modern and rather sumptuous reception room contrasted sharply with the dreary exterior. A sulky girl with a bad complexion announced Holmes into an intercom, then said to him automatically, "Mr. Lippencott will be with you in a moment," and turned back to her switchboard. Holmes looked about at the sky blue walls and the large photographs mounted on them. They illustrated company products, mostly cast metal components for a variety of mundane items. Lawn sprinklers, ornate door handles, plumbing fixtures seemed to predominate. At first, Holmes suspected he had come to the wrong place, but then he saw some photos that were more recent. A strange looking implement resembling a gaping mouth was titled "Deep Sea Bottom Sampler." Standing next to it was a workman pointing stoically at some unique feature of the jaws. Another appliance, a bottom corer, had the same man posing with it, this time staring directly at the camera. Holmes heard a sound behind him and turned to see the president of the company striding toward him with outstretched hand.

"Captain Holmes? Welcome aboard, as they say in the Navy. I'm Jack Lippencott."

Holmes grasped a wide hand and nodded. The president was a portly man in his mid-fifties, dark with small brown eyes set close to a heavy nose. His thick black hair was combed in a swelling dip in front and held in place by a sticky looking substance. The full, pistolgrip sideburns acknowledged a more recent grooming style, as did his mod fashioned suit.

"Come in the office, Captain. Coffee?" Before getting an answer, he said to the receptionist, "See if you can scare up a coupla cups, Nellie. How d'you take it?"

"Black and sweet." Holmes spoke for the first time.

"Like your women, huh?" Lippencott grinned roguishly and Holmes vowed to never use that expression again.

He was led to a surprisingly spacious office with the same blue decor. An enormous desk and high-backed swivel chair looked as though they belonged in a Park Avenue executive suite. Most incongruous were the two flagstaffs rising from the floor behind the desk. A gold fringed national ensign hung on one, and the other held the company colors, Holmes supposed.

"It's a pleasure having you stop by, Captain, we've been hearing a lot about you and this business with the . . ." He paused absentmindedly, looking toward the door. "The, uh . . . *Launcherfish*, is it? No, *Lancerfish*," he said, ducking his head slightly as he remembered. "*Lancerfish*. Boy, I take my hat off to them guys trapped in her. I wouldn't want to be in their shoes for all the tea in China."

"I assume you got my message concerning this call today to inspect the winch." Holmes was eager to get on with his visit.

Lippencott nodded with slow exaggeration. "Yessir, my plant manager has it ready for you to look at. No problem."

"Yesterday I was at the shipyard to check progress on the chamber," Holmes said. "The only thing holding it up now is the winch. When will it be completed?"

Lippencott turned when the receptionist came in carrying a tray with coffee. He answered Holmes, motioning to the girl at the same time with an outstretched arm.

"We're on target. It's about ninety percent done, I believe. Lessee, the delivery schedule on that was . . ." He opened a notebook, licked his thumb, and flicked through salmon colored sales orders. "June eleventh. No, that was the first quote. We got a change order on that, here it is, June eighteenth. A Friday, I believe. No problem."

"Yes. Next Friday." Holmes took the cup held out by the girl. "Sooner, if possible. Also, Mr. Edwards, the design engineer, needs the manufacturing drawings so the mounting studs can be installed."

Lippencott frowned slightly as he stirred his coffee. "Yeah, I talked with Edwards last week. We sent them sales drawings right after we got the contract. He should be able to go by those, they're to scale. You see, Captain, manufacturing drawings are company property, sort of confidential. We don't like to let those out of the plant."

Holmes struggled to control the rancor that was building in him. "Look, Mr. Lippencott, I'm told he needs the dimensions, or else the yard must wait until the winch arrives before welding the foundation studs. I don't want unnecessary delays."

"There won't be, I promise you." Lippencott put his elbows on the desk and pressed his fingertips together. "You see, this is a design that was developed 'in house.' The contract reads *design* and fabricate. The Navy supplied only the operational characteristics. This is our own design. It's proprietary information, Captain."

"You think the Navy is going to build winches and compete with you?" Holmes fought to keep a sneer out of his voice.

Lippencott raised his hands as though to ward off the protest. "Understand my position. I've had experience with the military before, on similar contracts. Our research and development department will bring out a new concept for an item to be delivered to the military, then the government turns around and has someone else fabricate the same thing, using our plans. We're just the little guy, Captain, this isn't

220

General Motors. I've got to protect myself, y'see what I mean?" He leaned back, adding, "Look, I'll get a drawing of the mounting bracket, with dimensions, sent up to Edwards, all right?" He got up smiling. "Would you like to have a look around the facilities?"

"I would like to see the winch. I'm due in Washington this afternoon." Holmes was a little curt.

The shop area contrasted sharply with the ostentation of the offices. As they proceeded through the plant, Lippencott explained that he had been in business for twenty-five years, though his company had been in oceanographic hardware for only the past two years. Previously, it had been the Lippencott Machine and Diecasting Company.

"There's going to be a boom in ocean technology," Lippencott yelled over the noise of a milling machine, "a lot of money to be made if the little guy can just keep his head above water, so to speak."

They slowed their pace as they came into a newer looking section. Lippencott paused with his hands in his pockets, looking around proudly. "This is our new welding shop —automated—cost me nearly a hundred thousand." He waved to a man carrying a clipboard, who joined them. Holmes was introduced to the plant manager, and they moved to a bench where the winch rested.

There was nothing especially sophisticated about it. The drum and frame were much like the smaller versions in service, except for a different drive mechanism and spooling device. Holmes learned that the only delay was the motor, which was coming from another supplier. Lippencott was optimistic, saying that the unit was to be shipped to them that day.

"It's coming from Philly, so we should have it tomorrow, or Wednesday. There's only a couple of hours work to install the drive motor, then it will be on its way to Portsmouth."

221

When they returned to Lippencott's office, he called in a drafting supervisor and instructed him to have the drawing made up. When the man had left, Lippencott became conciliatory. "That'll be no problem, Captain. Edwards will have his dimensions by tomorrow."

He was silent a moment, then in a different tone asked, "What's it like for them? You know, do they have plenty of food and water? How are they standing up to it?"

Holmes briefly described the conditions, following the same general accounts given by the newspapers. He wanted to leave; Lippencott's platitudes and banal questions annoyed him.

"They say the atomic reactor might be a danger someday," Lippencott went on. "What do you think, Captain? Or maybe you can't say." He looked quizzically at Holmes.

"The radiation danger is exaggerated," Holmes said. "The safety devices and fail-safe features in the reactor are designed to protect the nuclear core. But even if it were to be exposed someday, the amount of contamination would be negligible. You must remember that it is over a hundred miles at sea and quite deep. That reactor is surrounded by a tremendous volume of water, which would dissipate nuclear contamination."

This seemed to satisfy Lippencott's curiosity. But was it true? Holmes thought. This was the official position, and from what he knew about atomic energy, he could not challenge it. It sounded plausible.

Lippencott accompanied Holmes to the waiting sedan. "That's going to be a big event—when you rescue them guys, I mean." He placed his hands on the bottom of the car window and peered in at Holmes. "I guess a lot of pictures will be taken of that chamber when it comes out of the water." He looked at his feet a moment. "Any chance of getting one of those shots? You know, something I could put up in the office, might even get a little advertising mileage out of it."

222

"Better see if it works first." Holmes was short. "You'll have to go through the Chief of Information for photos." He gave a quick nod of farewell. "Let's go, driver."

Later, as Holmes was being driven to the airport, he thought about the nuclear contamination problem again. Who made the determination that exposure of a reactor at sea would be harmless, and with such assurance? He gazed at the opaque sky. It seemed that this part of New Jersey was always shrouded in a sulphuric haze, caused no doubt by the concentration of industry and the continuous smoke that poured from great stacks. The endless motor traffic, moving over the maze of highways, while overhead the multi-engined jets trailed black tracks in constant arrivals and departures; this too added to the effluvium.

From the vantage of a high viaduct Holmes looked down on brown water as it flowed through a dead marsh to the Hudson River, which would ultimately empty into the sea. This pollution of the sky and ocean was probably more dangerous to the ecology than a nuclear reactor. Somewhere he had read that traces of DDT had been detected in such remote locales as Antarctica, and that all living things were tainted with the insecticide. This contamination was showing up in the milk of mothers and was blamed for causing thinner eggshells, resulting in more spoilage. Even wild-fowl species were becoming endangered, because the shells were often broken during incubation. Some people believed that the chemical caused inferior fleece in sheep and that woolen garments tended to wear faster. It was nearly impossible to buy a knitted sweater that did not show early signs of nap-balling. Surely, when DDT was first used, no one anticipated this widespread effect.

It could be that the Navy doesn't really know the final consequences of nuclear pollution from a submerged reactor, Holmes thought. There could be a credibility gap here too, and by the time it was discovered that such contamination accelerates deterioration of the environment, it would be too late. There had been two U. S. Navy reactors lost in the sea with the sinkings of *Thresher* and *Scorpion*. Even the Russians had lost a nuclear class submarine off Portugal. Now, with the *Lancerfish,* there were four potential sources that could someday be exposed to the sea, all in the North Atlantic Ocean. This area contained the major fishing industries of the hemisphere, he reflected. The east coast of the United States, including the Grand Banks, one of the most prolific commercial fishing grounds in the world, now had two of these pollution sources in the general area. Such radioactive contamination could be carried by the Gulf Stream and North Atlantic Current to the British Isles, the North Sea, the Baltic, even the Berents Sea and beyond the Arctic Circle.

Holmes's speculations were interrupted by his arrival at the terminal building of Newark Airport. He dispatched the driver and hurried toward his gate. He was anxious to become airborne and get above the sour air that filtered out the sunlight, and to look upon the pristine serenity of the substratosphere.

Less than two hours later in Washington, Holmes's taxi swerved to the curb near the main entrance to the Navy building. There was a small crowd milling about on the sidewalk, and police barricades were necessary to keep them from the steps. Two patrolmen with portable radios looked on impassively. Holmes paid the driver and moved past a group of onlookers with his overnight bag, wondering what the protest was about; something directed at the Navy, obviously. He paused on the steps with curiosity and surveyed the orderly demonstrators. They were mostly young, though scattered in the slowly moving ranks he saw a few older faces and business suits identifying the Establishment. The signs they carried were crudely printed. One read: RESCUE THE MEN NOW! Another, carried by a young man with a tuft of beard and a wild mass of hair, proclaimed: BETTER SAVED BY A RED THAN DEAD!

Holmes was mildly surprised that the rescue operations were receiving this attention. The recent news stories and commentary concerning the possible Soviet involvement had no doubt precipitated this new issue. Next it will be the environmentalists protesting the dangers of nuclear pollution, he thought as he turned away.

The meeting was informal, involving a few representatives of the DSSP, Captain Shepherd, and Holmes in Admiral Moran's office. Holmes was the only officer in uniform, and he sat in the center of the room facing the Admiral's desk. The others occupied a deep settee at the opposite end of the room, giving Holmes a feeling that he was testifying before a court. When he finished his status report on the rebuilt McCann Rescue Chamber, he gave his appraisal of the Russians' *Bentos V*.

"There's no doubt it could make the depth. Dr. Gornin claims to have made recent dives to even greater depths than what we are confronted with. Actually, their bell could probably lock on to the *Lancerfish*. I really don't know what reason we can give to turn down their offer."

The Admiral straightened in his chair. "That won't be a problem," he said, looking toward Captain Shepherd. "Shep has come up with a good idea. We'll tell them that the *Lancerfish* has a hatch of special configuration and the *Bentos V* wouldn't be able to make a seal. In fact, we can say that's the reason we're modifying our own chamber. I think, Barney, it would be better if you communicated this reply to the Soviets first."

Shepherd, in a dark business suit, crossed his legs and flicked imaginary lint from his knee. "Really, I don't think this soul searching is necessary. With all deference to the Commodore," he said, smiling politely at Holmes, "I feel the Soviet chamber is inadequate. It is a shabby, rust-worn relic, most likely even dangerous. I don't think . . ."

"Not shipshape, to be sure," Holmes interjected, "but the basic features are there, crude though they may be. Let's not delude ourselves, the damned thing would probably work."

Shepherd shrugged. "Possibly, but as we discussed before, there is a security problem involved. Anyway, the survivors have been down this long—nearly a month—a few days more should make no difference, and we won't have to worry about classified material being compromised."

Admiral Moran pitched a pencil to his desk. "Shep is right, Barney, there is no point in going over this again. The decision has been made, we're ruling out assistance from the Russians. Admiral Calhoun concurs with me on this."

Replying to Shepherd, Holmes said, "When this operation started we had sixty-one men alive. Now there are twenty-six, maybe less. I've got another downhaul rigged, and still I must wait another four days for that chamber to come from Portsmouth."

Holmes realized that he was in favor of using the Russian device if he could deploy it from the *Kingfisher*. Those crewmen were waiting out the delivery of a drive motor, that's what it amounted to. Regardless of national pride, and even if only one day was saved, those survivors should be brought up. But he had to have the Admiral's support.

"Admiral, if we can get the Soviets to go along with transferring just the *Bentos V* to *Kingfisher*, we could make a rescue attempt tomorrow. That wouldn't jeopardize security."

The Admiral shook his head. "No, Barney, it wouldn't work. In the first place, the Russians would not agree to that. The very fact that we had made such a request would be our acknowledgment that their system is workable and we would have to agree to their terms." He paused thoughtfully. "Or face an outraged segment of the American public. Also, if their chamber fouled the cable, or was in any way responsible for delaying our attempt with the modified bell, we would catch even more hell."

"What if it succeeded?" Holmes's voice was clipped.

"We would still catch it—from a great majority in this country who would feel that we should have waited for the U. S. chamber and denied the Communists their propaganda. The only way we can win in this situation is to put our money on the reworked McCann chamber or"—he turned to Shepherd—"possibly even Shep's DSRV."

Holmes looked at the others for support, but their silence told him they sided with the Admiral. Shepherd sat with tightly folded arms, his chin pressed over his bow tie in meditation. Holmes knew he had probably been instrumental in the decision to reject the Russians. There was a perplexing atmosphere of antagonism in the others, as though they had lost faith in him. What was the reason for it? What had he done, or not done, to earn this lack of confidence? He thought over the events of the past weeks. Perhaps he should have foreseen the problems with the downhaul winch and corrected them earlier. Under the stress of the emergency, that had been overlooked. Should he *not* have made the first attempts? There had been no way to test the winch, if it had occurred to him, because it was attached to the hatch of the *Lancerfish*.

No, no one could fault him on the steps he had taken. The contention he felt in all departments of the Naval Material Command stemmed from an older resentment. During his earlier campaign to initiate research and development in submarine rescue devices, much of his vigorous prodding had been directed at this command.

The Admiral was talking to him again. "You've been at the site and not aware of the hornet's nest this sinking has stirred up. The public outcry at so-called ineptitude on the part of the Navy is loud and getting stronger. There's talk of a Senate investigation when this operation is over. And in addition, insofar as the Russians are concerned, there has been State Department guidance on this too. Go back to your ship, Captain, and inform Captain Vashenko that his bell lacks the capability to work with this American submarine. And, by all means, thank them profusely."

The Admiral stood up, signaling the meeting was ended. He smiled slightly and said to Holmes encouragingly, "Anyway, Captain, Friday is not far off."

Holmes noted the use of the less familiar "captain." The others were moving toward the outer office, and Holmes with cap in hand prepared to leave.

"A final question, Admiral. What if our new chamber fails next Friday and that DSRV gadget can't get all its problems solved?" He did not wait for a reply, knowing there was none.

As he approached the big glass doors in the lobby, Holmes observed the number of demonstrators outside had increased. Some were simply spectators, drawn by the activity and the presence of a television camera. When Holmes reached the sidewalk, he was confronted by a man with a microphone.

"Captain Holmes, when will you try to reach the men in the submarine again?" he said, cocking the mike to Holmes's mouth as though offering him a taste of it. People encircled them inquisitively, cutting off escape.

"As soon as the rescue bell is delivered from the shipyard," Holmes said, trying to sidle away.

"When will that be?" the reporter persisted.

Holmes stopped and turned fully to the man. Behind him stood a movie cameraman already focused on Holmes, recording the interview. The reporter's easy recognition of who he was made Holmes realize the amount of news coverage and public interest that had centered on the *Lancerfish* rescue attempts. They had a right to know what was being done and what hope existed for the survivors.

"We expect to start the rescue next Friday," Holmes said.

"Captain, there's a rumor that only one man is alive in the submarine now. Can you comment on that?"

"The last number of crewmen known to be still alive was twenty-six. That was a week ago, shortly before we lost communications. I think the source of the rumor was my statement that *at least* one man was still alive, because someone is pounding on the hull."

"Captain Holmes, you met with the Soviets to consider using their rescue device. Is it any better than the U. S. Navy's, and could it be used to bring the men out now?"

Holmes could hear the whir of the camera and was aware of the crowd's eyes on him. "No, it's no better. However, the one we are preparing is specifically designed for the depth."

"There seems to be some controversy over using the Russian diving bell. Some quarters believe that if it was the British government offering this assistance, the U. S. Navy would accept it. What is your view, Captain?"

Holmes shifted his bag to the other hand; he felt cornered by the probing questions. "I don't think that's true. The Navy would pursue the same course, no matter what country was making the offer."

"Then, Captain, as the one responsible for saving the men in *Lancerfish,* you would not hesitate to use the Russian bell if you thought it would make the rescue?"

"Not for a moment. The important thing is to save lives." Holmes began moving off, and the spectators made way for his passage.

That night in his hotel room Holmes watched the television newscast, wincing slightly at his last statement.

When Holmes returned to the *Kingfisher* on Tuesday, he found little had changed. There were still no communications with the *Lancerfish*; even the banging on the hull was

229

more sporadic. Jenkins reported that it was thought more than one person was providing this primitive signal. There was a variance in the manner in which the sound was made. Sometimes it was a rapid pounding, and on other occasions it would be a slower, methodical beat.

The officers of the *Kingfisher* were assembled in the wardroom, where Holmes brought them up to date on his visits. The status of the DSRV vehicle had not progressed. It appeared that if the modified bell was ready by Friday, that would be the equipment to make the attempt to reach the submarine. Though it had been decided the Russian bell would not be accepted, Holmes held off informing them of this fact. If he did, the Soviets would probably leave to continue their research program, taking with them the only operational chamber in the area.

As the Commodore reviewed the sonar log, he was reminded that the last voice transmissions with the *Lancerfish* had taken place on Monday of the previous week. At that time they had told the survivors that the modified chamber was scheduled to be on site by Wednesday. He wondered what the men did that day, with no communications to know rescue was still some days off. The disappointment must have been profound as that Wednesday slowly passed.

DECISION

13 – THE LOTTERY

JUNE 15

BY TUESDAY, JUNE fifteenth, the
conditions in *Lancerfish* were rapidly worsening. Since Sunday night four of the surviving men had died, which included Lt(jg) Langworthy. Also among the latest casualties
was Hazleton, an electrician's mate and the last technician
experienced in the life support system. The carbon dioxide
in the atmosphere was definitely increasing, reducing the
remaining nineteen men to almost total exhaustion. There
was little movement about the compartments and passageways, except to carry out vital activities. The only watch
maintained was the one in the machinery space and reactor
room.

Hayman had joined Fitzgibbons, Roche, and Chief
Benson in the wardroom to consider what steps could be
taken to prolong survival. That morning marked the beginning of their thirty-first day on the bottom, and Fitzgibbons
remarked on it to the others. "Or, to be more precise," he
said, studying his watch, "exactly seven hundred and fifty-
three hours." No one replied because of the effort it required.

Hayman contemplated the possibilities for extending

233

their endurance until the bell arrived. The last of the emergency CO_2 absorbent had been used the previous week. The lithium hydroxide crystals were still spread on blankets in the compartments. Occasionally they would be stirred by the watch for whatever exiguous effect they might have. The remainder of the breathable air in the banks had been bled into the boat during an earlier air crisis. The only means for clearing the contaminated air of their exhalations now was the one carbon dioxide scrubber.

As though he read his thoughts, the chief said to Hayman, "The life support gear is working, but just barely, not to rated capacity. It just won't handle this many men, and the CO_2 level is increasing." The operating manual for the equipment was open in front of him. "I've been troubleshooting the system," he said, shaking his head sadly, "but I can't find the problem."

"How many of us will it support?" Fitzgibbons asked.

"About half our number, if that. It depends upon how much carbon dioxide is already in the air." The chief thought for a moment, then hesitatingly said, "The air would've been worse this morning, except . . . there are four less of us since yesterday."

Fitzgibbons opened his journal, looking at the names of those who had finally expired. He sat in contemplation for some moments, then sat up with awakening interest. "There are just nineteen of us," he said, looking from one to the other with shining eyes. "Nineteen, and do you know who most of them are?" He directed his question to Hayman. "They're the ones with faith, Robbie. The ones that were not afraid to pray and believe God would deliver them." Hayman was perplexed at first, then understood Fitzgibbons' implication. Most of the men on the list that were still alive were those who generally assembled for the religious services. There were about a dozen men who comprised this regular coterie in the torpedo room.

"I think it means something." Fitzgibbons' voice lowered in wonderment. "A revelation, Robbie, you can't deny it—this power of faith."

"It's also a coincidence," Hayman said. "They're mostly from the torpedo room, where you conducted your services. You had a captured audience."

"You're wrong, Robbie, you won't accept divine power as the answer, and do you know why? Because you're afraid, afraid that your rejection of God has doomed you." Fitzgibbons leaned back, his breath spent. The others stared at him and Chief Benson shifted uncomfortably. Hayman said simply, "All right Fitz, have it your way."

Fitzgibbons stood up, moving toward the passageway. "I must tell them, give them hope. They're going to live!" He left and they heard him lurching along the tilted deck to the torpedo room. Hayman slid out of his seat to follow. "Can't let him get too wild," he said.

Fitzgibbons made his way to the front of the compartment and climbed up to the catwalk between the tube nests. He faced the bunks, gasping and swallowing, trying to catch his breath. "Men!" he said hoarsely, attempting to wake those that slept and get the attention of those who just stared into space. Hayman approached him.

"Fitz, don't roust them out, leave them be. It will just contaminate the air more."

"I'm getting them up. Men!"

He banged on the tube door with a spanner wrench. Heads began to pick up and eyes turned toward him.

"Listen, we're going to make it. Your prayers have been heard. Look about you. Who survives? The very ones that have consistently beseeched Him; the ones that have never let their faith falter."

His excitement grew, and he waved an open Bible to them. "Let me read you something from the first chapter of the second book of Corinthians: 'But we had the sentence of death in ourselves, that we should not trust in ourselves, but in God which raiseth the dead: Who delivered us from so

235

great a death, and doth deliver in whom we trust that he will yet deliver us.' " He had to pause for some time to recover, then in a lower voice he continued, "We shall pray. Speak the words in your hearts." He bowed his head. In halting, breathless stanzas he recited the Lord's Prayer. Dirksen pushed himself erect in his bunk and trance-like repeated the words, each phrase coming like a sob. Two or three others joined in the prayer, mumbling the words uncertainly.

Hayman turned back to the wardroom. A bitter anguish welled in him. Couldn't they see Fitzgibbons was irrational? Why must they die in this manner? There was no dignity in this groveling and pleading to an impassive God. If there is a God, why would he have compassion now? The men who had already gone wanted to live just as desperately. He took his seat at the wardroom table again, aware that the eyes of Roche were on him. They sat in silence and Hayman had the notion that they would never move from the wardroom again. This is where they would slowly die. He looked up once as Fitzgibbons shuffled by on his way aft.

He must have slept, for suddenly Hayman was aware that his head rested on the table. He sat up and looked around. Only Roche was still there, slumped in an exhausted drowse. What had stirred him? He listened to the silence but heard only the familiar singing in his ears, a phenomenon he had become accustomed to. The ringing persisted, much like the sensation one has after a gun has been fired too close to the ears. But there was something distinctive about it now, there was a rhythmic beat to it. It had a different aspect of familiarity. He put his hands over his ears and the rhythm stopped, leaving just the amplified sound of his respirations. He lowered his hands tentatively. There it was again, positive, undeniable units of dots and dashes. Morse Code!

He grabbed Roche by the shoulder. "Andy, listen!" he

heard himself say. The other man started up, staring at Hayman as though he thought he had gone mad. "Do you hear . . . anything?" Hayman demanded. Roche shook him off and listened, then bounded up.

"Yes, it's code wave," he said, searching the space above him as if to locate a buzzing fly.

They moved into the passageway but at first could not determine where the sound came from. It stopped for a moment, and when it resumed the sound seemed to be coming from forward. They went to the torpedo room and the emission became louder. Hayman saw Cruthers standing in the middle of the compartment. He too had heard it.

"Get Johnson in here," Hayman shouted.

The sonarman would be able to read the transmission. Cruthers held up a hand, batting the air for silence. Then Hayman saw Johnson bent over a pad on his knee, a pencil poised in his hand.

"It's our call letters," he said. "They just keep sending our international call, over and over."

Hayman picked up the wrench Fitzgibbons had used earlier and struck the base of the escape trunk several times. The dots and dashes stopped abruptly, then resumed at a slower rate, and Johnson began to write. Hayman moved closer to Johnson and watched him print out: BELL TO ARRIVE EIGHTEEN JUNE. The message was repeated twice and was starting a third time when Hayman again hit the escape trunk, acknowledging receipt.

The eighteenth! Hayman thought, God, that's Friday —three days away. He doubted they could hold out another twenty-four hours. He read the message to the men without comment and turned to Johnson. "Is there any way we can tap out a reply to them?"

"We tried pounding out code after the UQC crapped out. They can't make out the dots and dashes on their listening gear. Pounding on the hull causes resonances that mask the definition on the receiver end." He looked up at

237

the overhead. "They must be using a powerful transmitter to reach us down here in the audio range."

Hayman encountered Fitzgibbons at the door to the wardroom. He told him of the message from the surface, and a beatific smile spread over Fitzgibbons' face.

"You see, Robbie? You see . . . God speaks to us, He is with us." Fitzgibbons grasped Hayman by the shoulders.

"But, Fitz, we can't wait until the eighteenth," Hayman said with resignation. He pulled away gently. "They will be too late."

"No. It's not too late, not yet. Some of us will live after all, and it will be because we never lost faith."

For a while Hayman was alone at the table. A deep despair had settled over him. To come so close to escaping this fate, only to have it snatched away, was capriciously unjust, so damned senseless, he thought. It was like racing to catch a departing train that was already moving. No matter how fast you ran, the train gained speed, leaving you with some dark horror waiting just behind you. Life would soon be finished, and that stark thought terrified him. So, now it comes; it was ordained from the very beginning.

So deep were his thoughts that Hayman did not immediately notice Roche's return to the wardroom. He faced Hayman across the table. They gazed at one another, their chests heaving, as though competing for the rancid air. There was no fear in Roche's eyes. He smiled wistfully and gave a philosophical shrug.

"Well, that's that. How much longer do you think we've got?"

"A day, maybe. We'll begin to lose more men soon. By tomorrow night there could be nobody left." Hayman recalled he had not seen Evers since the night before. "Have you told Tom about the message?"

"I looked in on him just now. He's sleeping, so I didn't bother to wake him."

238

Fitzgibbons appeared at the other end of the ward-room. His face still wore the blissful expression with the faint smile, as though enjoying some inner amusement. He took a seat carefully, watching the other two cautiously.

"I just talked with Chief Benson about our life support system. He can't fix it."

"We know that," Hayman said, hoping Fitzgibbons would not start on his fanatical theme. "We have to face up to it, Fitz, no one will leave the *Lancerfish*."

"Yes, they *will*," Fitzgibbons said, drawing the last word out emphatically. Something in his demeanor, the fierce certitude, alerted Hayman.

"Fitz, don't begin with it now; all the prayers in the universe won't help us."

"The prayers have been answered." Fitzgibbons spoke slowly, almost threateningly. "For some, there will be life."

"In God's name, how?" Hayman felt the old exasperation. He leaned back, shutting his eyes.

"That's exactly it, Robbie, in God's name," Fitzgibbons said, pronouncing it *Gaw-id's*. "He moves in wonderous ways and He moves through me. There will be eight survivors. The scrubber can keep that many alive until Friday. But eleven of us must cease to exist, in order for the others to live."

Hayman opened his eyes, turning to Fitzgibbons in disbelief. Roche raised his head from the table and looked from one to the other.

"Who do you think will volunteer to stop breathing?" Hayman asked.

"No volunteers. Being the senior officer, I have made a selection. It wasn't easy, Robbie, I've prayed for guidance, and it came. You gave me the answer, Robbie, you with your antichrist superiority. Who *deserves* to live? Answer me that. Who but the ones that never lost faith in our Lord; who for the love of God shall be returned to life to tell the

239

world of God's power." He stopped, out of breath. Sweat glistened on his forehead.

Hayman's mind was in turmoil. Fitzgibbons was completely deranged; insane. He had to stop him, subdue him if necessary. He met Roche's look of amazement.

Fitzgibbons continued, "I have made up a list," he opened his journal matter-of-factly, "and I've told some of those that will live what must be done."

Hayman stood up, ignoring Fitzgibbons, and said to Roche, "Andy, give me a hand with Fitz. I'm going to lock him up in the ship's office, before he . . ."

"Sit down, Hayman!" Fitzgibbons commanded. In his hand was a .45 caliber service automatic, the hammer cocked. It was the same gun used by Schoenberg. Fitzgibbons had drawn himself to his feet, and Hayman saw three ammunition clips stuffed in the top of his trousers. "Your duties are done, and so are his," he said, motioning the gun toward Roche. Then, almost pleadingly, he said, "Do you think it was easy realizing what I had to do? If I don't carry this out, we all die." Hayman and Roche slowly took their seats, watching Fitzgibbons warily.

"How are you going to do it?" Roche asked, awe-stricken, "and when?"

"Today. Chief Harris and Dirksen are in the group that will survive. Dirksen will take the watch in the machinery room at noon. Then the chief and I will take one man at a time back there. They won't know what's being done, and their suffering will be cut short, as humanely as possible."

"Fitz, do you realize how silly this is?" Hayman said, trying to be casual, though a vague quaver in his voice could not be suppressed. "That gun isn't going to prevent me from resisting you, knowing we are to die anyway. If you shoot me now, it will be heard in the torpedo room, which will ruin your plan."

"Ah don't think you want your life cut off ahead of time. If you do, then it will be that much worse for those in the torpedo room that don't know they are to die." Fitzgibbons' eyes glittered menacingly.

Hayman felt naked fear, he had to talk him out of this. Christ, to die by a bullet slamming through his head! It was too brutal. He looked at the muzzle of the automatic, remembering the sickening sight of Schoenberg's head on the typewriter. He looked at his watch: 1140. Fitzgibbons would commence his hideous plan in twenty minutes.

Fitzgibbons cranked the telephone with his free hand and picked up the handset, keeping his eyes on the two officers.

"Harris? I'm bringing Mr. Hayman and Mr. Roche to the control room. Are you alone?" He listened a moment and said, "Yes, we've got to do it now, no one will hear it in the pump room." He hung the phone up and glanced quickly into the passageway, then ordered Hayman and Roche to precede him.

It was too fantastic. Hayman could not believe it was really happening. It was like a dream, like one of his grotesque nightmares. He felt Roche stagger into him from behind, as though in a hurry to have it over with. His mind spun and was curiously blank. Can't just let this happen, he thought, but could not formulate a course of action, his brain would not function.

They were all winded by the time they reached the control room. Hayman ducked through the watertight door and saw Harris standing by the ladder going down to the pump room. One foot was up on the railing around the hatch, and a hand rested on the hydraulic manifold. So many times in the past, before the sinking, Hayman had seen the chief-of-the-boat in this posture. This was his diving station, and Hayman could imagine him giving his laconic report that the boat was rigged for dive. As Hayman struggled to regain his breath, he looked into the sardonic face which regarded him steadily. How could Harris do this, even knowing it saved his own life? If the situation was

241

reversed, Hayman thought, could he kill a man in order to stay alive? There was no guarantee anything existed after death. Yes, by God, hell yes, he could kill to prolong his own life, particularly if the man was already doomed. In minutes he would be dead, this was worse than just a slow suffocation. There was a loud sound of breathing at his ear. Roche was just behind him staring at the hatch.

"Climb down," Fitzgibbons ordered. To resist here would only mean they would be shot here. Hayman moved down the ladder, following Chief Harris. As soon as he arrived in the crowded little compartment, he looked about for a weapon—a wrench, pipe, anything. He was not going to die without fighting. The others came down and Roche moved up alongside Hayman.

There was a scuffling sound, a casual but rapid movement by Harris. Then it seemed they were just standing there looking at one another. Harris held the automatic by the barrel, presenting the butt to Hayman. Fitzgibbons grabbed for the gun, screaming unintelligibly, but the chief held him back with one arm and handed it to Hayman. Fitzgibbons' eyes were full of hatred for Harris.

"You . . . you Judas, you lying traitor!" he yelled venomously. "Do you know what you've done? You have killed eight men."

"Sorry, Mr. Fitzgibbons, but I just couldn't do it. It didn't seem to be the way," Harris said. "I didn't want to live the rest of my life knowing I had killed shipmates to stay alive."

Hayman brushed past the others and climbed back to the control room. As torpedo officer he had custody of the small arms locker, and he wanted to make sure no one else was armed. The experience, added to his weakened physical state, had left him trembling violently, and he felt nauseous. He found that it was becoming more and more difficult to move from one place to another. One thing for sure, he decided: the automatic would stay with him.

Hayman inspected the small arms locker in the forward compartment and found that there was a full inventory. There was little likelihood of anyone getting at the weapons because of the bar lock that protected them. There were two other keys; one kept by the captain and one with the executive officer. He went to the captain's cabin and located the uniform the skipper had last worn. To his relief, the key was there, along with several others on a large ring. But Crawford's key could not be found, and was probably with the body in the torpedo tube. He was not going to open that up to find out, he decided.

Roche and Harris were in the wardroom when Hayman returned. Fitzgibbons was in his stateroom; Hayman could hear his voice raised in a beseeching chant. There was no need to lock him up now; they were weakening fast enough as it was.

"Thanks, Chief," Hayman said as he sat down at the table.

"For what, Lieutenant? Saving you from getting a bullet?" Harris looked down at his folded arms. "I didn't do you no real favor."

"You stopped an insane plan of mass murder."

"Maybe. But, you know, Lieutenant, until I got down in the pump room I was going to do it. When it got right down to doing it, I thought about all the guys we had to do the same thing to, just to save my ass . . ." He paused and shook his head in slow emphasis. "I just couldn't let Mr. Fitzgibbons do it." He smiled thinly as he wearily got to his feet. "Well, you're the officer-in-charge now, Mr. Hayman. Now you're responsible for what's left of the crew."

"There's not much hope, Chief. The rescue chamber won't be here until Friday, and we can't last that long. Only a miracle can save us."

The chief looked back as he departed and said, "Yeah, a miracle."

Hayman was surprised to hear a soft chuckle from Roche. "So, Robbie, you believe in miracles after all."

"Not the kind that come by blabbering prayers like an idiot," Hayman said, "or deciding who is going to have their brains blown out."

"You know, it's curious, in a way. Who's to say whether you or Fitzgibbons is right? Fitz was going to take it upon himself to eliminate eleven men in order that eight may live. You believe that's wrong, mainly because we had to do the dying. You're willing to let us all die because of your principles."

"But, goddammit, it's *morally* wrong," Hayman said explosively. "It's against human nature."

"I'm not sure what you mean by 'human nature,' unless you mean instinct, and there I disagree with you. Instinctually we want to preserve our lives, some lives. Fitz was going to do it, by the only moral code he knew." Roche, winded, was silent for a moment while he struggled to regain his breath, then asked in a barely audible voice, "What is your moral code?"

Hayman searched for a reply, looking from side to side at nothing. "But . . ."

"Objectively speaking, Robbie, your unwillingness to take some lives in order to save others is merely shirking a disagreeable task and you call it being human. In all fairness, it is selfish and egotistical."

"It *is* against instinct. I'm not an animal."

"But you are, that's precisely it. You are a human animal and as such have the faculty of reason. Look at the problem intellectually instead of emotionally. Reason tells us we have an environment that will support eight men. This means eleven must be eliminated. Look at the problem on earth now; too many people, a population growth that threatens to overcrowd the planet. Scientists are making predictions about a dire future where only so many children will be allowed to live. It's the same thing here."

Hayman's mind buzzed with giddiness. The conversation, the two of them sitting there discussing the morality of killing for the purpose of saving life, was unreal. Roche was right, he admitted. If that was the only means to save some of the crew—even one—then it should be done. God, what a decision for *man* to make. How could he ever make up a list, choosing who would live? Who would he be accountable to if there *is* something after death?

There was little time left, it was up to him to make a decision. But how? Logic had to be maintained, Hayman thought. Take it just one step at a time. So, okay, what do we have? Without doubt eleven men had to stop breathing, no getting around that. Who is going to decide? Then it struck him. Let fate make the selection, that's what they had been trusting themselves to anyway. They would have a lottery.

"You're right, Andy," Hayman said at last. His voice sounded remote and strange to his ears. "Okay, I've got a plan, and we've got to get it going. Get Fitz and Harris in here."

A few minutes later Roche returned with Fitzgibbons and Harris in tow. Since the traumatic event in the pump room a change had come over Fitzgibbons. The fire had gone out of him and he stared unseeingly at nothing. His jaw hung slack, as though in shock. Hayman relieved him of the ammunition clips and ordered the others to the opposite end of the table. Hayman sat at the head of the table, where the Captain used to sit, and later Crawford, then Ritter, and finally Fitzgibbons. It was the first time he had ever sat in the chair.

The first thing Hayman did was have Chief Harris make a quick inspection of the men in the torpedo room. He wanted to know the condition of the men. Harris returned shortly with the roster. There were still nineteen survivors alive in the submarine. Hayman went to the cupboard over the settee and took down a box of poker chips. He counted out nineteen white discs and put the box back. He resumed his chair, reaching for Fitzgibbons' journal as he did so. Obviously, the numbers that Fitzgibbons had assigned to the names were for his planned elimination of crewmen. The sequence started with Hayman as number one and ended with Fitzgibbons. The final eight names were those that would be allowed to live. In this manner Fitzgibbons had intended to work down the list, paring the survivors according to the atmospheric conditions, starting with Hayman.

With great care to ensure legibility, Hayman numbered the poker chips from one to nineteen. When he had finished he pushed the journal to Roche, who sat closest to him, and asked him to verify the accuracy and pass it to the others. He explained his plan. They would draw lots, using Fitzgibbons' numbers. The first eight names would be the ones to continue existing.

While the names and numbers were being checked, Hayman went to the small arms locker again and picked out another .45 caliber automatic. He relocked the retaining bar and moved down the passageway to the captain's cabin. Using the master key ring, he unlocked the medical and narcotics cabinet and removed several packets of morphine with disposable syringes, and a bottle of Seconal. He then returned to the wardroom. The journal was in front of his place at the table, and the white chips were neatly stacked nearby.

The procedure was explained. Upon completion of the drawing, Hayman would turn over one pistol to the senior man selected to survive. The second automatic would be given to the next senior survivor. The drawing, and the results, would not be revealed to anyone outside the wardroom, which included Chief Benson in the machinery compartment. The morphine would be used on those that had to be killed, administered by one of the men chosen to live. Before this could be done, however, the man had to be given two Seconal capsules. The administering of the sedation could be explained as medication for averting further lung congestion. Those that were already comatose could be given the morphine immediately.

Hayman waited to hear objections after announcing the plan, looking at each of the men. Roche gave a quick little nod and Harris stared at the pile of syringes in the center of the table. Fitzgibbons only looked at Hayman dumbly, as though lost in a deep reverie. The numbered chips were placed in Harris' cap, and Hayman held it high, shaking it for a long time.

"Well, here goes," Hayman said. He had to hurry, his legs felt as though they would not support him much longer. "Andy, you read off the names as I turn up the numbers, and . . . good luck."

He swished his hand around inside the hat, grasped a disc, and put it on the table, the numeral six showing. "Rumford," Roche said softly but clearly. Hayman continued. Two more from the torpedo room; Johnson and McGovern. The fourth number was Chief Benson. Hayman found himself staring at the next selection, the first that designated one of them at the table. Number nineteen, Fitzgibbons! When Roche read the name, Fitzgibbons released a brief moan that dissolved into a sobbing sound and reminded Hayman of hiccups.

Hayman stirred the chips for some moments. Only three to go to make up the eight survivors. There were three of them in the wardroom who had not been chosen. He pulled a number. "Dirksen," Roche said calmly. At least one of them sitting there was slated to die. The next chip was number one, and Hayman felt the sweet relief flush through him. The final number was Bartolla.

Hayman dropped into his chair. There it was, he

thought, fate or whatever it was, pure chance, had decreed who was to live. He looked at Harris, whose eyes were fixed on him. The face was pale and cynical. Roche gave a nervous smile and made a thumbs-up gesture to Hayman. His hand trembled noticeably.

Hayman laid one of the automatics on the table. According to his rules, he was supposed to give it to the next in line—Fitzgibbons. He hesitated, rubbing his hands over his face with exhaustion. Could he trust him? Fitzgibbons was completely irrational, and Hayman still considered him dangerous. If he returned the gun to him, he might use it to re-establish his own plan. Some of his religious followers had been selected to die. Fitzgibbons might look upon the turn of events as divine intervention, placing him in authority again in order to save them.

Hayman heard a movement and looked up to see Chief Harris handing the loaded automatic to Fitzgibbons. "I believe you're the senior officer, sir," he said quietly.

14 – ON THE BOTTOM

THE SUBMARINE RESCUE vessel *Kingfisher* had been at sea for a month and for twenty-eight of those days had been moored over the *Lancerfish*. During the first two weeks there had been diving operations on the downhaul cable and subsequent unsuccessful efforts of the McCann Rescue Chamber. Since June first, when the last attempt with the chamber almost proved disastrous, the crew had little to do. There were the routine chores and watches to be stood, but this demanded only part of their time and tedium was setting in. The destroyer *Frobisher* had kept them supplied with fresh provisions, movies, and occasionally mail. The crew had not been given liberty, or leave, though *Frobisher* made runs to New York City twice a week and there were daily helo flights. One exception had been made in the case of a cook who was granted emergency leave because of a death in his family. Under normal circumstances Commodore Holmes would have permitted the men to go ashore in rotation, but he felt it was wiser to keep them aboard. Better they should be isolated from the public until the rescue operations were completed.

When Holmes returned from Washington on Tuesday,

he was particularly anxious for communications with the submarine. He had hoped the men in *Lancerfish* had been able to repair the underwater telephone. He desperately needed to know the status inside the submarine. Was the reactor still providing the power to maintain the life support system? Would their atmosphere sustain them until Friday, when the modified chamber was due from Portsmouth?

Holmes went to the sonar room and listened to the sounds of the submarine that came from the depths. They were the same as before, but the sonar log showed that there were fewer times when pounding on the hull was detected. If only he could let them know there were just a few days more to wait before the bell arrived. He asked the sonarman if there was any way this could be done. The man thought for a while, then explained that if a transducer of sufficient strength could be placed near the sub's hull, they might hear code wave. Low frequency sound impulses would penetrate directly into the compartments. Holmes called the *Marine Explorer* and learned that not only did they have the proper electronics, but their submersible could carry it to the desired proximity as well. Within two hours this was done, and it worked. The men in *Lancerfish* now knew the bell was coming on the eighteenth.

After dinner in the wardroom that night the conversation turned to the Russians and their chamber. Lt. Morgan had been quite impressed with his visit to the *Nikolai Trunov*. "Might have been interesting to dive that bell," he said, rolling his napkin methodically. "Could possibly have made a seal on the *Lancerfish* hatch."

Holmes studied the cigar he had just lit and said, "Petrosky thought the winch looked a little unreliable. It probably hadn't been used in a long time, because they were only making scientific observations."

"Yessir, it looked a little neglected, but I don't think

they would have offered it without being pretty sure it would work," Morgan said.

Holmes stood up, knowing the other officers were waiting for this signal that the evening meal was over. Captain Jenkins inquired if Holmes planned to join him for the movie on the stern. It was a clear and balmy evening, ideal for a topside showing. Holmes declined, as he usually did. He would take his air on the bridge. As he was leaving, Holmes was met at the door by a radioman with a classified message addressed to him. He scanned it quickly, then read it over again with increasing exasperation. He handed it to Jenkins wordlessly, studying the effect on the Captain.

CONFIDENTIAL 152205Z
FROM: COMSUBLANT
TO: COMSUBRESFOR
INFO: CNO/COMNAVMAT/COMTHREE

DSRV ENROUTE NORFOLK BY AIRLIFT X ESTIMATE THREE DAYS FOR FINAL PREP X DUE AT RESCUE SITE ABOARD TENDER APPROX 20 JUNE X DSRV DESIGNATED PRIMARY RESCUE METHOD X CAPT G. G. SHEPHERD HAS BEEN ASSIGNED O-IN-C OF DSRV OPERATIONS.

Jenkins shook his head in thoughtful wonder, returning the dispatch. "What about the McCann chamber? It should be here before the DSRV."

"I know, but the Deep Submergence people have been pushing to complete the new vehicle so it can be used on the *Lancerfish*. They claim it's been adapted to mate with the hatch, but there have been a lot of problems. Dammit, Jim, they want me to hold off everything so they can prove the time and money spent on this gadget were worth it. It's a complicated piece of gear, and they have been having a hell of a time getting all systems in it operational." Resentment and frustration were evident in Holmes's voice. "I'm not waiting for anything. The first workable device that is available will be used, whether it's the DSRV or the chamber from Portsmouth." He turned to go. "If we get any more information, I'll be on the bridge."

Holmes paced from one side of the bridge to the other. He could imagine Shepherd's exultation in this opportunity to use the DSRV. It would be his chance to vindicate the cost and incredible length of time it had taken to achieve this first prototype. The cost overruns had skyrocketed the initial estimate of three million dollars to more than seventy-seven million! If the *Lancerfish* survivors could be saved with this costly device, it would take some of the heat out of that Senate investigation. Holmes was also chagrined by the fact that Shepherd was coming out to "take charge" with the new vehicle. It would make Holmes look as though he had bungled the rescue job.

Holmes stopped his pacing and sat down in the bridge chair. Faintly he heard the soundtrack of the movie on the stern. He looked out across the water at the lights of the other ships. He guessed the real reason for his anger lay in his resentment of Shepherd. Holmes did not want to see all of his effort usurped. The twentieth, he thought, that was five days away. It was bad enough waiting these three days for the modified chamber. No, by God, he would not wait any longer than necessary, he reaffirmed to himself. When that chamber arrives we're going after them. If the DSRV was going to make the rescue, the downhaul cable would have to be removed anyway; might as well put it to work.

He was not a politician, he was a sailor. His job was to save as many men as possible, using the facilities at hand, coupled with good sense and seamanship. He looked around the force again; he certainly had enough ships and technical personnel, even including that grotesque Russian bell. At least the *Bentos V* was here. He wished Admiral Moran had backed him on that. If he could have talked to the Russian, he might have cooperated and let their chamber be transferred to the *Kingfisher*. If it had worked, the survivors would be up by now. It had been worth a try, anything was at this point. And it still was, he thought suddenly, what harm would there be in talking with Vashenko? He peered at the distant lights of the force, trying to identify the *Nikolai Trunov*. There were two sets of lights on the line of bearing where the Soviet ship had last been seen.

Holmes called a signalman to the bridge and ordered him to try to raise the Russian ship. For several minutes the signalman banged out the international call, the brilliant light illuminating the night with staccato explosions. Finally an answering wink came from the Russian ship, and Holmes had the signalman request a visit in the morning. Holmes wanted to see and speak to Vashenko in person. He must get the Russian to let him have the *Bentos V* without putting the *Nikolai Trunov* in the mooring, as the Russian Naval Attache had stipulated. Whether or not such a tactic was for propaganda purposes, Holmes did not care. His objection to that procedure now was that it would be complicated and time-consuming. Holmes could imagine the confusion of American and Russian sailors as they tried to pass the mooring lines and adjust the *Nikolai Trunov* over the *Lancerfish*.

The answer came back shortly. It stated simply that the *Nikolai Trunov* was getting underway in the morning to resume her cruise. Holmes was disappointed.

"Any reply, Commodore?" the signalman asked respectfully.

"Yes," Holmes said with determination, "make to them, 'Request visit tonight. Most urgent. Signed, B. C. Holmes.' "

A half hour later Holmes was in the motor whaleboat cutting across a flat sea. Well, the die was cast, he thought; there would be some high echelon repercussions over this. It made no difference, he smiled to himself. He had gone about as high as he would ever go in the Navy anyway. If the men in *Lancerfish* were saved, there would be little the Navy could do to him. Failure, of course, would bring more serious consequences; a court-martial, most likely. Also, if

253

this succeeded it would put Admiral Moran on a spot. A lot of righteous citizens would want to know why the Navy waited a week before deciding to use the Russian bell.

It seemed to take a very long time to reach the *Nikolai Trunov*. Now, as they drew closer to the big ship, Holmes began to have some misgivings. It would be strange to Captain Vashenko that Holmes was obviously acting on his own. If the Soviet captain queried his embassy in Washington and they stuck by their terms, Holmes could count on being relieved forthwith. Then it would be all Shepherd's show.

The dark side of the ship rose above him. The accommodation ladder had been taken aboard in preparation for departure in the morning. Figures moved about the deck, dimly lit by the deckhouse lights. A jacob's ladder tumbled down, and the coxswain brought the boat alongside. Holmes scrambled up to the deck and was helped over the railing. He looked about, expecting to see Dr. Gornin or the Captain. But there were only sailors and one civilian Holmes had not met before. The man led him through a different passageway to a large compartment, or saloon. The officers' wardroom, Holmes guessed; there were several people sitting or standing about. The gathering had a club-like atmosphere with some engaged in conversation while others bent over a chessboard or book. He was surprised to hear a female voice and turned to see a woman with a broad face talking with a man in naval uniform. They both turned to look at him but continued speaking in Russian, which to Holmes sounded like a tape recording played in reverse. He was beginning to feel uncomfortable, his guide having disappeared.

Out of the hubbub of voices Holmes heard his name called and saw an arm wave. It was Dr. Gornin beckoning to him on the far side of the cabin, where he was engaged in a discussion with two men. Holmes made his way around chairs and people, feeling out of place and self-conscious.

254

He had supposed his meeting with the ship's captain would be in his quarters.

"Good evening, Commodore Holmes, Captain Vashenko is just here." Gornin's clear English words suspended other voices in the cabin, and Holmes felt many eyes on him. The Russian scientist stood before him with a glass in his hand, smiling affably. He was dressed in slacks, brown sport coat, and tie. He looked very academic and could pass for a university professor attending a dean's social. Holmes felt quite conspicuous in his work khakis and windbreaker with the bold "Barney" emblazoned on the back. He had been in too much of a hurry to change into a dress uniform before making his visit. Besides, he had expected to see Captain Vashenko under more informal conditions.

"Good evening, Commandant." Holmes recognized the broad accent of the Soviet captain. He was sitting on a short couch with another man just behind Dr. Gornin. He got to his feet, setting his glass down, and approached Holmes. "And your submarine, Commandant, you have progress with her?" he said, smiling politely, then added, "You drink something?"

"Thank you, Captain, nothing." Holmes said, "I must return to my ship soon." He was no longer the center of attention and conversation resumed. More than ever he felt unsure about how he would present his request. What would Vashenko be able to do? He had probably received his instructions to proceed with the cruise. Apparently, this gathering of scientists and the ship's officers was to mark their sailing in the morning. Best to be direct, lay it on the line.

"Captain Vashenko, the situation in the *Lancerfish* is grave. Some of the crew are still alive, but it may be three or four days before we can start another rescue attempt." Holmes paused, he had spoken too rapidly and Gornin had to translate. Holmes continued, "I have been instructed to

255

remain in the mooring and to await the arrival of a new device. In the meantime we have the cable to the submarine which could be used with the *Bentos V.*" He stopped to let Gornin speak, but Vashenko waved a finger at the scientist, indicating he had understood. "I think we could bring the survivors up with your bell," Holmes hesitated a fraction of a second, "from the *Kingfisher* tomorrow."

Vashenko asked Gornin a brief question, frowning, then comprehending said, "Ah, you wish to launch the *Bentos V* from your ship?"

"Yes, with your technician, of course," Holmes said. Vashenko started to speak, but lapsed into Russian directed to Gornin.

"Captain Vashenko says the *Nikolai Trunov* is better equipped to handle our chamber because we have a big crane and the *Bentos V* is very heavy. There would be many problems to adapt your fittings and communications to the chamber. It would be much simpler for us to take a position over the submarine and make the rescue, you understand?"

"The *Kingfisher* has a boom that can lift the *Bentos V,* and we have connectors that are compatible with your fittings. It would require considerable time to position your ship in the moorings." Holmes heaved a great sigh and continued. "I'll be frank with you. I do not have authorization to accept the offer made by your embassy—that is, to turn over the rescue operation to the Soviet government. I'm taking a risk in making this request. My superiors will not be pleased. I am asking for the use of your chamber because it is the only alternative I have at the moment. The time is critical for the men in the submarine, and I want to save as many as possible."

"Ah, to be sure, Commandant," Vashenko said, "bot I also have orders. Admiral Mikhailovsky has instructed me that your Navy does not want Soviet assistance." He became thoughtful, cocking his head to one side. "I can ask to them what you want."

256

"No, Captain, I doubt that it would be approved. We must recognize these negotiations are political. I am asking for your help as one seaman to another." Holmes felt his arguments were having no effect and he was losing ground. "Captain, I appreciate that what I am asking may have risks for you as well. But it is also an opportunity to demonstrate something unique: Americans and Russians working together to save lives."

Gornin spoke up. "Commodore, you are naïve," he said, tempering his remark with a smile. "It is not us you must convince, it is your own Navy. They have made their decision, knowing fully the consequences to the survivors. It is impossible."

Vashenko gazed at his feet in meditation, his hands clasped behind his back. He looked up at Holmes but said nothing, then turned and took a few steps away, only to stop as though by command. He spun around.

"Da. Yas," he said, with a confirming jerk of his head. "We are to sail at eight tomorrow morning. I will proceed to your position, nearby, and put to the water the *Bentos V*. Your little boat, she can bring to you the chamber?"

Holmes had not expected the sudden decision by the Russian captain and, looking at Gornin, realized that he was surprised as well. A feeling of relief swept over him. What had made Vashenko change his mind? Perhaps he too was about as high as he could expect to go in the Russian Navy. Holmes wondered who would catch the most hell, and decided that he would rather be in his position than in Captain Vashenko's.

All the way back to the *Kingfisher*, Holmes planned his operations for the following day. The first thing was to brief Captain Jenkins, Morgan, and Petrosky. The adapters for the air line would be made up during the night, and the boatswain's mate could make up a towing bridle for bringing the *Bentos V* alongside. He wondered how many men he

257

could bring up on each dive. Four or five, he guessed, recalling the equipment inside the bell that would limit space. No time for unrigging it. That would mean six to seven dives to get them all out if the same number of men still existed down there.

Breakfast the next morning was animated, the atmosphere electric with purpose. Holmes had turned in very late and even then had not been able to sleep for some time. In spite of this, he felt rested, and much of his vitality had returned. He was anxious for the time to pass and had the lookout maintain a watch on the *Nikolai Trunov* since sunup. He ate a big breakfast. It would be quite a day.

Before going to the wardroom Holmes took a turn about the deck to inspect the preparations. The lifting boom was already rigged out and looked like a giant fishing pole suspended over the water. The motor whaleboat waited alongside with the bridle coiled on the bow. The weather had remained calm and the forecast predicted it would continue.

Holmes was just finishing his third cup of coffee when a messenger brought the dispatch board to him. There was a message from the Naval Material Command detailing the preparations of the DSRV in Norfolk. Apparently there were problems yet unsolved in connection with the navigating and positioning system. Also, there was a short dispatch from ComThree stating that the Associated Press was sending Edgar Lewis back to *Kingfisher* on the morning helo flight. Holmes looked down the table to Lt(jg) Watkins, the information officer from district headquarters.

"Your friend Ed Lewis is coming out, Mr. Watkins," he said. "I think the TV networks will be a little annoyed that I didn't tell them about the rescue attempt today—with the assistance of the Russians."

But he could not tell them, Holmes thought, at least not until he sent his situation report to Admiral Calhoun. He would hold off sending that sitrep until just before the actual operation. Holmes took a message form from his pocket and passed it to Jenkins.

"Jim, when I give you the word, send this off. Better make it confidential. It covers my intentions to use the Soviet chamber. I'll let the top brass break the news to the press." He looked at his watch: almost 0730. "Let's go ahead and adjust the mooring lines to put us over the *Lancerfish*, and take the downhaul cable in hand," he said, pushing away from the table.

From the bridge the *Nikolai Trunov* looked ghostly in the morning haze five miles to the west. Holmes inspected the ship through his binoculars but could discern no activity or preparations to get underway. Well, it's still early, he mused. But suppose Captain Vashenko had second thoughts about letting him use their chamber, and just steamed away? He could, without even letting him know.

By 0810 the Russian ship still had not moved, though a smudge of smoke came from her funnel. Jenkins reported the downhaul cable was secured on deck and the ship was almost directly over the sunken submarine. The latest current data had been received from the oceanographic ship, and a velocity of 2.7 knots was reported on the bottom.

"Okay, Jim," Holmes said, raising the binoculars again, "what the hell's taking them so long to weigh anchor?"

"At least she's there, Commodore. I had some fears she might be gone this morning."

"They could still do just that," Holmes said.

The signalman reported from above Holmes's head: "Small boat standing out from *Frobisher*."

Holmes swung his glasses around to the destroyer and noted the helicopter had returned. "Must be bringing Shepherd and Ed Lewis," he said. He could see several persons in the boat. He asked for the latest sonar information on the *Lancerfish*. The reply was disconcerting. The machinery sounds were still evident, but there had been no banging on the hull since the night before. Suppose we finally reach the survivors and they're all dead, Holmes thought. All this time spent on station, the other ships and personnel involved, the fantastic amount of money spent to rescue them would all have been in vain. Holmes could not dwell on that possibility now.

As the boat from *Frobisher* turned to make the approach on the accommodation ladder, Holmes saw Captain Shepherd look up to the bridge and touch the peak of his cap in a jaunty salute. "He's in for a bit of a shock," Holmes muttered to himself. The other passengers turned out to be Leonard Wright with a cameraman, in addition to Edgar Lewis. They had several camera cases and boxes with them, and Holmes wondered if they had been told of the rescue attempt. Perhaps the Russians had alerted them to this turn of events.

"The Russian ship is underway, sir, and headed this way," the signalman yelled down to the bridge.

Holmes turned to Jenkins. "I'll take them to the wardroom and break the news. Let me know when the Soviets are close aboard."

"Aye, sir," Jenkins nodded and as Holmes started down the ladder added, "in case I don't get a chance to say it later, Commodore, good luck."

Shepherd bubbled with congeniality as they took seats at the table and the steward started pouring coffee. He was eager to speak and sat with ramrod back on the edge of his chair and his elbows on the table. He pressed the palms of his hands together pontifically as he waited for the others to settle. "Gentlemen," he smiled to each of them, "the solution for the *Lancerfish* rescue will soon be here. The vehicle is being checked out in Norfolk and should be on its way here by the weekend. Admiral Moran sent me out today to brief Commodore Holmes on this first mission of the DSRV. I realize the media's interest in this operation," he nodded at

260

each of the reporters, "and we'll try to provide the facilities and cooperation you require. I know Leonard is particularly anxious to shoot some background scenes aboard the *Kingfisher* today if that is convenient for you, Commodore. We will return to the site on Saturday, when the DSRV is expected. At that time I will be bringing additional members of the press and the Navy's Mobile Photographic Team. The Admiral wants the rescue covered as thoroughly as possible." He opened his briefcase. "I've made up a schedule of events," he said, "sort of an operation order." He handed mimeographed pamphlets around the table.

Holmes had listened with patience, watching Shepherd through a haze of cigar smoke with half closed eyes. The *Nikolai Trunov* should be getting close; he would drop his bomb.

"We can discuss the DSRV at some other time if we need to. At the moment we are preparing for a rescue attempt with the *Bentos V*, the Soviet bell. The *Nikolai Trunov* is heading for us now to make the transfer."

Shepherd, who was about to read from his schedule, turned to Holmes. He adjusted his heavy-rimmed glasses, as though disbelieving what he saw. "The *Russian* bell?" he said incredulously, all traces of the Oxford accent disappearing. "Admiral Moran didn't mention it was even being considered. I've seen no dispatches on this. Who and when was this decided?" he asked with growing suspicion.

Wright put his cup down quickly. "Are the Russians taking over, Commodore?" He looked from Holmes to Shepherd and whistled softly. Lewis let the front legs of his chair drop back to the deck and he straightened. The attention of every man in the compartment was focused on Holmes.

He answered Shepherd, his voice becoming hard with authority. "Who? *I* made the decision. You haven't seen a dispatch on it because one hasn't been sent yet. The Russians aren't taking over, they're only lending us the *Bentos V*," he added, turning to Wright.

"You can't do that," Shepherd interjected. He searched through his briefcase for the message from the Admiral. "The DSRV has been designated the primary method for rescue. I'm sure you've seen . . ."

"Of course I've seen it. But I'm also the commander of rescue operations. I am only interested in saving the sailors in *Lancerfish*. I am not going to use this disaster to demonstrate the feasibility of a new and untried concept."

"With all respect, Commodore, I object, as officer-in-charge of the DSRV deployment . . ." Shepherd's voice rose in pitch. "There are certain preparations that must be carried out in order to employ this submersible. The downhaul cable must be removed and the area around the hatch on the submarine cleared of obstructions."

"Captain Shepherd, you know damned well there's nothing to clear—you've seen the *Lancerfish* yourself from the *Seasearch*. The cable can be cut just prior to operations with your vehicle if it is needed. Until then I intend to use that downhaul. If the Russian bell doesn't work out, we'll try the new McCann bell when it arrives."

The telephone next to Holmes yelped, and he picked it up. It was Captain Jenkins reporting the *Nikolai Trunov* was half a mile on their beam, approaching slowly. Holmes told him to release the message to ComSubLant and ComNav-Mat. He got to his feet and said to the newsmen, "You can cover the rescue operations from the boat deck or bridge. Please stay clear of the main deck."

Wright had already given his cameraman instructions to get set up, and was busy assisting him with the cases. Lewis and Lt(jg) Watkins followed Holmes out of the wardroom, leaving Shepherd sitting at the table holding his schedule.

The forecastle of the *Nikolai Trunov* seemed to tower above the stern of the *Kingfisher*, though the ship was 200

262

yards away. She was dead in the water, turning slowly to reveal her full length. Many of the Russian sailors on the main deck and the scientists on the second level were merely spectators. Most were armed with cameras and snapped pictures of the American vessel. On the after deck of the *Kingfisher* men were laying out the lengths of hose and line that would be used with the bell. From time to time they looked up from their work to gaze soberly at the impressive Russian ship. The turret crane on the *Nikolai Trunov* lifted the *Bentos V* and swung it smoothly out over the water. At that moment a motorboat set off from the side of the Russian ship and headed for the *Kingfisher*.

Holmes searched the figures on the bridge of the Soviet vessel and recognized the stocky form of Captain Vashenko speaking into a voice tube. When the Russian captain looked up, he saw Holmes and raised an arm in silent greeting. The motor whaleboat cast off with Lt. Morgan to supervise the towing of the bell to the *Kingfisher*.

Edgar Lewis, the AP reporter, moved to the side of the bridge where Holmes was standing. "Strange, isn't it, working with them?" he said, watching the Russian motorboat as it approached. "It seems like only a short time ago we were shaking our fists at them during the Cuban missile crisis, and now the Reds are helping us save our men."

"This ought to be a big story for you, Ed. I hope it works out." Holmes said.

"Yeah, for your sake as well as the guys in the sub. But whatever the outcome, I think you did the right thing."

Holmes regarded the reporter. He looked better than the last time he had seen him. Those first weeks moored over the *Lancerfish* had seen quite a few stormy days with rough water, and Lewis had been frequently seasick.

Holmes went down to meet Dr. Gornin. The main deck was crowded with ship's company; they too had turned out with cameras to photograph the Russian ship. Shouts of "gangway" preceded Holmes as he made his way aft. The big orange and white dome of the bell was almost alongside. They might be able to commence the first dive within the hour, Holmes thought.

Dr. Gornin wore coveralls, obviously intending to be one of the crew for the chamber. What would the men in the *Lancerfish* think when the hatch opened and a Russian greeted them? Holmes thought. For the moment Gornin was absorbed in the activities in the water as the chamber was eased under the boom. The motorboat from the Soviet ship was lying off a little distance, and Gornin yelled to them in Russian. The boat moved closer to the bell, ready to help ward it off the side of the *Kingfisher*. Holmes looked back to the boat deck and saw a gallery of onlookers gathered around Wright and his cameraman. They were men from the "black gang" mostly, though here and there an off-duty radioman or messcook watched the proceedings. Much of the scene would be witnessed by television audiences, Holmes realized. He hoped they would also see the remaining crewmen of the submarine safe at last.

When the *Bentos V* had been shackled to the lift wire of the boom, Holmes gave instructions for it to be left in the water. There was no point in it swinging from the boom while he conferred with Gornin and his personnel. The *Nikolai Trunov* had moved off a little distance, and Holmes could see Captain Vashenko watching him through binoculars.

Holmes and Gornin were followed to the wardroom by Lt. Morgan and Chief Petrosky. The compartment was empty except for Shepherd, who had watched the transfer of the bell from the weatherdeck doorway and returned to the wardroom when he saw the group approach. He did not get up as they entered and acknowledged Dr. Gornin's presence with only a short nod. When Jenkins had joined them, Holmes introduced the Russian scientist and motioned for them all to sit.

"We'll make the first run as soon as we're rigged," he

said, "but before we do I'll review the situation on the bottom for Dr. Gornin's benefit."

Holmes unfolded a large chart that showed the shelving depths where *Lancerfish* was sunk. After a short presentation he said, "I would like to send Chief Petrosky as the assistant operator. He's familiar with the submarine and will maintain the communications with the surface." He looked at Gornin questioningly.

"As you wish, Commodore. I could manage alone, except for the lower hatch. It is heavy for one man, and the block and tackle is not installed."

Holmes spread open a large line diagram of the *Lancerfish* which showed the details of the topside arrangement. In the lower right corner was a conspicuous CONFIDENTIAL. Holmes caught Shepherd's concerned frown and smiled to himself. What anguish this must be for him—revealing classified information to the Communists. If Shepherd had anything to do with it, this would be another charge against him at his court-martial.

Holmes pointed out the forward escape trunk hatch, explaining that probably it would not be seen during their approach. The alignment of the viewports on the *Bentos V* were such that only the hull would come into view during the last few feet. Holmes also explained that there had been no communications with the survivors in several days. The condition of the internal atmosphere was not known. To safeguard the bell operators, emergency breathing apparatus would be taken with them. Gornin studied the diagram with interest but asked no questions. When Holmes had finished, Gornin launched into a description of the bell. It was intended for Captain Jenkins more than anyone else, because he had not seen it before.

"Oh, we're quite familiar with that," Shepherd said from his end of the table. "After all, the *Bentos V* design was derived from our old McCann chamber."

Gornin at first seemed not to have heard, then smiling

quickly he turned to Shepherd. "There are many differen-ces, Captain, most notably it will reach your submarine. The McCann bell will not."

"Perhaps, but I have reservations about using such a primitive means for such a deep mission. If the rescue oper-ation continues after today, which I rather expect, you might have the opportunity of seeing a more sophisticated concept." Shepherd turned to Morgan, adding in an aside intended for all to hear, "And no doubt the Russians would not long afterwards have a deep vehicle of sorts too."

Shepherd's blatant attempt to provoke the Russian in-furiated Holmes. "Captain Shepherd, I'd appreciate it if you would confine your observations to our objective," he said.

"It does not matter, Commodore," Gornin said. "I am very sorry the Captain cannot use his new device now."

Morgan opened the wardroom door in response to a knock and saw that it was a messenger. "Is it important?" he whispered.

"Yessir, a classified dispatch for the Commodore."

"Let him come in," Holmes said, catching a glimpse of the reporters behind the man in the passageway. "Also, tell Mr. Wright and Mr. Lewis they can join us if they want." Holmes stuffed his cigar back in his mouth and took the clipboard from the sailor. The dispatch was from Com-mander Submarine Force Atlantic and read:

USE OF USSR RESCUE DEVICE DENIED REPEAT DENIED BY THIS COMMAND AND SOVIET EMBASSY X ACKNOWL-EDGE X SIGNED T. CALHOUN.

A direct order from the Admiral himself. The Navy must have informed the Soviet Embassy, hoping they would order Captain Vashenko not to cooperate. Holmes won-dered if the Russian captain had received instructions and was at this moment preparing to recall the *Bentos V.* There was no time now for conjecture, Holmes thought as he wrote out his reply on the bottom of the message:

266

CANNOT COMPLY X SOVIET BELL HAS BEEN DEPLOYED X HOLMES.

When the meeting ended they all returned to the stern, and the order was given to prepare for the dive. The boom picked the bell out of the water, letting it hang for a moment over the side while it drained. It twisted slowly, looking like some denizen fished from the sea. The bell had been repainted since Holmes had seen it last. Lettered conspicuously above the viewports was: CCCP БЕНТОС V. Steadying lines were attached and the big yellow chamber was swung aboard. Chief Petrosky climbed to the domed top and installed the hose adapter and connected the communications and backhaul cables. Meanwhile the lower hatch was opened by Gornin so that extra oxygen flasks could be passed to the interior. These would be transferred to the submarine in case additional oxygen was needed. Holmes knew that if the *Bentos V* was able to mate with *Lancerfish*'s hatch, it would be many hours before the last survivor was out.

After the downhaul cable had been secured to the winch, Petrosky reported to the diving officer. "We're ready, Mr. Morgan, but there's going to be a small problem. I'll be manning the phones to relay information, but I can't read the gauges. They're calibrated in the metric system and labeled in Russian."

"It doesn't matter, Horse, just pass up what Dr. Gornin tells you; we'll make the conversion from meters to feet up here. How does that winch behave?"

"Oh, it works," the chief boomed in his loud voice, "but it's slow as hell. One good thing about it, there's plenty of power to pull us onto the hatch. What's the current down there now?"

"The oceanographic ship reported nearly three knots about an hour ago."

Gornin paused in the hatch before following Petrosky

267

into the chamber. He looked toward Holmes and the other officers standing around him on the boat deck. "We are ready, Commodore."

Holmes glanced down to the dive control panel and Morgan nodded. "This is a deep dive," Holmes said, turning back to Gornin, "and the bottom current is strong. You may have some difficulty seating around the hatch."

"I am confident. The *Bentos V* was designed for such depths," Gornin said and started to back into the chamber.

Shepherd, who leaned on a railing nearest the bell said, "Our rescue chamber would have made it two weeks ago, except for the failure of the winch."

The Russian stopped and fixed his eyes on the tall officer. "There is an old Cossack proverb, Captain: 'Blame not your horse in defeat, or salute yourself in victory.' " He pulled the hatch shut and dogged it.

The *Bentos V* jerked into the air and was swung over the water once more. Two gangs of sailors paid out the air hoses and communications line. The rigging quivered as the creaking lift cable eased the bell into the water. Halyard blocks on the mast squeaked as the international flaghoist went up, signaling that diving operations were in progress. Holmes consulted his watch; it was 1108.

Inside the *Bentos V* Petrosky watched Gornin manipulating the valves. When the tanks were flooded he cinched the valves shut, checked the oxygen flow once more, and seemed satisfied. To Petrosky, sitting by one of the viewports, the life support equipment appeared rudimentary. The carbon dioxide absorbent was spread in containers resembling pie plates and held stacked in a bracket. Gornin, who noticed the critical look, said, "We have a better system than this, normally. It is the same type of atmospheric monitor that is used in the Soyuz spacecraft. It is being refurbished aboard ship now, and so we must be content with this older method."

Gornin started the winch and a muffled growl came from the flooded compartment below. Petrosky reported the dive had commenced and watched the hand of the depth gauge jitter to life. After some moments Gornin said, "Ten meters," and Petrosky repeated it into the transmitter on his chest. The next ten meters took a little over a minute. At this rate, Petrosky calculated, it would take them nearly forty-five minutes to reach the *Lancerfish*. He looked at the Russian making an entry in a little book. Funny, he didn't seem like a Commie, the chief thought; he could almost pass for an American. His English was perfect, though he did sound a bit like a Limey. He peered through the small viewport, but there was nothing to see except a few stray little bubbles wobbling upward.

At a hundred meters the bell began to lean more with the increasing current. Petrosky's reports were given monotonously as they passed each new depth, but now he added the angle of the chamber. The interior became cooler and moisture condensed on the uninsulated walls. They put on the foul-weather jackets that had been brought along for that purpose. Outside the viewports it was totally dark, and they were only one third of the way down. Petrosky's thoughts turned to the men sealed in the submarine below. He knew many of them were dead, perhaps even all of them by now. How had they spent all this time? After all these weeks they must be damned near crazy. He hoped they would be able to make a seal on the hatch and get those poor bastards out.

"Two hundred meters," Gornin said. Petrosky made his report, adding, "We're picking up more vibrations now. The chamber angle is about ten degrees."

"Topside aye." Lt. Morgan's voice sounded remote. "The vibration is caused by vortex shedding of the cable in the current; should decrease as you near the bottom."

Slowly the hand crept around the depth gauge. It was getting colder inside the bell. The outside water tempera-

269

ture was forty-eight degrees. When they reached 300 meters, Gornin stopped the descent. He turned off the interior lights except for the illumination on the control panel, energized the exterior floodlights for a moment, then tested the winch despooling mechanism again and found it functioned as expected. There was about 200 feet to go to the hatch. They resumed descent at a slower rate. It seemed they were inching down the cable. Petrosky massaged his cramped thighs; his feet felt completely numbed.

The exterior lights were turned on at 320 meters, or nearly 1050 feet. The chief pressed his face close to the viewport; the light was dazzling at first. Small specks of marine life drifted up past the ports. "Pteropods," Gornin explained, "a small mollusk." Petrosky made no reply, continuing to stare downward into the halo of light, reluctant to even blink, in case the hull of the *Lancerfish* should suddenly appear. He checked the depth gauge quickly; only about thirty-five feet to go, should see something soon. His straining eyes played tricks on his imagination, and twice he thought he saw the sub's deck.

But, it was Gornin who first caught sight of the superstructure. His viewport was on the side of the chamber that was canted downward. "By Jove, there she is!" he suddenly exclaimed. He stopped the winch and Petrosky moved to his side to look.

"Wait, I'll winch down a little more. We are about twenty-five feet above her." Petrosky reported the sighting to the surface and heard Lt. Morgan repeat it to the Commodore.

The forward deck of the *Lancerfish* was now clearly visible from both viewports. Their field of vision encompassed the walkway and the area around the hatch. It seemed to grow into focus as they got closer to the deck. Now they could see the shadow of the *Bentos V* creeping across the hull, and a flatfish the size of a frying pan jumped to life and sped into the gloom.

270

The winch was stopped again, and high-pressure air was blown into the lower compartment. This would create a bubble, or air pocket. After the seating gasket was firmly in contact with the sub's hull this air would be vented, and the tremendous sea pressure would cause them to suck down. Then the remaining water in the lower compartment would be pumped out. There would then be a free access to the torpedo room.

They started moving down very slowly; in a moment they would touch. Petrosky felt a slight jolt and presently saw a small cloud of sediment roll out from under the chamber. Gornin was busy with the winch now, applying power, then off, a little more, and off again. The chamber felt as if it were in the grip of a giant that was slowly rotating and righting it.

"I think that's it, Doctor. I think she's flush," Petrosky said.

Gornin opened the vent and the air roared for a moment, then abruptly changed in tone. They had sealed.

The remainder of the water was removed until a gurgling was heard. The lower compartment should be empty. Gornin opened an equalizing valve, and the upper and lower compartments now had the same internal pressure. The strongback was removed and the hatch was lowered into the lower skirt. The two men stared down upon the hatch of the *Lancerfish,* momentarily awed by the sight, as though it were some object exhumed from a grave. About an inch of water remained around the hatch. Petrosky cautiously lowered himself into the compartment, maneuvering around the cable and attachment bail. There was a strong brinish odor, and water seeped into his shoes. His phone cable was extended to its full length. He would have to remove it before trying to open the sub's hatch.

He reported into the transmitter, "Topside, I'm standing on the *Lancerfish.*"

Petrosky handed the phone set up to Gornin and knelt

over the hatch. It was icy cold and his hands slipped when he applied pressure, cracking his knuckles in the quadrant of the handwheel. He took another purchase and heaved mightily, but it was solidly immovable. He was wet from his feet to his knees and he began to shiver. "I'll need some help," he yelled to Gornin straddling the hatch above him. Gornin climbed down to Petrosky's side. Together they leaned their weight against the handwheel. It moved tightly at first, then became easier. The thin layer of water around the lip of the hatch bubbled as air from inside the sub vented to the bell.

"Hold it," Petrosky ordered, bending over and trying to smell the escaping air. The atmosphere inside the submarine might not be capable of sustaining life any longer. He was about to return to the upper compartment for the breathing appliances when he heard a noise and felt a tingle in his fingers on the handwheel. Had something broken? Then two more blows; it was someone hitting the handwheel. Someone inside the submarine was alive! He gave the handwheel another turn and the rush of air increased, splattering water up around them. In a moment it began to subside and the residual water around them disappeared. They were equalized with the *Lancerfish*.

Petrosky swung the hatch open and looked down into a brightly lighted compartment. A heavy, sickening odor welled up around them, and Petrosky stared into a face just below him. It was thin and heavily bearded. Dull eyes sunk in dark hollows gazed back at him, and Petrosky was not sure whether the man was dead or alive. Then the mouth worked and a voice croaked, "Hayman . . . I'm Lieutenant Hayman."

15 – JUNE SIXTEENTH

L<small>T.</small> H<small>AYMAN</small> <small>COULD</small> <small>NOT</small> take his eyes off the two strangers who looked down at him. He was afraid that if he did, they would disappear, dissolving into another mocking fantasy. He wanted to touch them, or hear them speak, to verify they had come at last. Only minutes before, he had been in the control room and McGovern had called to say he heard sounds above the hull. A few men were gathered under the escape trunk hatch when he arrived in the torpedo room. Others had heard it too and were struggling out of their bunks. Hayman had opened the lower hatch and gone up in the trunk to listen and stare at the handwheel of the upper hatch. Then the wheel moved a trifle, and air whistled around the gasket. The hatch was opening! He had called for a wrench and struck the underside, and the sound of venting air became louder. The pressure differential between the submarine compartments and the bell was only slight, but there was a considerable volume. The whistling continued for an interminable time, the men's ears popping with the decreasing pressure, and finally diminished into a long sigh. Water dribbled around the hatch lip and cascaded down the walls of the trunk. Then they were there, two faces gaping speechlessly.

Hayman spoke first and one of the strangers said, "I'm Petrosky, sir, chief master diver from the *Kingfisher*." He lowered himself into the trunk. "How many survivors, Lieutenant?"

"Fifteen. You'll have to make two trips," Hayman heard himself say. His voice sounded remote to him, disembodied, as though he stood apart from himself. Was he already dead? The chief shook his head. "Four, sir, we can only squeeze four or five men in at a time." He lowered his loud baritone and explained, "That's not a navy chamber —it's Russian, on loan to us. The operator is Doctor Gornin, a Soviet scientist."

Hayman looked up, perplexed, and saw that the other man had returned to the upper compartment to communicate with the surface. No time to ask questions now, he thought. It would be explained later.

Petrosky followed Hayman back down the ladder to the torpedo room. Emaciated, bearded men crowded about eagerly, jostling one another to get under the hatch and look up at the rescue bell. The atmosphere was rank and nauseous to Petrosky, and already he was beginning to pant. He was anxious to get the first evacuation started and explained that oxygen had been brought down. While the flasks were being unloaded, fresh air from the high pressure supply in the bell would be flushed through the compartments.

Over the babble of voices Hayman heard the familiar accent of Fitzgibbons. He was in the after end of the compartment on his knees, offering up a sing-song prayer of thanksgiving. Hayman explained to Petrosky that on the previous day the carbon dioxide had reached lethal proportions. Four of the survivors had succumbed. The latest of these had been Lt(jg) Evers, who died that morning. Hayman did not describe the survival lottery or the morbid consequences it had nearly brought about.

Hayman went to the wardroom to get Fitzgibbons'

journal, which contained a list of crewmen still alive. He would use this to determine the order in which the men would go up in the bell. The weakest would make the first ascent. He saw the morphine ampules piled in the middle of the table and thought of that eventful day.

After the names of those who would survive had been selected, the four men sat in silence for a long time, reluctant to do anything. Roche was the first to speak.

"Chief, I think you and I should do the administering for each other," he said slowly to Harris. "but first I will tend to the others." The chief continued to stare at his cap on the table, then almost imperceptibly nodded concurrence. "Robbie, I would like you to accompany me," Roche went on, "but not to give injections. I don't think any of the eight survivors should be involved in this."

Hayman looked down the table at Fitzgibbons. He had not moved since the drawing and sat slumped in his chair. He seemed withdrawn, even ignoring the gun on the table in front of him.

Roche placed the morphine in the chief's hat along with the bottle of Seconal. "Robbie, bring the list and give me the name of each man, alphabetically," he said as he got to his feet. Hayman put the automatic in the top of his trousers and followed.

Roche turned to Hayman questioningly when they had reached the torpedo room. Hayman opened the journal, ran his finger down the names, and said, "Cruthers." Cruthers? Why did it have to be him, his leading seaman? Almost anyone else would do; why not someone like Dirksen? It wasn't fair, this haphazard selection.

Roche was inspecting the bunks, trying to locate the one that contained the first man. He stopped by a bunk and peered down intently at its occupant. It was Bartolla, sunk in a stupor and barely conscious. "Where's Cruthers' bunk?" Roche asked in a low voice. Bartolla rolled his eyes

275

to the officer uncomprehendingly. Roche repeated the question and the man lifted a finger, pointing to the bunk above him.

Hayman watched Roche climb back down from Cruthers' bunk after a moment. There was a strange expression on his face.

"He's already dead, Robbie," he said placing the unused syringe back in the hat. "He must have gone just a short time ago. He was alive when the chief checked the men earlier."

Hayman and Roche made a survey of the remaining bunks and found one other new casualty. Rumford. The steward had been one of the men chosen to live, but now it was too late. Hayman looked at the terribly still form that stared unseeingly, and wanted to yell at him. He wasn't supposed to die. God dammit, Totem, you've screwed up the whole plan.

Hayman rested against the warhead of a torpedo. Everything was changed now. Who would take Rumford's place? Would he and Roche go back to the wardroom and conduct another drawing to see which of the condemned men could now live? Hayman realized that what he had thought was such an intelligent decision was wrong. What right had they to provoke fate? He looked up at Roche.

"We can't do it, Andy. This isn't the way. We don't really know that the scrubber can support eight men, or two, or even seventeen."

They had returned to the wardroom. Hayman had dumped the ampules back on the table and picked up the second automatic. He said to Harris, "We either make it together or die together, but no one is going ahead of time."

Hayman tore the page from the journal and returned to the torpedo room. Now it was over, he thought, as he watched the last of the big green oxygen bottles being lowered. Air from the surface was already making it easier to breathe. He read the names of the men who would make the first trip. Most of them had to be helped up the ladder. Fitzgibbons, as Hayman had decided, would be in the second group, but first he had to gather his classified publications to take with him. As operations officer, Fitzgibbons was the custodian of cryptographic and top secret documents. What a strange irony, Hayman thought, safeguarding secret papers while being saved by a Russian chamber. Three of them would make the last ascent—Chief Benson, McGovern, and himself.

Sending up the first load of survivors was difficult for those that had to stay behind. Something could go wrong with the bell, or the downhaul cable could part again. Even the weather could blow up. It was with relief that McGovern reported to Hayman the second mating of the bell. When preparations were being made to close up the chamber for the third trip, Hayman told Petrosky to ask Commodore Holmes for any final instructions. The reactor would be shut down by Benson and the electrical power taken from the battery. A thought occurred to him. If the Russians were able to get a chamber down to the *Lancerfish* now, they could do it at some later date as well. It would be a risk worth taking in order to gain first-hand intelligence of the U. S. Navy's most advanced undersea weapon. The sub was in international waters; what was to prevent them? Maybe they should flood the compartments as they left on the last trip. He ripped a page from the journal, wrote a message to the Commodore, and gave it to Chief Petrosky. The chief could not ask about such a procedure on the telephone with the Russian listening in, Hayman thought.

When the *Bentos V* came down for the last time, Petrosky dropped into the torpedo room and handed Hayman the same piece of paper. Scribbled below his message was: "Secure nuclear reactor only. Leave compartments as they are. Salvage or demolition will be attempted later."

Chief Benson reported to Hayman that the reactor was

shut down and the lighting and ventilation load had been shifted to the battery. Hayman ordered the last two men into the bell. Then he went aft through the empty, silent compartments to make a final inspection. The ventilation blower still hummed softly and the lights cast his shadow on the bulkhead for the last time. It occurred to him that once before he had thought he was performing everything for the last time. When he passed through the berthing space and saw the bunks swollen with the bodies, he had a vague feeling of guilt. He thought of the Exec, Ritter, Langworthy, and Evers; so many men he was leaving behind. Somehow it didn't seem right that he should now be able to escape.

He paused at the wardroom and saw the journal. Fitzgibbons had forgotten it. He picked it up and started for the escape trunk. Outside his stateroom he stopped again. Should he take anything? He picked up his handbag, considered it for a moment, then set it down again, turned, and hurried to the torpedo room.

It took less than fifteen minutes for the *Bentos V* to surface. Just before the bell broke out of the water, Hayman felt the motion of the sea once more. The light in the viewports became lighter, and then they burst from the sea. He looked at his watch. It was a little past 1700, June sixteenth.

As he was helped from the top hatch of the bell, Hayman was aware of a great many people surrounding him. Cameras were trained on him, and a flashgun momentarily blinded him. Many people seemed to be talking at once. He answered questions automatically and looked about. Everything was *level,* and the cool, late afternoon air was deliciously sweet, tanged with salt. On the boat deck above him he saw a crowd of men gathered behind a heavyset Navy captain. The four-striper regarded him enigmatically as he stripped cellophane from a cigar.

Hayman was taken to the sickbay, though he wanted to spend a little more time on deck to see the late afternoon sun hanging just above the horizon. After a brief check-up he would join the other survivors on *Frobisher*. From there, helicopter flights would take the men to New York.

Holmes entered the tiny compartment, followed by Captain Shepherd. He introduced himself and said, "You were the last one out, Mr. Hayman, fifteen rescued all told." He looked at the extremely thin officer, sitting in just his trousers having his pulse taken. "Do you think you people could have held out until Friday?"

"No, sir. We wouldn't have lasted another day. For us you came just in time."

Holmes said nothing, thinking to himself that at least he was off the hook for going against orders. Tom Calhoun would not press charges against him in the face of that fact. But what about Captain Vashenko?

"Well, I guess it was a good thing the Soviet ship was in the area," he said, turning to look at Shepherd. "I'll get a message off to the Russian Embassy to thank them for the assistance of their Captain Vashenko."

Later, before embarking in the boat that waited at the quarterdeck, Hayman looked out across the water. So many ships. Had they been up here all this time? The massive outline of the *Nikolai Trunov* loomed nearby, her red ensign billowing for a moment and catching the light of the late sun. Between the Russian ship and the *Kingfisher* a tall nun buoy was surging in the low swell. The paint had started to peel, and rust nearly obliterated the lettering that spelled out *Lancerfish*. A seagull banked steeply and dipped for an instant to the dark Atlantic water.